Kept Waiting

By E.N Holmes

Chapter 1

Mr. Finley slowly made his way down the hall, faltering with every other step. Three times a day he walked from the dining room to the bedroom. Three times a day for the last four years he performed this daunting trek. 4,380 times, to be precise, he had shuffled down the hallway with a lonely and indifferent look on his face.

But today it was different. He was optimistic, confident. He stood taller and shuffled faster. The nurses looked at each other with curiosity. Each wondering the reason behind his sudden change in attitude.

"Mister Finley!" A voice called. He paused and turned as the nurse quickly came down the hall, with his cane in her hand. A smile graced his aged face and he reached out towards her. She wrapped her hand around his, and offered him the cane. He waved it off but kept hold of her hand. The isolated old man from previous years had disappeared before her eyes.

"You're in a cheery mood today!" She tried to coax information from him as the two continued down the hall.

"Wonderful. Just wonderful." His eyes shined as they met hers. He went on to mumble nonsense about the weather, the date and needing to check on the clocks. She led him across his room and helped him into his chair.

"Can you help me face it towards the window?" He gestured to his seat. Outside his room the world was frosty. Snow dusted the window sill and passersby slipped on the thick layer of ice that coated the sidewalk. She swiveled him into the light and walked towards the window to shut it.

"No dear, leave it open. I quite enjoy the cold." He fumbled with the blanket for a few moments before she came and tucked it around him.

"You've got to stay warm. Climate change is real, Mister Finley, and with the strange winter we've been having, the snow is going to fall hard again soon I think." She looked from the window to him and their eyes met again. He raised his hand to her face.

"You remind me of her. She had beautiful eyes too." His smile grew and she quickly broke his gaze. "She was so beautiful. One of those stunners who could stop traffic. She actually did stop traffic once. I was driving the car, but-" He trailed off into laughter, "and that laugh. Oh I can't wait to hear her laugh again." He turned his face to the window again.

"I wish I could've met your wife Mister Finley. She sounds amazing." She placed her hand on his shoulder, as if on instinct his hand reached up and wrapped his fingers around hers. "Happy New Year Mister Finley." She said, and placed a gentle kiss on his hand before she made her way towards the door.

"Nurse, umm -" he paused searching for the name.

"Liza." she filled in.

"Thank you. Nurse Liza, can you call my daughter?" He requested.

"Of course. Anything specific I should say?" She replied, before opening the door.

"Ask her to bring all the clocks from the attic." He said and turned his face to the window.

"Of course Mister. Finley." Liza made her way to the phone, and began to dial.

"Hello? Mrs. Finley-Swan? Something is happening with your father. I think you should come down. Also, he asked that you bring the clocks. Whatever that means."

"Which one?" The voice asked.

"All of them?" Liza said to a stunned silence on the other end of the line.

The Cape was by definition a small town; 3,607 people living in 2.7 square miles. All your basic amenities, but no extravagance. As small as it was it still had a certain charm; everyone knew everyone, and everyone was always welcome. The way those who spend their time there describe it as, "if you lived there you wouldn't want to stay, and if you visit you'd never want to leave." Beauty was the real draw of the Cape. Victorian era style houses lined the streets and stunning beaches surrounded the town on three sides. During rush hour you could make it from one corner of town to the other in 15 minutes.

But between loading over one hundred and twenty-one clocks into multiple vehicles, and navigating the slippery roads it was more than three hours before the Finley-Swan clan had reached the nursing home. The clocks were loaded into his room one by one, and after some thorough direction from Mister Finley, all the clocks had been piled or hung. His collection consisted of regulators, schoolhouses, tambours, carriage, bracket and mantel clocks, and one single six foot tall grandfather clock. Every other clock was well taken care of; they were polished, wound, and free of any evidence of their age.

His room had undergone a complete transformation. Before, when you entered you would be engulfed by a hazy beige, which covered the four walls, and a smell of sickness hung heavy in the air. Now, you were greeted by the bright light of the window and the rich deep colours of the wall of clocks surrounding it. The smell of sickness and age was now replaced with the smell of the freshly polished wood which adorned the walls.

Mister Finley walked the span of the clocks, slowly inspecting each one as he went before he settled into his chair.

"I'm pretty sure you have more clocks in this room than there are in the whole Cape Dad." Bea said plopping down onto the couch under the window.

"Yes, I have acquired quite the collection." He beamed at her. "Thank you for taking such good care of them all these years." He turned to face the clocks again, the light from the window shone on his face.

Her father had aged during the years since her mother had passed. Five years prior his wife was diagnosed with ALS. Slowly it worked its way through her body, and every step of the way he was there to take care of her. Two years later she passed. The loss took a toll on their whole family, but no one was hit harder than Mister Finley. They had been together for 51 years, grew old, and raised a family. Now, he was alone; loneliness written all over his face. His black hair had thinned and faded to grey. His frown lines were more defined and dominant than ever before.

"What's so special about the clocks Dad?" She paused. She watched him very closely. Just as the nurses had before, and she noticed a change. A type of excitement could be seen in his eyes.

"This is going to be an exciting year. Important things are going to happen. I just want to make sure I don't miss a minute of it." There was something he wasn't saying. He was always excellent at talking around a question, a skill she knew well. Ever since Bea was a little girl he always managed to avoid explaining awkward or important things to her.

"Whoa." Two teens entered the room gasping at the site of the clocks.

"Too cool for digital Gramps?" Grant said, carefully eyeing up the stack.

"Well those of us who can actually read an analog clock are too cool for digital. Right Grandpa Charles?" Charlotte said, grasping at the opportunity to poke fun at her brother. The two of them stopped to give their grandfather a hug before joining their mother on the couch.

"What can I say? I'm a traditional man." Looking at the three of them, the family relationship was evident. Their brown eyes, thick dark hair and slender faces, made each of them three carbon copies of his former wife. After a moment Grant broke the silence.

"I have to ask, why are there so many clocks, Gramps?" It was unclear whether this was a rude question or not, but it was something all three of them were wondering.

"Some of them were from important moments in my life." He stood up and sauntered over to the wall.

Using his cane, he pointed up towards a medium sized, rectangular mantel clock. It was made of cherry wood, had a small handle at the top, and large script numbers on its face. "This one was in the back room of the church where Grandma and I got married." He took a few steps forward and moved his cane to a small antique brass alarm clock with roman numerals that hung about six feet up the wall. "This was our bedside alarm we bought when we moved into our first house." He sighed thinking back. "Kept us on our toes for a good five years."

"Oooh, tell them about my clock Dad." Bea called out. Charles chuckled and made his way to three identical perfectly lined up clocks in the bottom right corner.

"These are from the day each of the kids were born. Theodore, Freddie and Bea." He pointed as he listed off their names. The three clocks were all plain round black plastic clocks. "I stole them from the hospital rooms that they were born in."

"Clearly you don't love us enough Mom." Grant commented. "You didn't steal anything when we were born."

"I gave you life," Bea retorted. "Be grateful." Charles laughed and returned to staring at his collection.

"Almost all of them have a story. I guess it would take a long time to go through all of them." The kids made an audible sigh which was quickly cut off by a dirty look from their mother.

"Don't worry you two, I won't bore you with that." He paused and watched their faces relax. "For today at least." He let out a chortle and settled back into his chair. "The ones that don't have a story, well," he paused for a long time, as if trying to find the words to explain them. "They were just too beautiful to pass up. I had to fill out the collection." He said at last.

Time passed quickly as Charles and Bea sat and chatted about work, the kids after school activities, and what Theodore and Freddie were getting up to lately. Grant and Charlotte sat quietly, chiming in every so often. As the conversation was winding down Charles sat up straighter in his chair and leaned towards Bea.

"Can I ask another favour of you?" He grabbed Bea's hand. "Can I get the kids to stay, help set the clocks?" She looked at her children. Both their eyes filled with an urgent plea for help.

"One second Dad. We just have to call Patrick. You know, to make sure he doesn't need them for things around the house today." She dragged the kids into the hall.

"Mom -" Charlotte began to whine but Bea quickly cut her off.

"Oh no, you're staying. He is 91. And this whole clock thing is making me nervous. It gives me a feeling that he may not have much time left with us." The tears started to fill her eyes.

"Don't give us the pity tears. You say that every year, and he is still alive." Bea wiped her tears. Her son knew her too well, and could clearly tell when the tears were fake.

"The man is going to live forever." Charlotte stated in agreement.

"He's your grandfather." Bea firmly stated.

"And we are teenagers. Spending all day with him doesn't sound like fun." Grant pouted.

"You're right. You *are* teenagers." Grant and Charlotte sighed in relief. When Bea blinked a light shone in her eyes. "And I am your parent, your ride, the wallet that holds your allowance. You're spending your day here."

"Oh that's cold, Mom. You just want a kidless saturday." Charlotte accused.

"That's not entirely untrue." Bea said with a laugh before pushing the two of them back into the room. "Good news! They are all yours!" She kissed her father on the cheek and scooped up her purse. "Just give me a call when you're done with them and I'll rush back over to get 'em." She lightly tapped both kids on the shoulder as she passed them on her way to the door. As she looked back over her shoulder she could see the look of sheer disappointment and vengeance on her children's faces. She made a sarcastic boo-hoo face as she closed the door behind her.

An awkward silence settled in the room. Charles had begun to stare at his clocks again, almost unaware of the kids in the room. His grandchildren watched him. They had a dilemma. They didn't want to spend their afternoon sitting in silence, but they also didn't want to speak and spook him. They looked to each other for a hint of what to do. They ultimately decided that the fear of giving him an accidental heart attack was greater than their fear of sitting in silence.

"Pop quiz!" Charles blurted out. The sound of his voice in the silence elicited a surprised jump out of the two. "Who knows how many time zones there are in the world."

Charlotte's hand shot up causing Grant to jump for a second time. "24," she said.

"Your teachers must be very fond of you." Charles said, giving her a thumbs up.

"Her teachers must *tolerate* her, is the phrase I think you are looking for." Grant clarified. Charles stifled a laugh.

"24 time zones. 121 clocks. That is our mission for today." Charles declared. Grant and Charlotte's gracefully thin faces reflected confusion and disbelief. "Pop quiz again!" Charlotte was on the edge of her seat. But Grant interrupted him before he could continue. "It is Saturday gramps. Please, no more quizzes."

"Fine, fine. I want to set the clocks so that I have quick access to each timezone." With that, Charlotte brought out her phone, opened up her calculator and quickly did the math.

"Five! Should be five per time zone." She paused. "Damn it."

"Language young lady!" Charles interjected.

"Sorry." She sounded frustrated. "It's just that there is going to be one clock left over. It would've been perfect if there was just one less clock."

"It doesn't need to be perfect. It just needs to be." He reassured her.

"That is my kind of motto." Grant said high-fiving his grandfather. Grant settled on a chair next to Charles to discuss sports while Charlotte began to plan out how they would organize the zones. A few minutes later she produced a drawing identifying which clocks would be which time zone.

"We will start on the left in Alaska, work our way right in strips, until we reach the farthest corner of Russia." She explained, gesturing as she spoke. "Exactly like how they are laid out around the world." Grant scoffed at the excitement in her voice. After some arguing, he went and asked for a ladder from the nursing home staff and returned to set to work.

"Did your mother bring the box of watches?" Charles asked before they had finished the first time zone. Grant scooped up a box from the bed and placed it in Charles' lap. They watched as he gingerly opened the box and gently moved his hands over them. They returned to their task, leaving him alone with the watches.

After every 5 clocks Charlotte would glance back and find him closely analyzing each watch. As he went he muttered to himself. "Right colour...wrong face. Right face...wrong chain" or most often he looked at it and simply said, "not engraved" and then moved onto the next one, becoming more frustrated and sad as he went.

"Did mom bring the wrong box?" She finally asked, hoping to calm his frustration. He looked up from the watch in hand.

"Oh no, it's the only box of watches I have. It has just been a while since I have seen them. I just wanted to double check."

"What are you looking for?" She questioned again.

"I've been looking for an extremely special pocket watch for a very long time." He paused. The kids could see a serious sadness in his eyes. "It belonged to her. She left it with me before she -" the words caught in his throat. "Before she went away. Lost them back in the

50's. I spent years looking. It completely disappeared. I never found it." Tears had started to roll down his cheeks. Charlotte came to her grandfather's side, reached out, and took hold of his hand. He squeezed it, as if to say thank you. He looked up from the box and wiped his tears. "Never mind that now. I've got my brood here, this is not the time for being sad." Charlotte smiled trying to remind herself that he was old. He was allowed to confuse things.

Grant had made his way down the ladder and was beginning to move it eastward across the map of clocks.

"What about this one?" He pointed to the largest clock in the room.

Directly in the center of the collection was a massive round, lightweight steel industrial style clock. The face was bright white with only black lines for reference of the time. It stood out not for its size, but because it was the only one in the room that wasn't ticking, the face was shattered as if it had fallen to the ground.

"It doesn't work. Should I take it down?" Grant reached out to play with the clock hands. Before he could move the hands from their permanent 1:28 position Charles quickly spoke out. "Just leave that one. It doesn't work."

"If you took it down it would fix the time zone plan. Plus, why keep a broken clock?" Charlotte motioned for Grant to take it down.

"Please, do not touch that clock." There was a slight sound of anger in Charles' voice when he spoke. The two backed away from the clock and went back to work. They fell back into their awkward silence. Charles picked himself up from his chair. He stood in front of the big broken clock, eyes closed tight, and hands behind his back. The teens stood on either side of him, arguing through silent gestures, trying to decide who would speak. After a quick and silent game of Rock-Paper-Scissors, Grant spoke first.

"The attic is going to be so empty now with the clocks here. Maybe I can move my room to the attic with the extra space." He said, trying to fill the silent void.

"Yeah, it'll be the perfect place to lock you in." Charlotte agreed and laughed. "Life will be so much better. Why did you have to wait and ask for the clocks until now, we should've done this years ago." It was a humorous rhetorical question, but Charles answered anyway.

"She could be here any day. I don't know where she is right now." He wrinkled his brow. "But I want to be sure I know all possible times in the day. That way I won't miss her." His voice trailed off. Grant and Charlotte's bright brown eyes met. They exchanged looks of concern. "We have completed 10 time zones. I think that has earned us a break. So gramps, what's so special about the broken clock?" Grant pestered. It wasn't because he wanted to know the story or distract his grandfather, but more for the selfish reason of wanting to take a break.

"It is a very long story. I promised I wouldn't bore you today." He meandered back towards his chair.

"You said each clock was an important story. And clearly this is the most important." Charlotte stated. With that Charles perked back up. He loved to tell stories, and it was about time that he told this one.

"Well then, if we are going to get into it, I guess we should have something to eat." He called for the nurses to bring them lunch in his room. After a few minutes the two settled on the couch, sandwiches in hand, trying their best to look enthusiastic.

Charles had moved into the storytelling position. The kids remembered the position from when they were younger and would sit at his feet waiting to be told an epic tale. Charles sat forward with his hands on his knees as if to brace himself for the rollercoaster he was about to ride.

"It was 1945. The war was over and we had just arrived home."

Chapter 2

Elizabeth sat atop the staircase with a newspaper in hand. In large bold letters the headline read 'Welcome Our Boys Home!' She casually flipped through the pages, skimming the articles; one summarizing the aftermath of the atomic bomb, and multiple announcing celebrations of peace around the globe. She flipped through the pages a couple of times before closing the paper. She stood and began to pace around the second floor landing. She paused as she caught a glimpse of herself in the nearby mirror. She studied her face. Her chocolatey wavy hair formed her face nicely, and detracted from her round cheeks and freckled face. She gave herself a once over before shrugging and moving along. She continued pacing and fidgeted like she always did when she was impatient, nervous, angry, or just simply bored. The time was passing much too slowly. At last, somewhere down below she heard the pounding of feet followed by the jostling of coats being hung; for two people it sounded more like a stampede of cattle. She struck a sarcastic pose at the top of the stairs, tapping her foot and looking at the spot on her wrist where a watch should've been.

"You could've started without us." A voice echoed from the bottom of the staircase. Two shaggy heads of dark black hair popped around the corner and upon catching sight of her Michael laughed.

"Don't be so dramatic." The two bounded up the stairs two at a time. Their long slender legs made easy work of it.

"I thought I would read the paper instead." Elizabeth joked and Kenneth snatched the paper out of her hand.

"Thought you get all caught up on world events." He chuckled and handed it back to her. When they both reached the top of the stairs, she realized how tall they really were. Elizabeth was by no means short, but standing next to Michael and Kenneth she was a munchkin of oz.

"Honestly, I didn't want you to miss out on all the spring cleaning fun." She laughed, stretching her arms to embrace Michael in a hug. His arms rested easily on her shoulders and her head just grazed his chin. "Stop growing, you're making me feel so old."

"Oh auntie, you may be 24 but you barely look a day over 19." Kenneth said and flashed her a charming smile.

"There's a reason you are everyone's favorite." She said before she was hugged tight against his chest.

She wrapped her arms around the both of them and steered them towards the narrow, rickety ladder. She watched the two climb the ladder into the attic and waited for their reaction upon seeing what they had in store for them this evening.

"What? No!" Kenneth called out. "I said I would help tidy up some family heirlooms. Not cleaning and organizing the Cape Historical Society Museum."

Elizabeth made her way up the ladder with boisterous laughter. She stood between the two boys and tried her best to wrap her arms around their shoulders. She sighed as if to say, 'you poor naive boys.' The three of them stood facing the mammoth piles of knicknacks, boxes, trunks, books and furniture.

"I didn't think Gran really had this much stuff." Michael gasped as he made his way into the antique labyrinth.

"This isn't just Gran's things. It is her's and her mother's and her mother's mother's. It is about time you boys have learned our family's deep dark secret," she paused for dramatic effect. "You come from a long line of collectors."

"Hoarders are more like it." Kenneth said in a tone of disappointed amazement as he gazed around the room.

The three set to work under Elizabeth's instruction, organizing the collection into four piles: Keep, Garbage, Sell/Donate, and Take Home. Gran had given them very specific guidelines, "Keep anything that looks like it is important." To Gran that meant keeping every single item. To the three doing the cleaning that list included, family photos, clothing from special occasions, and any book or record that looked like a collectors item. Anything they were unsure of they put note on to ask Gran about later.

The mountain of tasks started out fun. They enjoyed going through the memories, laughing at the silly photos and listening to the old records they came across. Elizabeth stumbled across a box of old clothes from the 1920s. She began pulling out an outfit for each of them. She threw two fine pinstripe black suits towards the boys demanding they put them on. She drew out a white, low waisted, flapper v-neck dress with a wide bulky ribbon around the hips.

After the three of them had dressed they each took turns poking fun at the fashion of the time and striking goofy poses in the mirror.

"We have to commemorate this beautiful moment." Michael announced jokingly. He hiked up his too-big pants and went looking for a camera. Elizabeth and Kenneth began discussing possible poses for their picture and settled on what they considered to be a 1920s mob pose. The boys stood arms crossed and the brims of their panama hats slightly tipped over their faces, and Elizabeth in the middle hand on Kenneth's shoulder and one on her hip. They checked their pose in the mirror and snapped the picture.

"We look like we could smuggle whisky straight into New York." Michael cheered. "Clearly we should drink to -"

"Ha!" Elizabeth interjected. "No underage drinking in this house. Back to work." She took off Michael's hat and gently smacked him with it.

Over the next few hours the only sounds in the attic were record player static and the occasional sliding of furniture and trunks across the floor to their respective piles. The pile of things for the garbage was growing much faster than the others in the room. The second largest pile was that of Elizabeth's. Gran had told her if she cleaned the attic she could keep anything she wanted, as long as it didn't fall into the important items category. She had found an old dresser, desk, record player, box of books, clothes no one would want, and records, all that she wanted to keep for herself.

Elizabeth was making quick work of a box of books. Throwing all tattered covers and ripped pages into the garbage. When at the bottom of the box a slight gleam caught her eye. She reached in, elbow deep and grasped hold of a chain and slowly drew it out of the box. At the bottom of the chain was a round, gently used, faded gold pocket watch. Its face was stunningly white and the roman numeral numbers were a crisp black. Aside from slight scratches on his back and around the area where it was wound, it was in surprisingly good condition. Elizabeth passed the pocket watch between her hands, looking at it closely. On its back, engraved, were the words *Be Wise, Be Careful, Be Brave.* She walked across the room and added it to her pile of things she wanted to keep for herself.

"Hellooo?" A voice called and a head popped up through the attic floor door. "I'm here to pick up a dinner order?" Mary entered the room and began to clap. "Nicely done so far!" She walked around the room, similar to a supervisor in a factory, hands clasped behind her back and a scrutinizing look upon her face. She found Elizabeth hidden behind a pile of boxes, sprawled out on the floor, looking through an old yearbook. Elizabeth pointed to a picture of their Grandpa and began to read.

"Have a great summer Wallace! Thanks for including us in all of your 'adventure'." She paused and continued to read comments silently to herself. People described her grandfather as a loner with his head in the clouds.

"Wow, people were mean." Kenneth said while he read over her shoulder. "Grand-paps wasn't that delusional was he? They all make fun of him, but-" he paused and flipped through the pages looking for something positive. "I mean look around, he had all of the adventures he said he would."

"No honey. He didn't." Mary pipped from the other side of the boxes. From where Kenneth stood he could see Elizabeth giving a deep eye roll. "Your Grand-Paps did none of these things, he was a collector and delusional, just like everyone said he was. The majority of these things should be sent back to the museum he stole them from."

"Wrong." Elizabeth said and pulled herself up from the floor. She rushed over to the pile of photos they were saving for Gran, "no we won't and some of it he did." She quickly started showing the boys photos from his trips to the pyramids, the desert in Australia and the tearing down of the Berlin Wall. "He did what he could, all things considered."

"Yeah three of the three thousand things he'd claimed he'd done. And what do you mean, 'all things considered'?" Mary retorted.

"He had a family, he had to give up his adventure for something else. He settled down and financially adventuring just wasn't an option." When she said it she knew she'd regret it. She knew how touchy her sister was, and Elizabeth was certain Mary would have something to say.

"So he gave up his adventure to have a family? Having a family isn't adventure enough?" Mary responded defensively.

"No, I don't think it is." Elizabeth spoke honestly, which caused Mary to cross her arms and roll her eyes with frustrated exhaustion.

"Ha! Clearly you and Grandpa are more alike than we thought." She said quietly to herself as she let her eyes wander over to Elizabeth's pile of items to take home.

"Hey boys! Can you help me carry a load of this garbage down to the car." The three of them left and Elizabeth continued to look through the yearbook, brow furrowed thinking about her sister's comment. Shortly after loading the car, the boys returned to announce that burgers would be arriving in an hour.

The atmosphere had changed yet again. She thought the promise of food would brighten up the mood, but it felt colder.

Elizabeth had moved on to another box of papers, in which she found a collection of newspapers from the end of World War 1. She scooped them up and added them to her slowly growing pile papers to keep.

"Keeping another ancient thing?" Michael scoffed as he watched her. "Your pile is bigger than the things we are actually letting Gran keep."

"It's history. It's important we remember the past, it helps plan for the future, that's what your Grand-Paps said." Elizabeth said, brushing off his curt tone. The atmosphere had changed from fun to annoyed. The attic was hot, they were hungry, and they were nowhere near being finished. She assumed he was simply becoming frustrated.

"Where are you going to put all of that anyways? Your house is way smaller than this. You're going to be a hoarder too aren't ya auntie." Kenneth joked trying to cool the mood.

"Yup, and delusional like Grand-Paps," Michael whispered with an accusing and disappointed tone.

"Huh?" Elizabeth was unsure where this was coming from. She had always been on good terms with her nephews and this was out of character for them.

"You're just as bad as him. I've been to your house, it's full of unlived adventure garbage." His voice was slowly growing louder as he gestured to her pile in the corner. "You know what, this is not how I wanted to spend my sunday. Yet mom made us come here to keep an eye on you, to make sure selfish Elizabeth didn't take everything."

"That is just what mom says." Kenneth interjected and smacked his brother. "Auntie, she is just moody, she doesn't... she just wants to protect you."

"From who?" Elizabeth knew the answer but she wanted to hear it.

"Yourself." Kenneth confessed and winced when he spoke. He then stopped talking and lowered his eyes. He didn't want to make eye contact with her. He didn't want to see the anger in her eyes, let alone be the one of the ones that caused it. Elizabeth picked herself up from her position and retreated to the back of the room. The boys could see her seething as she walked. Kenneth caught Michael's attention and gave his brother a shameful, disapproving look.

A blanket of silence fell over the room as Elizabeth sat and stewed over what the boys said. The boys thought they were going to go deaf from the noiselessness, until Mary's head popped in again. Before she could even hand out the food Elizabeth's voice broke the silence.

"You think I'm selfish?" She spoke quietly from her seated spot in the corner.

Mary shot an angry confused look towards her sons. She put down the bags of food and took a defensive stance.

"You think so little of me, that you tell my nephew's basically not to trust me, all to 'protect me from myself'." The anger was building in Elizabeth's voice, but she was trying her hardest to stay calm.

Mary looks at the boys again.

"No, don't blame them. I'm sure they are just repeating what they've heard before. Auntie Elizabeth is just like Grandpa head full of fantasies she'll never accomplish." Elizabeth paused to take a breath before continuing. "I'm sure you're just jealous of my freedom, that I even have the option to do any of the things on my list. You're just scared that *you're* actually like Grandpa, giving up your freedom to settle down."

Elizabeth and Mary had had this argument before, in small bits and pieces throughout their lives but today it seemed to spill out in full.

"I am having my adventure. My adventure and your adventure are different. I have kids, I have to put my family's needs over everything else, living like you isn't an option! You don't have kids, you have the whole world to explore and you just sit there, collecting things. You made a selfish and lonely choice to only ever have to look out for yourself, you push everyone away and then brag about going it alone, like it is some competition you've won. Even if you wanted to do the things on your list you'd be too afraid. And God forbid you find someone to do them with you, I am certain that your sarcastic attitude would get in the way." Mary's monologue was long as she got all of her feelings off of her chest. Her words cut through Elizabeth.

Michael and Kenneth sat quietly in the corner watching the women scream at each other, unsure if they should step in or not. Slowly Michael grabbed the bag of food, and the two quietly retreated out of the attic.

Mary and Elizabeth argued nonstop for 45 minutes. They touched on all subjects from their lives together; who pushed who outside the Pizza Hut, the real reason the dog ran away, how Elizabeth has never done anything selfless in her life, how once Mary had children she expect the world to stop for her, and how neither of them has had the life they wanted.

"You're right Mary, I'm a lonely, selfish, hoarder who will never accomplish anything and will die alone." Mary opened her mouth to speak but Elizabeth continued her rant. "But don't just sit there on your high horse pretending you're happy with what you have either!"

"I am happy with my life! I love my boys, I love my husband, and the life we have has been built with work and loss."

"Yes Mary you've had it so hard, perfect boys, big house on the water, never having to work because David is so wealthy." Elizabeth rolled her eyes.

"Oh please Elizabeth, be better than you are now, make a choice that is for more than just yourself and then tell me how easy it is! Oh I forgot, you won't because you'll never have anyone to share things with." Mary screamed in response.

Elizabeth shook her head in hurt and disappointment. She walked to her pile of antiques, scooped up the pocket watch and all of the newspapers sitting below it and quickly retreated down the attic ladder.

She stood in the entryway contemplating her options. She could march back up the stairs and give her sister a piece of her mind. Or she could leave, calm down, and then give her sister a piece of her mind when she had had time to come up with a more elegant way of expressing herself, without using the many diverse curse words she had on her tongue right now.

She began to pace around the entryway. Talking to herself, she fidgeted with her rings, spun the dial on the watch in her hands, picked at the paint on her fingernails. With a deep calming breath, she decided she didn't want to be here anymore. She grabbed her coat from the bottom of the stairs and flung her arms into it. She caught her reflection in a nearby picture frame and let out a frustrated sigh. She had completely forgotten about the ridiculous flapper dress she was wearing. Her clothes were upstairs. As she made for the stairs she paused and thought better of herself. If she went to retrieve her clothes, she would run into Mary and she would lose all common sense.

Luckily her jacket was long enough to cover the low hanging lace of the dress entirely. She pulled it tight around her, shoved the watch into the pocket and piled the newspapers under her arm, and marched out of the house, tightly slamming the door behind her.

Chapter 3

Charles, Freddie and Lennie were dressed in their formal naval uniforms as they casually strolled down Beach Street. If you didn't know them you would assume they were brothers. Each of them had a sturdy military build, short and well maintained dark hair, and each of them stood just taller than six feet. The only difference was in Charles. Freddie and Lennie possessed the blue eyes that came with their fair complexion and bright laissez-faire attitude. Charles however had dark brown eyes, as smooth as polished mahogany, and a focused and level headed attitude which balanced out their group nicely. The three of them had been friends since grade school, but bonded while training at the naval base in the Cape. Their commanding officer referred to them as Huey, Dewey, and Louis. Not because they were inseparable, but more so because the officer believed they had the common sense of adolescent ducks.

The boys were luckier than most, they spent their service at home in the Cape. After their naval training, they were scouted by the coast guard for coastal patrol, and anti-submarine warfare. They remained close to their family, and never had to see the bloodshed that was happening in Europe. They wore their uniforms with pride but without the tragic understanding of why they wore them.

A block ahead, the three noticed a woman storming out of a nearby house. It was hard not to miss her with her furious slamming of the door and visible huffing and puffing as she walked. She stood on the sidewalk looking around, getting her bearings. As they approached they noticed a flash of white from inside her coat and a large stack of newspapers under her arm. Freddie and Lennie elbowed, winked and whistled at each other. The meaning of this was beyond Charles' understanding and interest. He rolled his eyes and returned his focus to the frustrated girl ahead.

The wind had begun to pick up. She was struggling to try to keep herself in order as it whirled around her. One gust hit and flung open her coat. In the motion of trying to catch it, the newspapers from under her arm took flight. Seeing her turmoil, the three men began running up the street. Before she knew it, they were there on the ground gathering as many papers as they could before they danced away in the wind. She didn't have time to fully process the entire event before the gentlemen were standing in front of her papers in hand.

"I'm really sorry." Charles spoke first, gathering the papers from the others and organizing them into a stack. "I think some ran away with the wind." Freddie scooped up her hand in his.

"Frederick Marcus." He winked and shook her hand furiously before passing it down the line.

"Leonard Knox." He tipped his hat to her and kissed her hand. The three gentlemen were clearly charming, if she hadn't been so flustered she would have taken the time to appreciate it more. Her main concern was thanking the gentlemen, getting her papers, and getting out of there.

"Charles Finley." His shake was gentle, and his smile almost knocked her off her feet. His charm was less put on than the others, and there was something genuine in how he looked at her directly in the eyes. At last she took her chance to speak.

"Elizabeth." She stopped. Charles had not let go of her hand, he was looking at her like he was waiting for more.

"Whitley." She finished. To her disappointment he dropped her hand. She shook her head to refocus herself in the moment.

"Thank you for saving my papers." He passed the papers back to her and she held them tightly in front of her. Their eyes were locked. Freddie and Lennie were not unaware of this. Freddie let out a very audible, disappointed sigh while he ran his hand through his hair. His sigh knocked the two out of their shared moment.

The three of them stood in front of her looking very formal, feet together, backs straight and hands at their sides, as if waiting for something.

"At ease, soldiers." She joked. Confusion flashed across their faces.

"Sorry miss, but these are naval uniforms." Lennie corrected her, looking at her like she was stupid.

"I was making a joke." She gestured to them hoping they would notice their formal stance.

"Ha!" Charles let out a chuckle when he noticed. "I guess we haven't lost our habits yet." He placed his hands in his pockets and relaxed. The only one looking confused was Elizabeth.

"I think we better be going." Freddie announced. The two blue eyed boys tipped their hats to her, turned and began to walk.

"Thank you again." She said waving as they went. Charles tipped his hat, and shot her a wink.

"Hopefully the wind leaves you alone." He turned and followed after his friends.

"Hopefully not." She sighed when the three were safely out of earshot. Maybe if the wind picked up he would come back. She shook her head again attempting to clear it. She wasn't the damsel in distress type, but she would find the closest train tracks to lay on if it meant having him save her.

Elizabeth plopped down onto the curb and began to look around. She had been so distracted by the wind, and then the boys, that she hadn't taken the time to notice that something was different.

An old classic car sat across the street parked directly where she had left her car this morning. The boxy vehicle was staring at her, almost daring her to notice it. It was strange, not because of it's horrible orange colour but because it didn't seem out of place. It was as if that was the place it parked everyday, like it simply belonged there. Quickly she started to notice other changes, the trees, the newly paved street, the houses or lack thereof houses across the street.

She brushed the strangeness off as flustered confusion. She reached her hand in her pocket to find her cellphone.

"Damn it!" She said when she realized she had left it up in the attic when she stormed out.

Elizabeth turned to go back into the house and what she saw left her bewildered. From where she stood she had expected to see her childhood home. A two story, navy blue, victorian style house, with white trim and a red door. Fear began to slowly grow in the pit of her stomach. The house behind her looked like the house she grew up in; well it looked like her house if someone had cut off the top floor and painted it a pistachio green. She sat, staring at the house in disbelief. This had to have been some kind of mistake.

"I must've come out and walked down the street." Elizabeth stood, turned and faced the row of houses. She paced up and down the street a few blocks in each direction. As she walked she scanned for the red door that would reassure her she hadn't lost her mind. Every door was white, and the house she left was simply gone. She stared closely at the green house in front of her and she began to panic. Maybe she hit her head on the way out of the house, this had to be a dream. She closed her eyes and pinched her arm.

"God damn it!" She cursed after she opened her eyes to see the house had not disappeared. Her heart had started to race and she felt dizzy. Slowly she sat back down on the sidewalk. She closed her eyes and took five deep breaths.

"Okay." Her heart had slowed and she began to talk herself through her possible options.

"I am dreaming, someone is playing a horrible prank, I have hit my head and I am living in a coma, I have travelled back in time, or I have simply gone insane." Every idea sounded worse than the one before. She began to think through her possible options.

"Dream?" She had already proved she wasn't dreaming, but pinched herself again just to be sure. Nothing.

"Prank?" She didn't have enough friends, let alone know anyone with enough money to pull off a prank this big. No.

"Coma!" She frantically ran her hands over her body looking for cuts or bruises to show some kind of accident. She held her breath to hear if someone outside of her coma was telling her not to go into the light. Nothing.

"Time travel? Not possible." She thought, "Stupid idea. Next."

"Clearly I have lost my mind." She sighed. "I mean I know I was mad, but not mad enough to black out and slip into a delusional fantasy. Maybe I am more like Grandpa than I thought."

She sat still trying to take in everything around her. The old cars laughed at her as they roared down the street. There were two young boys playing in the yard next to her and they looked like something out of an old timey movie with their high socks and string toys. At last her eyes landed on a lonely phone booth she spotted sitting in the distance, something about it made her brain itch.

Exhausted with confusion she rubbed her eyes and tried to make a sensible plan. "Hey, phone booth. I'll just call for help." She shoved her hand in her pockets to search for change but nothing could be found in her pocket except for the watch she had found in the attic. "Nope."

"Maybe if I just go back into the house everything will reset." She stood up, turned and marched back up to the door.

She gave the handle a giggle only to find it was locked. She dropped her head back and sighed. "Frickin' white door." She whispered while she gave 5 quick raps against the wood.

"Hello?" A small elderly woman opened the door. She stood a head shorter than Elizabeth with a pink cardigan and white hair haloing around her head.

"Mary?" Elizabeth questioned.

"No dear. I am Matias." A smile grew across the old woman's face.

"Matias Walker?" Elizabeth asked, her eyebrows scrunched towards each other in anguish on her forehead. The old woman simply nodded.

"No shit." She said and sat back onto her heels with a look of confusion and amazement. Elizabeth remembered the name from the stories her grandpa used to tell about the previous owners of the house, but she was certain they died in the 50's.

"You're still alive?" The words slipped out of her mouth but before she could apologize the woman looked taken-aback by what Elizabeth said and slowly closed the door in her face.

"Elizabeth," she spoke to herself as she made her way back to the sidewalk, "how does this option make the most sense?" Pause. "It makes more sense than having completely lost my mind. I hope." She retorted.

She stood, facing the house she had literally walked out of minutes before. "It makes sense, but it doesn't make sense." She said at last. "Not possible." She pinched herself and checked her body for signs of trauma wanting to finally rule out any other option. "So you're seriously believing this?" She asked herself again.

But part of her mind kept whispering *it could be possible.*

"I need help." She stated. She reached again for the cellphone in her pocket, only to be reminded it was gone. She looked down the street and a smile grew on her face.

"I know just the man." She paused and looked down the street in the direction the boys headed off in. "Gentlemen," She corrected herself, "who could help." She closed her coat tightly around her, gripped her papers tighter and began running down the street after them.

"Hey! Soldier boys!" she called out hoping to get their attention. "Could one of you, dapper gentlemen," she panted, trying to catch her breath after she caught up to them four blocks down the street, "point me in the direction of a library or post office. Or some other place I could find a newspaper?"

Freddie chuckled and pointed to the stack under her arm. "Looking to add to the collection?" She scrunched up her nose in embarrassment, trying to think of a better way to explain. "Oh, I mean, I'm looking for today's paper." She laughed through the confusion.

Charles reached out towards the pile. "I think," he paused, taking the pile and shuffling through them. "Yah, I saw it in the paper tornado earlier." He pulled out the paper and handed it to her. "You've already got one."

She gently took the paper and turned it over in her hands, the fear on her face did not go unnoticed by the men in front of her. In large bold letters the headline read, 'Welcome Our Boys Home!' She quickly flipped through the pages, skimming the articles; quickly recognizing the one summarizing the aftermath of the atomic bomb, and multiples announcing celebrations of peace around the globe.

Frantically she flipped to the front page and read the date aloud, "September 21st, 1945." The words caught in her throat as she said them. She couldn't catch her breath, she felt like all the blood was rushing out of her head, her limbs had gone numb and the colour was fading from the world around her. She dropped. If she was conscious she would've been extremely pleased to know that she had fainted directly into the arms of Charles Finley.

Chapter 4

Elizabeth woke up feeling hazy. Outside the room she could hear the sound of familiar male voices.

"One second she was standing, looking terrified, and the next moment she was out in my arms. I've never seen her before, do you know her?" His voice was unsteady.

"She doesn't look familiar." A woman's voice spoke. "She seems okay right now, no cuts or bruises. But I'll check again when she wakes up."

Elizabeth considered moving and calling out to let them know she was awake and okay, but the place she was laying was much too comfortable. She laid there trying to figure out where she was and how she got there. Her ridiculous time travel theory began to swim in her mind once more and she chuckled at the thought.

Okay, I must've hit my head when I stormed out. The boys clearly brought me back inside and I'm on Gran's squishy couch. She thought and reasoned herself back to sanity. She opened her eyes and blinked trying to focus her vision but the room was unfamiliar, this was not her Grandparents living room.

"Hey!" A voice called out, "I think she's awake!" She looked towards the voice. It was one of the tall, blue eyed naval boys from before. She recognized him but couldn't remember his name for the life of her. She heard the pounding of feet from somewhere down below.

The sound of footsteps brought her back to the present. Back to cleaning out the attic with the boys, fighting with her sister, storming outside, Frederick, Leonard and Charles, the claim of 1945, and then black.

She shot up into a seated position. She had moved too fast causing all the blood to rush out of her head making her dizzy all over again.

"Hey hey hey," Freddie said and kneeled by her side. "Slow down." He helped her lay back down on the bed. Charles entered the room followed by Lennie. Charles scooched Freddie aside and seated himself next to Elizabeth on the bed.

"You okay kid?" Charlie asked. Elizabeth attempted to sit up again, Charles wrapped his arm around her for assistance, while Freddie moved the pillows to help prop her up against the headboard.

"I think so. Thank you." She looked at the three of them. "You've rescued me twice in one day. I swear, I am really not this clumsy all the time." She paused to think about it for a moment. "Okay, I'm pretty clumsy, but I usually don't have someone there to witness it." Her joke began to lighten the heavy atmosphere in the room.

"So, what is your story?" Lennie said laying across the foot of the bed.

Elizabeth paused. She honestly didn't know what to say, *"I think I've accidentally travelled back in time,"* they would have her committed. Her pause lasted too long and the silence in the room was becoming awkward.

"Running from your wedding?" Lennie joked and pointed to her dress. She quickly tightened her coat close around her, trying to hide the bright white flapper dress peeking out from underneath.

"No. Umm," she paused to try and find a normal way of saying she was playing dress up.

"Is it really any of your boys' business, Lennie?" A tall, round faced woman had entered the room. She moved in and stood next to Freddie. He placed his arm snugly around her waist. Elizabeth exhaled and smiled a relieved smile, her relief did not go unnoticed by the woman.

"This is Alice." Charles looked in her direction. "My sister." He sternly stated. When he finished, Freddie awkwardly removed his arm from around her waist. Alice rolled her eyes at him and crossed the room to Elizabeth. The four of them surrounded her, staring. She felt the overwhelming need to fill the awkward quiet.

"So," she let out a big sigh. "How did I get here? And better yet where exactly is here?" Elizabeth questioned. *And when is here,* she joked to herself.

The boys went on to explain how after she fainted and that they stood on the sidewalk for fifteen minutes fanning her and debating what to do. Freddie and Lennie began talking over each other as they recounted the tale.

"We were too far from the hospital to-" Lennie began.

"And we didn't know where to take you home to." Freddie interjected.

"Charles scooped you up and brought you to me." Alice said, effectively silencing them.

"Alice is a nurse. I wanted to make sure you were okay." He grabbed her hand and gave her a reassuring smile.

"Well thank you, all of you." Elizabeth looked around at all of them.

She had to figure a way out of here and how to get back to ~~where~~ when she came from. "Really, I need to get going, and I'm feeling perfectly fine." She attempted to stand up to gather her things.

"I'll be the judge of that." Alice ushered the boys out of the room and began checking Elizabeth's pupils and pulse. After she finished she sat next to Elizabeth and kept hold of her hand. "Everything seems to check out. Your pulse is a little fast, but seems appropriate all things considered." Sadness welled up in Alice's eyes.

"We see it, too often, at the clinic. Women running away. I've never been in the position to help before but I know how hard it is to start all over again. I know it's not my business, but," Elizabeth shot her a concerned look, "whatever reason you are running, you're welcome to stay here until you have it figured out."

"Thank you, Alice." The two girls hugged, and for the first time since she stormed out of her mother's house, Elizabeth felt calm.

"I really have no idea what I'm doing." Elizabeth said with all honesty. If this really was 1945, Elizabeth had nowhere to go. She had watched enough movies to know she needed a McFly family or Doc Brown to shelter her. She needed a safe place to sort everything out, and this dropped into her lap. Or well, she dropped into its lap.

"I promise I won't be in your hair for very long." Elizabeth promised. Alice smiled and popped out of the bedroom and quickly headed down the stairs.

"Leave." Alice announced. "Everything is fine. Go." Elizabeth could hear them shuffling around the front door. "Yes, even you, Freddie. No, I don't know how long she is staying. Yes, you can come back for dinner." Alice said firing off answers to questions Elizabeth couldn't quite hear through the crack in the door.

"It's safe to come out now. They've gone." Alice called out as the door closed with a bang. While Elizabeth came down the stairs, Alice eyed her up and down. "Not that I don't love that vintage dress, but do you have anything else to wear? You'll stick out like a sore thumb if you wear that around town."

Elizabeth thought of the ripped denim skirt she was wearing earlier, but it would make her stand out, more so than the dress she was sporting now.

"No." Elizabeth shook her head. "Would you believe me if I told you I didn't plan for any of this?" She said in a joking tone, even though she was being completely honest. Alice gave her a pitiful look before she grabbed Elizabeth by the hand, and took off back up the stairs dragging her along into Alice's room.

"I've always wanted a sister to share clothes with." She said with a big sime and flung the closet doors open. "Pick something out, and then we will head to town. I have a few things to pick up for dinner." Elizabeth said nothing but began sifting through the clothes. "The boys demanded that you get a welcome dinner, and I agree. Though, now that I think about it, they were probably using you as an excuse to have me cook them dinner."

"Should really pick up all the ingredients and leave it for them to cook, it was their idea after all." Elizabeth said casually sifting through the clothes.

"Ooh, I like you!" She chuckled and left Elizabeth in front of the closet.

Elizabeth turned into the skid. She allowed herself to be completely swept up in the new world around her. If this was all real she was damn well going to appreciate it.

Alice gave Elizabeth a thorough tour of the town, taking her down each street and showing her every shop and tourist attraction. Even though this was the same Cape she was in only hours ago, Elizabeth felt like she was visiting it for the first time. Everything looked familiar; the Melen Estate, the lookout tower, and the beaches were all in the same places but in Elizabeth's memory they had never looked so new.

"There are talks that they are going to build an amusement park up the beach." Alice explained as they headed out from the dress shop.

"You mean Piper's Pier?" Elizabeth responded not thinking and quickly regretting the words as they came out of her mouth.

"You are from around here, aren't you?" Alice had been watching her as they walked.

"Huh?" Elizabeth said feigning surprise. "Nope."

"You know everywhere I show you, but you are still so astonished when you see it." Alice didn't want to push her to explain why she was here, but it was clear now that she had been here before. Elizabeth had tried to explain earlier that she was from a town further north, but she danced around the specifics.

"It's complicated. I've been here but when I was, it was never like this. Brand new, freshly built." Alice looked at Elizabeth trying to process what she had said.

"I should look you over again. Maybe you hit your head when you fainted."

"I do fall quite frequently, I wouldn't be surprised if I've knocked something loose." Elizabeth joked. *I need to be more careful, she* thought, but the girls laughed off the confusion and continued through town.

The girls spent hours walking through town, talking about the sights, sounds and fashion they saw in the shops. Elizabeth enjoyed spending time with Alice, she had never really bonded with her own sister or girl friends back in 2012. They returned home with bags in hand. As they were unloading the bags she caught a glimpse of herself in the mirror, 1945 looked good on her.

The high waisted black skirt and white tied off blouse made her waist look sizes smaller, and not to mention they were superbly comfortable. She took a moment to remember all of her ill-fitting clothes in 2012 and thought when she made it back she was going to raid the vintage clothing shops.

Then it hit her. In the hours she had spent out with Alice she had completely forgotten that she was stuck in 1945, stuck with no idea how to return. She felt dizzy again when reality set in, she had no memory of how she had gotten here and no way of knowing when or how she would get back.

She told Alice she was still feeling a little woozy, but okay, and that she was headed upstairs to lay down for a bit. She lay on the bed and slowly processed her thoughts.

She needed to figure out three things:
First, how she got here.
Second, how she was going to get out of here.
Third, what she was going to do in the meantime.

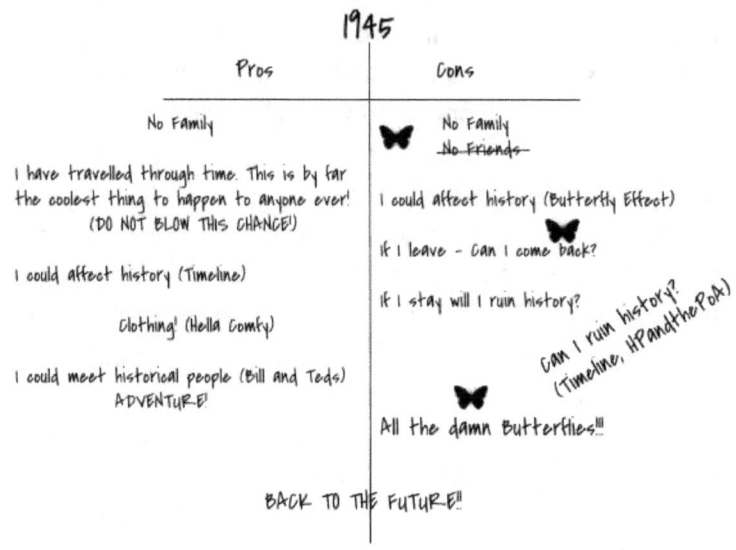

1945

Pros	Cons
No Family	No Family
	~~No Friends~~
I have travelled through time. This is by far the coolest thing to happen to anyone ever! (DO NOT BLOW THIS CHANCE!)	I could affect history (Butterfly Effect)
	If I leave - Can I come back?
I could affect history (Timeline)	If I stay will I ruin history?
Clothing! (Hella Comfy)	Can I ruin history? (Timeline, HP and the PoA)
I could meet historical people (Bill and Teds) ADVENTURE!	All the damn Butterflies!!!
	BACK TO THE FUTURE!!

Need to find photo or something to see if I have altered history. (Back to the Future)

"Okay. Number 1." Elizabeth began, after she endured the door had been securely closed. She laid out all of her things she brought with her. Scattered across the bed in front of her were her flapper dress, jacket, and antique papers. Elizabeth stared at them blindly, looking for something to lead her to how she got here. She picked up the pile of newspapers, "not so antique anymore." She said and scoffed at the idea, "like a newspaper would send me back in time." She pushed all of them aside, but left the infamous September 21st paper laying in front of her taunting her incessantly.

She stood and began pacing around the room trying to retrace her steps that morning. As she paced she reached for her nails to pick at the polish and a thought came racing back. Standing in the entryway of the house, she picked at her nail polish, toyed with her rings, and then shoved her hands in her coat pockets to fidget with the loose strings inside.

Elizabeth dove across the bed and scooped up her jacket. As she pushed her hand into her right pocket she hit something hard and metallic. She slowly drew it out of her pocket and sat down on the bed.

"Nah." She stared at it, allowing it to hang from the chain in front of her face. "I mean, it makes more sense than the papers." She shrugged.

Elizabeth passed it between her hands like she had done the first time she saw it. The faded gold was cold in her shaking hands. She bit her lip trying to remember; a memory flickered in her brain. She had spun the top dial when she was seething with anger that day.

She gently placed her thumb and forefinger on either side of the dial. Holding her breath she slowly turned it. She watched the hands on the face changing and the date dial flickering, "nothing abnormal," she sighed, "that's how watches work."

She layed with a thud back down on the bed, her head hanging over the edge and upside down. She toyed with the chain of the watch, running it between her fingers and tried to think of something else. Out of the corner of her eye she spotted the ticking hands of a clock resting on the bedside table. Quickly she popped back up and locked her eyes on it.

"I have to check." She placed her pointer finger and thumb around the dial of the watch, her eyes still locked on the clock beside the bed.

As she twisted the dial, the hands on the wall clock wound backwards 5 whole minutes. She dropped the watch and it crashed onto the floor.

"No shit!" She squeaked out, scrambling to pick it up. She quickly checked the clock opposite her to make sure she hadn't jumped through time again. She looked around the room. The papers had gone from their pile and were now scattered across the bed again. She looked around and nothing else had changed. She herself hadn't moved but everything else had reset to what it was five minutes prior.

"Whoa!" Her heart was racing. Thinking that her mind was playing tricks on her she decided she needed one more test.

Quietly Elizabeth opened the door and creeped down the stairs to look in on Alice cooking in the kitchen. Alice moved gracefully around the room from washing dishes to removing pasta from the oven. As she carried the dish from the oven to the table she slipped on a puddle that had formed under the sink. Her feet came out from underneath her and both Alice and the pasta dish crashed to the ground.

Elizabeth held the watch firmly in hand and wound it backwards slowly again. Elizabeth's eyes blinked rapidly at the scene before her, she couldn't believe what was happening. As she turned the watch's dial Alice began to move in reverse. Alice bounced up from the floor and the dish did the same, reassembled, and sat itself back into Alice's hands. Elizabeth sat on the stairs stunned. She removed her hand from the dial and watched Alice go about her cooking in the exact same manner. Alice slipped, the dish broke.

"Whoa. Deja vu." Alice said before she started cleaning up the pieces.

"One more time," Elizabeth thought. She turned the dial back again and watched Alice remove the dish from the oven. Not thinking Elizabeth called out as Alice was nearing the water.

"Watch out!" She darted across the room, dropped a rag over the water and caught the glass dish before it dropped out of Alice's startled hands. The dish slightly burned Elizabeth's hands before she could place it on the counter. Alice quickly grabbed her and guided her to the sink.

"Some reflexes you've got there." She said gently rinsing Elizabeth's hands.

"Just quick on my feet." While Alice was treating her burns Elizabeth remembered what happened as she turned the dial and thoughts flew through her mind. *I changed things. What did it mean? What did I do? How does time work?*

"Do you have a spare piece of paper?" Elizabeth asked once her wounds were covered and was struck with a sudden idea. Alice pointed to the desk in the sitting room. Elizabeth nodded thanks and took a blank notebook and pen, and quickly retreated back up the stairs.

A thousand thoughts rushed through Elizabeth's mind. She had just solved two of her three problems. She knew how she got here and figured out how to get back.

She grabbed the notebook and began to journal about her journey so far. She wrote about the clothes, the people and how different the Cape was. She gathered all of the things she had acquired in her short time here, she wanted to make sure she had some way to remember this when she went back home.

After she finished writing, she sat back and looked around her. She took a deep breath and then she quickly picked up the watch and wrapped her fingers around the dial prepared to spin it until she was back in 2012, but suddenly a weight pushed against her chest. She dropped the watch on the bed, disappointed in herself.

The third problem lingered heavily in the air around her; What should she do in the meantime, should there be a meantime?

"This is your moment Elizabeth and you're just going to waste it?" Elizabeth whispered harshly. She was suddenly reminded of her argument with her sister. It felt like it had been weeks ago, but in reality it was only a few hours ago.

"In reality, it hasn't even happened yet." Elizabeth joked through her thought process.

"Even if you wanted to do the things on your list you'd be too afraid." Mary had made a point, Elizabeth hadn't had many adventures yet and now she was just plopped into one and suddenly she was ready to leave.

"I'm not afraid." Elizabeth announced and stood up triumphantly. "Find then I'll stay."

Staying to prove a point? That's petty. It was as if she could hear her sister's voice calling her out to her across the decades.

"I don't care if it is petty or spiteful, it is an adventure. And like she said I don't have anything to rush home to." She argued with the imaginary thought of her sister, and began to pace around the room. A thought itched at the back of her mind. *If you stay, what happens?*

As she paced around the room she thought through her dilemma aloud.

"If I stay, I get an adventure. Which no one back home will ever believe I had. Who says I even have to go home? What if I don't go home? Who would miss me? Honestly, I could just travel back to the exact moment I left and no one would be the wiser." She sighed with relief.

"What if I change something? What if I have already changed something? I should just go back so I don't break the future. Is Hitler already dead? Yeah dummy, world war 2 is over, he died months ago." She thought of all of the famous time travel tropes she knew and her head began to ache and her stomach began to gurgle uncomfortably.

She jumped back onto the bed and began to draft out a pro and con list for staying in 1945.

All of her understanding of time travel came from movies and books, and who knew if they were accurate, "had any of them actually travelled through time?" She mumbled to herself as she wrote. She continued writing down all the mechanics that she had discovered so far and added them to the journal of her adventure in 1945. "I could make a killing off of this," she said, but then stopped herself. She ruffled through the pages she had already written. She wasn't sure if she should write it down after all, in fear of what Alice or anyone else would think if they came across it, they'd think she was crazy.

There was a knock at the door and quickly she stuffed her writing under the pillow. Butterflies began to flap their wings in her stomach. She opened the door to find Charles standing, hands in his pockets in the doorway. Seeing him standing there caused a lump to catch in her throat and the butterflies in her stomach began to flap more violently.

"Hi." She said casually sweeping open the door and leaning against the door frame.

"I've been sent on a mission to tell you dinner was ready." He said.

"Well, mission accomplished soldier." She returned with a smile. She quickly realized how inappropriate that comment could be at this time. "Oh I'm sorry. I really shouldn't make soldier jokes." She nodded to his uniform. "Clearly too soon, I am so sorry."

"Oh, don't let what the guys say fool you. We were part of the coast guard, and never saw a battle." He chuckled and gave an 'after you' gesture towards the staircase.

The five of them sat down to dinner, Freddie and Charles at the heads of the table, Alice and Elizabeth between them on one side and Lennie opposite the girls. They ate, drank and told stories. Elizabeth sat in silence for most of the evening. Quiet on the outside, but inside her head was reeling. Her thoughts kept bouncing around, "*I need to be on my toes. No slip-ups about the future. There can't be any mistakes like earlier. I don't want them thinking I'm crazy.*"

As the night progressed Elizabeth learned a lot about her crew of rescuers. They were all in their mid twenties, never married, and lived in the Cape their entire lives. This hit home with Elizabeth, 24, single, and living two streets over from her childhood home.

"During the war," Lennie said and screwed up his face, feigning sadness, "we lost a lot of good men out there. It was terrifying, never knowing if you were going to be coming home at the end of it."

Then Lennie and Freddie made eye contact and Freddie nodded at Elizabeth in confirmation. This was clearly a line he had been planning to use since the announcement of the end of the war. Stone faced, Elizabeth responded.

"It must have been terrifying. The things you boys must've been through." She reached across the table taking Lennie's hand, and his face lit up. "Even where I am from I know that the Cape coast guard and training base was the most dangerous place to be stationed." The sarcasm in her voice and the look on her face was subtle, but the comment sent Charles' drink flying up his nose as he laughed. "Plus it must've been terrifying not knowing if you would get to go home. Especially when you are literally stationed at home." Laughter erupted around the table while Lennie pouted.

"You had to tell her didn't ya." Lennie said, and shook his head in embarrassment and frustration at Charles. Elizabeth laughed and apologized stating that she just couldn't resist.

Slowly Elizabeth was coming out of her shell. She made jokes and talked about her family. She quickly realized that there wasn't much she knew about 1945, shy of World War II. It was hard to talk about books, music, movies, and hobbies when you had zero clue of what there was to do in the 1940s.

As dinner came to an end Elizabeth leaned back on her chair, completely relaxed and looked around.

Never in her life had she felt this comfortable or welcome with a group of people. She didn't feel like she needed to put on an act like she did with her friends in 2012, the four people seated around the table accepted her regardless of her sarcasm and no one laughed at her when she asked stupid naive questions. Though she was from a completely different time she fit here.

The boys cleared the table while the girls headed into the sitting room. Alice turned on the radio and before the sound of Helen Forrest and Dyck Haymes could fill the room Freddie came in, swept Alice up in his arms and the two began waltzing gracefully around the room.

Elizabeth sat on the sofa watching. She tried to picture what this would've looked like in 2012, instead of two people moving as one, gracefully swirling around the room, she remembered it being something more akin to two apes grinding against each other while the sounds of Pitbull pulsed in the background.

She basked in the simple beauty of this moment, Alice and Freddie moved so easily together. He held her tight to him, looking deep into her eyes singing along with the song,

"With all your faults, I love you still." She sang jokingly.

"It had to be you, wonderful you, it had to be you." Freddie said, and placed his hand under her chin and kissed her. There was a cough from the doorway, they all turned to see that Charles had entered the room, Freddie moved to separate himself from Alice, but she held tight to him.

"Brother, we survived a war. I'm celebrating" She waved Charles' off before giving Freddie a quick peck on the lips and returning to dancing. The look of comical disdain on Charles' face sent Elizabeth into a small fit of laughter. When she opened her eyes after laughing she found a hand out flat in front of her.

"Mam?" Lennie bowed slightly as she took his hand. The music had sped up and the two couples were flying around the room. Charles stood against the wall watching, his eyes glued to Elizabeth. The joy in her face as she was whipped around the room was refreshing to him. That type of bright optimism wasn't something he was accustomed to seeing in the past few years since the war began.

"May I cut in?" Charles said, tapping Lennie on the shoulder.

"She isn't the only girl here." Lennie argued.

"The other one is my sister," Charles raised his eyebrows proving his point.

"Who said he wanted to dance with me?" Elizabeth chuckled and placed Lennie's hand in Charles'. Lennie admitted defeat and replaced his hand with Elizabeth's, and went off to cut in on Freddie and Alice.

The two flew around the room, moving quick and easy to the fast paced lyrics of the Andrews Sisters. Elizabeth was clumsy, but with his arm around her waist she felt like she didn't need to worry, if she fell he would catch her.

"Whoa, Charlie, slow down. You're making me dizzy." She said as he spun her back into him.

"Charlie?" He wasn't used to being called Charlie. Lately it was always Charles, Cadet, or Cadet Finely.

"Ya, Charlie." Elizabeth clarified and smiled as he spun her back out. After a moment the music slowed and the sweet sound of Sinatra swooned out of the radio. Charles wrapped his arm around her waist pulling her in tight and they moved slowly around the room. As they swayed Elizabeth became lost in the moment, and the music triggered a memory she had from the future. She remembered her music shelf at home, covered top to bottom with records she had stolen from her grandparents or purchased at second hand stores. She smiled realizing that there was finally something she knew about and loved the 1940s, and that was the music. Not fully thinking she let herself get caught up in the music and began singing.

"Won't you tell him please to put on some speed. Follow my lead, oh how I need someone to watch over me." Elizabeth rested her head on Charles' shoulder, reminding herself to add the music and this moment with him to her pros column.

Charles listened as she continued humming to herself. When the music stopped he looked at her and smiled.

"What?" She exclaimed defensively.

"Surprised is all." He said, and she looked at him with little understanding. "You seem to not know much, but you sure knew that song." Elizabeth tried her best to keep her cool.

"I may not be from around here, but music is pretty universal. My mom raised me right. Grew up with all the classics, Nat King Cole, Frank Sinatra, Ella Fitzgerald, and the Beatles."

"The Beetles?" He gave her a confused look. "Like a bug?"

"No, Beatles, like B-E-A-T." She corrected, his confused look transformed into a pondering thought. "Beatles, like rock and roll, Hey Jude, Back in the USSR, Revolution, I Am The -" and then it hit her.

"They're British. The world is gonna love them." Elizabeth said as casually as possible trying to brush off the comment. She was so angry with herself for making such an obvious slip. To her relief Charles asked no further questions, and changed the subject.

"Alice said you weren't sure how long you would be staying? She mentioned that you talked about leaving soon." There was a gleam of hope in his dark deep eyes, and the look in his eyes hit her heart like a freight train. Elizabeth quickly ran through her pros and cons list in her mind seriously thinking over her answer, after a long pause she said,

"Actually, I think I may hang around. At least for a little while longer." The two shared a relieved and pleased smile before they went back to twirling around the room.

When the boys had left Elizabeth returned to her room. She opened the drawer and pulled out the watch, and then she shoved her hand under her pillow to find the watch and notebook. Sitting on the bed she passed the watch between her hands as she read over her pros and con list. When the watch moved from her left hand to her right, the writing on the back caught her eye. *Be Wise, Be Careful, Be Brave.* She took it as a sign.

"I'll watch my mouth, I'll be careful of the butterflies, but I won't let this opportunity go out of fear. This is my adventure and I'm taking it." She made this promise to herself before carefully placing it in the dresser along with her newspapers, flapper dress, and pros and cons list and shut the drawer.

Chapter 5

A few days later, Charles showed up on their doorstep promptly at 8:00am.

"Charles?" Alice was confused to find it was him knocking rapidly on the other side of the door. "What are you doing here?"

"There was a family emergency," Charles said with uncertainty before he stepped into the house.

"Is everyone okay?" Alice's attention piped up. "Is it Mom? No, Dad?" Alice was starting to panic. She was frantically running around the house looking for her coat to follow her brother to their parents house.

"I'm kidding Ali. Today is my scheduled leave." While he spoke, Alice caught him eyeing up Elizabeth in the sitting room.

"You can't be serious." She grabbed Charles by the arm and dragged him into the kitchen. "Can we all leave the poor girl alone? She just got here, running from who knows what, she may still be concussed from her fall," to Charles it sounded like she had already rehearsed her list of excuses to why he should leave Elizabeth alone.

"She doesn't need one more person, ugh, Lennie was already here this morning, she shot him down. Why would she go with you?" Alice said exhaustedly.

Out of the corner of her eye she spotted Elizabeth walking in their direction. "I'm not sure I would classify Elizabeth as a family emergency, you shouldn't lie to your captain. Go to work." Alice over exaggerated and pushed him towards the door in hopes Elizabeth would shoo him away too.

"I have to say Alice, I disagree. I would classify an adorable creature falling into your lives as an emergency worthy of a day off of work." Elizabeth said, as she casually entered the entryway. "In my personal history, I've skipped out on work for less than that." Elizabeth mumbled and crossed to sit on the stairs to look at the two of them. Charles chuckled and nodded good morning to Elizabeth.

Before Alice could protest any further, Charles had stepped back out onto the porch and reached for something laying on the ground. Alice took the opportunity to quickly shut and locked the door behind him.

"Hey, Alice!" Charles called out through the door.

"Good. Now." Alice ignored him and turned quickly, which caused her auburn bob to continue to bounce back and forth around her face. "As much as I would love to stay, I am off to work. I'm sure you'll be just fine, but if you need anything please - "

"I don't need anyone to look after me. It's okay. I'm okay." Elizabeth said, and gave Alice a reassuring smile. "I'll mill around the house for a while, and maybe go to the corner store, or heck maybe I'll find a job." Alice started to open her mouth to speak, "but I can find my way back, don't worry. I have the key you gave me. I'll be fine." Elizabeth reached to unlock the door to shoo Alice out just like she had done with Charles. Through the door Elizabeth could hear Alice and Charles still bickering on the porch, after a minute the voices were muffled as Alice dragged Charles away from the house.

Once Alice had gone Elizabeth retreated to the living room again. In the silence of the living room she had realized how much she relied on technology everyday, from scrolling mindlessly through her phone, or watching the TV, or simply having it on for background noise. She turned on the radio and walked around the room a couple of times, looking at the pictures and singing along to the slow tunes. Not sure what to do with herself, she repeatedly paced back and forth between the kitchen and living room until eventually she admitted defeat to the couch.

Half an hour had passed as she lay draped over the couch, Elizabeth knew that if she was going to stay she needed to find a form of entertainment. Then she was struck with an idea. She quickly slipped on a pair of sneakers, her jacket, keys, and stepped out the door.

When she stepped onto the porch she felt crunchy-squish below her foot. Elizabeth looked down to see a small bouquet of white daisies laid at the foot of the door. She quickly looked out to the street, swinging her head left and right searching for who left the flower delivery. She peeked gently through the petals and stems looking for a card, but there was nothing to be found.

"Cute." Elizabeth said and took a sniff of the flowers. She ran through the various possibilities for the flower's origin.

"Freddie for Alice is very likely, they're cute. Also equally as likely they could be from Lennie." Elizabeth scrunched up her face. "He did say he'd be back after I sent him away." She looked around half expecting to see him hiding in the bushes. "They could be from Charlie?" She questioned aloud and a small smile started to bloom across her face. With a shrug she tucked the flowers under her arm and continued on her mission to find entertainment.

Elizabeth had been through town with Alice yesterday, but when she was alone it was different. She took the time to notice each and every miniscule difference. She had grown up listening to her grandfather tell stories and share his collection of historical documents of the Cape post-war, but she had never expected to see it like this, crisp and new.

"I wish I could tell him. I wish I could tell everyone." She stood looking in a shop window and chewing on the inside of her cheek, deep in thought. "Ugh, they'd never believe me."

Though she was staring absentmindedly she caught the reflection of someone driving fast behind her and then they suddenly hit the brakes and veered into a nearby parking spot.

"Oi! Charlie." Elizabeth called out when she spotted Charles getting out of his car across the street. Not thinking she dashed out into the street.

"Elizabeth!" Charlie screamed. Quickly he stepped out, grabbed her by the wrist and yanked her off of the street as a car went rushing through where she had just been.

"Damn!" Elizabeth loudly exclaimed, even though she was muffled by Charles' chest, where he had caught her when he had pulled her onto the sidewalk. The two sat uncomfortably for a moment, the both of them catching their breath. "You can let me go now Charlie."

"Oh. Yeah." He let her go, slipped his hands back into his pockets and watched her while she fixed her hair and skirt.

"Thank you," she said, "again. I told you I was clumsy. But I'm lucky I've got you to save me." Elizabeth winked. She turned away from him, suddenly ashamed and panicked. *Did I just wink at him? You aren't a good flirt, Elizabeth. Ugh. Stop.* She thought to herself.

"You got my flowers I see." He tapped her on the shoulder and nodded at the daisies still in her hands. He had a nervous look in his eyes and Elizabeth's small smile from the thought of Charles bringing her followers earlier bloomed once more across her face.

"You should really leave a note next time. I wasn't sure if they were for me or Alice."

"Who would be giving flowers to Alice?" He sounded genuinely puzzled.

"Uh, Freddie?" Elizabeth responded dumbfounded.

"Nah." Charles shook his head and tucked his hands into his pockets.

"Yah," Elizabeth said, matching his dismissive tone.

Charles stopped in his tracks confused, thinking over the situation. "I mean they flirt but," he then stopped and shook the idea out of his head.

"I'm new here and likely slightly concussed, but even I figured that out." Elizabeth shook her head in shock. "They fit, the two of them. Like peanut butter and jelly, Jim and Pam, Sonny and Cher, Ross and Rachel," Elizabeth tried to list off famous duos she could think of completely forgetting that most of these duos didn't exist.

"Who?" Charlie asked.

"Nevermind." Elizabeth said when she realized her mistake. "They are good together. Have you ever just fit with someone? Where it all comes easy?"

Charles stood on the sidewalk still trying to accept the relationship between his friend and sister. "Nah." He said with finality.

"Where are you off to?" He continued to walk down the street.

"I was actually headed to the library." She explained.

"Would you like some company?" Though Charles had his hands in his pockets Elizabeth could he his hands tighten nervously.

Typically Elizabeth didn't like to be accompanied to bookstores or libraries. She didn't like the pressure of being rushed or judged. She'd prefer to be alone rather than inconveniencing someone with her idle book selecting process. But Charles looked at her with such fascination and nerves that it gave her butterflies. "You can accompany me if you'd like."

"Did you want to drop the flowers off? I don't mind circling back." Charles asked while he watched her struggle to find a comfortable way to hold them.

"No." Elizabeth said confidently once she had them nestled in the crook of her elbow. "I am going to carry them. I want to show them off."

Charles looked at her curiously.

"You probably find this hard to believe but no one has ever given me flowers before." When she said it she felt rather sad. "Well, unless you include my parents who gave me some after I was in a play in middle school, but those weren't from a dashing gentleman, so those don't really count." When she spoke Charles' cheeks turned a gentle pink. Elizabeth felt a bit of joy when his face went flush.

They weren't far from the library when they had met, so within minutes they were already there.

"Are you looking for anything in particular?" Charles asked, while he eyed up a section in the distance.

"Not really. I was just going to look around." Elizabeth watched him look off in a direction opposite from where she was interested in heading. She knew he didn't want to be rude, and she so badly wanted to know what he was interested in, but her urge not to be an inconvenience to anyone got the better of her. "If you have a section you want to go to, by all means don't let me stop you. I'll find ya." He nodded and the two took off in separate directions.

Elizabeth wound her way through the shelves at a snail's pace. The collector inside her leapt with excitement every time she'd stumbled across an original copy. She stared in awe at the original covers and crispness of the pages. She skimmed through each of them so gingerly, in fear of wrecking the antique quality of the book. Then she had to remind herself.

"Oh shit! Of course they're original, dummy." Elizabeth remembered her situation and cursed at her idiocy.

After almost an hour of perusing, she reached the section that had stolen Charles' attention. She found him leaning in the frame of a window. He leaned against the windows edge, with his ankles crossed, with one hand holding the book, the other tucked causally in his pocket, only taking it out to flip the page. His eyes were steadily moving over the page, completely transfixed by the words. Elizabeth almost dropped her collection of books at the sight of him.

"Daymn." She whispered. "This might be the sexiest thing I've ever seen." She stood a moment waiting for him to notice her but he didn't flinch.

"What did you find?" Elizabeth said as she nosed forward towards him trying to spy on the book in his hand.

"You found a few, I see." Charles said and quickly tucked the book behind his back, and Elizabeth caught a glimpse of shame in his eyes. He changed the subject when, one-by-one, he grabbed the books off of her pile asking questions about each one. "So you're a reader huh?"

"I could say the same about you." Elizabeth said and she reached around behind him and found the book he had kept hidden. "The Hobbit!"

"I just found it, the cover looked interesting." He feigned disinterest.

"Just found it huh. Seems to me," she spotted a small paper bookmark labeled CF hidden in its pages, "You've read it before."

Elizabeth teased by slowly pulling at the bookmark.

"Don't lose my page!" Charles called out urgently. He went on to mumble something about the boys making fun of him, nonsense fantasy worlds, and lack of pictures.

"I loved the Hobbit." Elizabeth confessed once he had finished his thought.

"You've read it?" Excitement filled Charles' tone. At her words his face lit up like a bulb.

"Totally. I read it in gr-" she caught herself. "In the last, recent, years?" She had read it back in grade six, but she had no idea when the book had been actually published. "Recently." She said with a nod.

"It's a really fascinating story right! I am really liking the trolls and the 'music', well I have an idea of what it should sound like, but-" Charles rambled on for minutes, showing Elizabeth different parts of the story he was so fascinated by. Elizabeth listened diligently, smiling ear to ear, thinking about how excited he would be to know the movie was coming out in the year she had just left.

"Charles Finley, you're a geek."Elizabeth said with her mouth a gape.

"A what?" Charles furrowed his brow in confusion, unsure if he should be offended or not.

"A proper 1940's geek." Elizabeth stared at him in wonderment. He said nothing, still confused. "It's cool. Me too."

"What's a geek?" He asked again.

"A geek is like a nerd. Sort of." Even though she was explaining, he still had a hazy look in his eyes. "It's different for different people, I guess. I've been called a geek derogatorily, but it's kind of a badge of honor. To like something enough that you know everything about it is pretty impressive. For me, a geek is someone who is passionate about things of the science, math, science-fiction, fantasy genre. But you can really be a geek for anything." Elizabeth explained and took a breath, and Charles simply nodded. "Now I'm a geek for books, like Agatha Christie," she pulled one from her pile, "Hercule Poirot, be still my heart. Or anything fantastical, dragons, dystopian futures," she paused a moment and she tested the waters, "time-travel," he didn't flinch. "But I was never a full geek for Lord of the Rings, watched them, loved them, but never read them. If you like this though, oh my boy, you are in for it."

"Huh?" Charles finally caught something she was rambling on about. "Lord of the Rings?"

"I mean, I heard he is writing more. Apparently they are going to be really good." Elizabeth ended the conversation and started to pick up her collection of books.

"Do you want some help carrying all that?" Charles said, watching Elizabeth struggle as she stacked book on top of book on one arm, and then neatly tucking two more under her other arm, all while still gingerly holding her daisies in her hand.

"Nah. I've got it." She said while making a face trying to balance everything she had, while she tried to open the door to exit the building.

"But how will you carry all of that, plus ice cream?" Charles asked with seriousness and cocked his eyebrow.

"Ice cream?" She questioned and Charles nodded.

"If you'd like." He offered out an arm in hopes to receive books.

"You sir know the way to a girl's heart." She didn't give him any of the books, instead she dropped The Hobbit back into Charles' hands, "you should sign this one out."

"The boys are going to-"Charles began.

"Screw 'em," Elizabeth said matter of factly, and Charles stood still contemplating her as she walked towards the front of the library.

While they walked from the library Elizabeth explained her love of Hercule Poirot, his glorious moustache, and how she had made it a goal to read all of Agatha Christie's books in her lifetime. "I knew they were old, like 50s or 60s, but I didn't know they were this old." Her words caused a confused look to flash across Charles' face, but Elizabeth's eyes popped wide for a moment but she continued hoping to brush it off. "I like the era they are written in, it's a little bit of historical fiction, plus I always try to figure it out before it's revealed."

"And do you?" Charles asked.

"Rarely. But if I could figure it out easily it wouldn't be any fun to read now would it." When she spoke she had a glow about her, and Charles noticed and he hung on her every word.

"You'll have to let me borrow them when you're done. I need to hear about this beautiful moustache." Charles requested and Elizabeth nodded in agreement and twirled an invisible moustache with her mostly free hand and they both chuckled.

Charles held out an ice cream cone to Elizabeth and she paused, trying to figure out how to hold her books, flowers and ice cream all at once.

"Now you have to let me carry some of your books." Charles demanded this time. "For the safety of your ice cream."

"No, I got this," Elizabeth said and fumbled some more before she sighed. "For the safety of the ice cream." Elizabeth agreed and plopped half of her collection into his open arm. "I'll need to remember a bag next time."

"Or I can come, carry them for you again." Charles offered tentatively.

"You don't have to do that. I can handle it myself, I just need to be better prepared. I wonder if Alice has a tote bag." Elizabeth was thinking out her plan and Charles let out an almost unnoticeable sigh and then Elizabeth spotted the disappointment in his eyes.

"My siblings are all older than me," Elizabeth suddenly felt the urge to explain. "and we never really had much in common. By the time I was 10 they had already moved out, and my parents both worked. So I've gotten really good at getting by alone, unless it's financially, financially I am a disaster, but that's something else." She stopped her thought to chuckle at herself. "Honestly, I don't like relying on other people for stuff, I always feel like I am inconveniencing them."

"You could never inconvenience me, I mean -" he stammered trying to find the words, "you let me carry your books." Charles reminded her optimistically.

"Well you did demand it," she began, "and threatened the life of a poor innocent ice cream. I couldn't say no, not that I wanted to." There was a silence in the building that made Elizabeth feel uncomfortable, she felt like she still had more to say. "I guess what I am saying is I've always been pretty good at being responsible for myself."

"Well maybe you need to let someone else be responsible for you too. To lighten the load." His words stopped Elizabeth in her tracks, there was something unspoken behind them. For the first time Elizabeth felt seen.

Chapter 6

Almost a month had gone by since that very first night when Elizabeth had tucked away the pocket watch. Every morning she woke up and had to remind herself that she wasn't dreaming, and she really was living in 1945.

She had settled into her new life easily. Every morning her and Alice would sit and have coffee before Alice rushed off to work. During the days Elizabeth would walk through town looking for work; before she left 2012 she had begun schooling for her teaching degree. On her fourth day she stopped in at the local schoolhouse and after casually saying that she was new in town and that the Finley's had sent her, she had scooped up a small position assisting in the classroom.

"Lucky to know that some things don't change, getting a job is still about who you know." She said as she successfully marched home that day.

Every night when they were both home, Alice and Elizabeth sat and discussed any crazy injuries or diseases that came into Alice's clinic, and gossiped about the people around town. Charles would visit the two of them daily, to fix things around the house or to simply sit and chat. And like clockwork at 6 pm, every night, Freddie and Lennie would show up on the doorstep to discuss dinner. Quickly she grew close with her little group of friends.

Alice had taken her on as a sister, sharing clothes and townie gossip. Freddie took the time to teach her how to drive stick and cook a proper italian lasagne. When Lennie wasn't trying to woo Elizabeth, he looked to her as a wingman. She'd helped him catch the eye of eligible ladies and she had mastered the alley-oop with his military pick up lines.

And Charles was something else entirely. He was military regimented and a complete geek before the term had even been created. Daily he'd bring over a new book or record as a gift to Elizabeth. They'd have long conversations about books, music or radio programs. Charles would try to joke with her, though he rarely understood her quips. He'd challenge her opinions and sarcastic attitude, and when no one was looking he'd let his eyes linger on her face for slightly too long after she laughed. He never pushed Elizabeth to explain her past, but he was always willing to listen.

Though her time in 1945 had been short, she had developed a life there. She had a home, a job, and friends who felt more like family than any family she had back in 2012. Slowly over time she woke up in the mornings and didn't have to remind herself that her life now wasn't a dream.

Each night she would slip her notebook out from its hiding place in the drawer and she would write about her day. The journal simply started as a way to track her journey. She knew that when she went home, if she went home, she would have wanted to have some proof that she was here, some way to remember her adventure in time - even if no one would ever believe her. She filled the notebook with stories about her new found friends, their adventures, and her wonderment with the 40s; It all started out pretty simple.

September 25th, 1945

This still doesn't feel quite real. I keep catching myself listening to see if someone on the outside of my coma is calling to me, but nope. I'm super happy about it.

September 30th

OH! Freddie and Alice are 100% sleeping together. They play it like they aren't but they are - I will write to confirm again later.

Also, Lennie could be transplanted to 2012 and fit right in. Last night at dinner, AFTER I tried setting him up with our waitress, he asked me on a date 11 times. It was 10 and then I was a smart ass and said '10 times that's just not enough, once more and I'll say yes.' This may never end.

October 1st

Charlie and I went to the library yesterday. He also got me flowers and ice cream. Is this what it is like to be wooed or courted? I feel like a teenage girl.

Charles, Charlie with a butt that sailed a thousand ships - I don't think that is the right quote but it's accurate because he is a naval officer and his butt is outstanding. Plus he is like the perfect nerd. Yesterday he called just to tell me about a radio drama he heard a few years ago he'd thought I'd like. He didn't know how to find it again, so he gave me a run down. It was War of the Worlds - I knew it. We talked for an hour.

I like it here, I like him.

October 3rd

I'm still here in 1945 AND I got a job today! It's kind of cool, I mean it's literally the same job I would've had in 2012. Did I mess this up? I should've taken the opportunity to be something else? It's 1945, can I be something else? I need to do some research.

I just feel like I need to do something to help out Alice. She took me in with no questions asked, she clothed me, fed me and I can't just freeload off of her. Honestly, if I was living with a stranger in 2012 I'd be murdered and on the news by now, but Alice is wonderful. I don't know what urged her to bring me in but damn I'm grateful.

Eventually her stories turned from fascination filled anecdotes to paragraphs of worries about her actions and its effects on the future.

October 10th,

What if I'm not supposed to be here? I haven't really questioned it before, but something has been nagging at me.

I was out with Alice and Charlie a few days ago. We were leaving the cafe and Charlie put out his elbow for me to take. He still hasn't let go the day I ran across the street and almost got hit by that car. We were laughing and I saw some old lady watching us.

This little old lady, with this long gorgeous grey hair - an icon look, note to future Elizabeth for when you go grey - she was following us down the street. Alice and Charlie turned to go into the corner store and when I went to follow them a door opened, smacked me in the face and I hit the pavement hard.

Now Alice says this didn't happen, but it feels too real to not be real. That little old lady who was watching us came to help me. But she didn't help me, she just crouched down next to me and stared at me, she had these really old greying eyes that burrowed into mine. She said, 'You can't do this. You shouldn't be here.' I remember trying to sit up but she pushed me back down, then she said 'someone always gets hurt, go back to where you belong before it's too late.'

I asked about Charlie and then all of a sudden he was just there, appearing like magic. Alice said I was pretty concussed and I asked where the old lady went and she said there wasn't one. She said they watched me hit the door, then my head hit the ground twice, so clearly I was imagining it.

But it felt real. I spent all day going around town looking for her, but I came up empty. I have a bunch of theories, all of them are ridiculous. That crazy coma idea from when I first got here is feeling more and more realistic.

Each night when she tucked her notebook back away into its hiding place, she would see the watch glistening on-top of her white dress, but she never felt the itch to spin the dial and go home.

That isn't to say Elizabeth never used it. The first time she used it for personal reasons gave herself a stern lecture.

She stood in the mirror fiddling with her hair when she realized she was going to be late for work at the school. She was about to run out the door when it hit her.

"Nothing big. The watch says to be wise. But honestly, I have phenomenal cosmic powers right now and I have been so well behaved. A little punctuality check won't hurt." Elizabeth said to reason with herself.

Since then she used the watch twice more for other minor fixes. Once on September 30th undoing a hole she accidentally put in the wall after tumbling down the last two stairs on the staircase, and the last time was on October 15th when she prevented a disastrous kitchen fire of her own doing.

"Will you let me cook you dinner?" Elizabeth pleaded with her friends on the evening of October 14th. They nervously exchanged looks of concern. "It's the least I could do after you have taken me in and made me feel so welcome. I want to give something back."

"Well the very least you could do is let me take you out to dinner. Let me take you on a date and we will all be grateful, then you'd let me take you home, and I'd treat you right. I'm sure you'd be grateful too." Lennie boasted which elicited an audible groan from the others. With a nod from Alice, Freddie walked behind Lennie and bopped him on the head.

"Yeah, you should let him take you out, we'd all be grateful." Charles said disgruntled and a stunned silence filled the room. "It'd make him finally shut up about it."

"Sorry, you're right." Elizabeth nodded to Lennie, and out of the corner of her eye she could see Charles' eyes filled with panic, and his hand tightened around his water glass. "That really is the least, bare minimum, bottom of the barrel thing I could do. And I'd still rather do this instead." Lennie let out a defeated chuckle. "You should try the girl at the diner, she swoons everytime you walk in."

"That's no fun. Where is the chase?" Lennie said.

"Maybe you shouldn't chase women. If they are running from you, they probably don't want to be caught." Elizabeth jested.

"Let the dream go." Charles added quietly and loosened his grip on his glass.

"I feel the need to also inform you, that I am not above smacking you, right across the face, if you keep pushing this." Elizabeth said with finality.

"Is she ready?" Alice said to change the subject and she looked at Freddie.

"No." Freddie said, and then quickly held up a hand to stop the pillow Elizabeth had thrown at him.

"Hey! The last time it wasn't burnt or undercooked and without the cottage cheese it doesn't smell like feet." Elizabeth defended herself.

"Stop talking." Lennie warned. "You really aren't building confidence here."

"Let her do it." Charles said. "How bad can it be?"

"It could be pretty bad." Elizabeth and Freddie said in unison. "But if it is bad-" Elizabeth continued, "I'll take you all out for dinner instead - the nice place downtown."

With that she had them convinced and the next day she went to the grocer and picked up everything she needed for a 5 star lasagne dinner. The gang gathered around 4 o'clock, to find Elizabeth standing confidently in the kitchen, her hair perfectly quaft and an apron causally wrapped around her waist, she told them she was challenging her inner 'Donna Reed' but none of them knew who she was.

Elizabeth was working frantically in the kitchen Lennie and Charles sat in the living room having a drink and listening to the radio, while Alice and Freddie paced back and forth by the kitchen door. Every 5 or 10 minutes one of them would pop their head into the kitchen to check on her, and everytime she would shoo them away,

"I've got this." She'd say to Alice, or "I'm a strong independent woman who doesn't need a man," she'd sassed when Freddie offered help. Every time someone went to check on her, she was slowly becoming more and more disheveled. Her hair had slowly gone from its perfectly coiffed bun of curls to frizzed out loose pigtail braids, and her perfectly white apron was streaked and stained with the blood of tomatoes and garlic.

While the four nervously sat in the living room listening to Elizabeth putter around in the kitchen.

"Someone should go in and help her." Alice said while she made her way towards the door again, but Charles stuck his arm out, grabbing her by the waist and pushing her back across the room.

"Leave her be." Charles said and took a defensive stance in front of the door.

"Why don't you go in and offer her help, loverboy." Freddie joked and caused Charles' face to go red.

"Excuse me?" Charles looked taken back.

"He's right, if she is going to accept help from anyone it would be you." Alice said.

"Why me?" Charles questioned.

"Don't play dumb." Alice said exasperated. "You two talk daily. For hours." Alice reminded him, but this seemed to be news to the others.

"Hey, we made a deal. We shook on it." Lennie said standing up offended. But when Charles opened his mouth to retort; but Lennie interjected to clarify "I mean, I asked her out and joked with her but she'd never actually say yes."

"Well I'll have you know Mr. 'why me' over there was here for 4 hours last night chatting her up on the porch about some weird book or other." Alice explained.

"Not that science-whatever radio show you've tried to get us to listen to." Lennie said. "Don't do that to her. She is pretty, smart and funny, don't make her weird."

"Well I'll have you know," Charles began mocking Alice's previous tone, "she was already weird and interested in that science-whatever stuff before I came along. She's a geek." A pleased smirk bloomed on Charles' face.

"A what?" Lennie was confused. Charles just waved it off not wanting to explain, and his cheeks went flush with enjoyment that he and Elizabeth had their own private joke. The two continued to loudly bicker over their promise to stay away, until Alice grew frustrated with their argument.

"Both of you just stay away like I said in the first place." Alice said in a harsh and demanding whisper, and then Alice turned to Charles with a pleading look in her eyes. "Please Charles, I love the girl too, I just don't want her to burn down my kitchen."

"Or poison us." Freddie added. "I've cooked with her, she tries her hardest, but it's not good."

A moment later there was a large crash, causing Alice's eyes to bulge in panic, then the door between the kitchen and the sitting room slowly swung open. Elizabeth calmly stepped out into the room to find them all pretending not to have heard the large cacophony moments ago.

"Dinner is almost ready." Elizabeth announced. She stood calmly folding down the edge of her apron that had popped up. "I just need a little bit of help, setting the table." The lie was obvious but no one pushed it.

"Charlie?" Elizabeth looked at him, her eyes almost filled with tears. Lennie rolled his eyes, and both Freddie and Alice nodded at him in an 'I told you so fashion.'

"My help?" Charles said feigning confusion before Elizabeth grabbed him by the wrist and yanked him into the kitchen.

"I don't want to disappoint Freddie, and I can't tell Alice, and Lennie is Lennie. And I trust you." Elizabeth instantly confessed the second the door had closed behind them and she looked at him with desperation in her eyes.

"Where do you need me, chef?" With that he rolled up his sleeves, and grabbed an apron off of the door.

"It's a disaster. All of it." Elizabeth was in shambles. She had begun to spin around the room pointing at everything which had failed. "The yorkshires are still in the oven, they won't poof. I would just google another recipe but I can't." She had been talking so quickly that she didn't hear Charles' comforting words. "And they are just sitting out there, waiting. It's making it worse. Ugh!"

Charles reached out, grabbed her by the shoulders to stop her from moving. He then placed his hands on either side of her face, focusing her gaze on him. Her cheeks squished under his touch, causing her distressed face to pucker adorably.

"Everything is going to be okay." He said stifling his laughter at the squished up look on her face. "How much time do you need?"

"An hour? I mean I've timed it all out. Dinner isn't supposed to be until 6 anyways." Elizabeth said while staring at the clock.

With a nod, Charles left the kitchen. "Leave." He told them firmly. "Leave, come back at 6, when dinner will be served." Alice opened her mouth to protest and Charles put his hand over her face. "Nope. You're leaving. Dinner was supposed to be served at 6 and it will be. But sitting here, listening and worrying isn't helping anyone." He threw their shoes and jackets at them and pushed them out the door.

"This is the plan." Elizabeth sighed with relief when he had re-entered the kitchen. She pointed to the counter where she had laid out bread, vegetables for a salad, and a device that Charles didn't recognize.

"What is that?" Charles said, eyeing up the beige pot-like device plugged into the wall.

"Slow-cooker." Elizabeth confirmed. "I bought it. Gift to Alice. You can cook anything in it, it'll just cook all day and you don't have to worry about it."

While Elizabeth explained, Charles inspected the device. When he lifted the lid a beefy-cheesy aroma filled the air.

"Smells good." Charles gave her a proud smile and she did a little triumphant fist pump in the air.

"And this is the back up plan." She swiveled Charles to face the kitchen table. On it sat a myriad of vegetables and baking powders. "I have lasagna in the slow cooker, and yorkshire puddings in the oven, which are being rude. But I don't think it's enough."

"Not enough?" Charles questioned, eyeing up the size of the lasagna.

"I typically cook for one, and the three of you eat like, well, sailors who have been starved at sea, and Alice can be such a picky eater!" Elizabeth complained. "I just want everyone to be happy. I don't want to let you guys down."

"You're not going to let anyone down." Charles reassured her. "Thank you for trusting me. Now why don't we do both?" Charles said, understanding Elizabeth's plight. "With the two of us we could have all of this done in half an hour?"

"Sweet, then we drink." Elizabeth joked.

"I'll peel, you cut?" Charles said and picked up the bag of potatoes.

The two worked easily together, tossing potatoes, dicing carrots, shaking salads, but they didn't let the time pass in silence.

"Have you finished the Poirot mystery I gave you?" Charles asked once they had developed a system. He had given Elizabeth a copy of *Death on the Nile* earlier that week and Elizabeth didn't have the heart to tell him she had already read it.

"Did you like it?" The light lit up in Charles' face again and he looked eager to discuss.

"My only issue with it was, nothing. It was perfect, start to finish." Elizabeth bragged. She knew it wasn't one of Charles' favourites based on the notes he had left in the margin.

"So which was more believable, Orient Express or Death on the Nile?" Elizabet egged him on, and the two tumbled into conversation comparing the realisticness of the plots, depth of the characters, and the big solve moment. 20 minutes later their simple discussion had turned into heated debate.

"It is more realistic that two people orchestrate a crime together, rather than a whole train worth of people." Elizabeth said, defending her stance.

"But the fact that every guest on the train was in on it; that made the Orient Express more monumental." Charles said and stopped stirring the gravy and frustratedly dropped his spoon onto the counter. "Plus everyone got off free at the end. Happy ending."

"By that standard, Death on the Nile is a happily ever after two, both of them died, murder suicide, no one convicted either." Elizabeth reminded him, and Charles stared her down frustrated with her correctness, but a smile still filled his face .

"You're going to burn the gravy." Elizabeth reminded him as he steamed at her logic. "Plus, I think I am just more of a boat person, easier way to lose the weapon." Elizabeth said while she added butter to the pot in front of her. "I'm right, admit it. You look as steamed as those veggies." She joked. "You know I wonder, how he is really a great detective if -"

"If he solves all the big mysteries and no one ever really knows?" Charles finished her thought.

"So why is he so great!" The two exclaim in unison.

"Maybe we just need to read more." Elizabeth said. "Library tomorrow?"

"I like having you here Elizabeth." Charles whispered in small confession.

"I like being here." Elizabeth said and bumped him with her hip.

"It's nice to have someone to talk about these things with." As he diced he slowly moved closer and closer in her direction. He placed a small kiss on her forehead and extended his arm to the other side of her. Elizabeth looked up at him and they lingered, eyes locked, bodies pressed closely together, lips inches apart.

"Heads up Liz." Charles said, breaking their moment, grabbed the pot on her left that was about to boil over. He moved behind her to strain the pot of boiling water.

"Damn it." Elizabeth whispered and cussed under her breath. "Wait, Liz?" Elizabeth said caught by surprise, Charles had only ever used her full name.

"You have a nickname for me. It's only fair I have one for you." Charles justified, and Elizabeth pouted slightly. "Well that's a double standard."

"I just like the way my name sounds on your lips. Elizabeth." She mimicked the tone in his voice when he spoke her name and her face turned pink with embarrassment. "I did not mean for that to sound so flirtatious."

"You sure?" Charles joked.

"Nope." Elizabeth said and started gathering kitchen scraps and throwing them into the trash trying to distract herself from her embarrassment of flirting.

"I get it though." Charles agreed. "I won't ever let anyone else call me Charlie."

"Just me, Charlie?" Elizabeth said to relieve his stammering embarrassment.

"Yes, just you Elizabeth." Charlie let her name slowly linger on his lips teasing her. Charlie moved closer to her, he slowly reached his hands out towards her. She was shorter than he was, so he had to crane his neck downwards to look her in the eye. Elizabeth's heart raced as his hands wrapped around hers and lifted them so her hands were draped over his shoulders.

"Oh shit!" Elizabeth squealed suddenly when steam from water boiling over on the stove broke their gaze. The two split apart, both of their faces flush with fliration.

"5:45," Elizabeth said after the steam had died down and she eyed up the clock and breathed a sigh of relief. "Wanna drink?"

Charlie reached towards the coffee maker, but Elizabeth shook her head, and pointed to the top shelf above the fridge. "Whisky or vodka?" Charlie asked, pulling them both down and brought them to the table and sat down.

"Why so worried?" He asked while he poured them a drink. "You know we all love you, and we don't care if you can cook."

Elizabeth sat down at the table across from him and casually tossed her feet up into his lap while she sipped on her vodka.

"Thanks for helping me today." Elizabeth said and she poked Charlie gently in the leg with her foot.

"Thanks for letting me." He placed his hand on her leg reassuring her. "It's nice to share the responsibility, right?"

"It's nice to have someone to share it with." Elizabeth leaned back, resting her head on the chair.

Their moment of reprieve was short. Minutes later the stomping feet of Alice, Freddie and Lennie came bounding into the house. Jumping up at the sound of the steps, Elizabeth passed Charlie the plates to finish setting the table. She leaned against the counter, tossed off her apron, and stared at the spread they had created.

"Charlie Finley, I could just kiss you." Elizabeth said in thanks with a sigh of relief, and rested her head against his shoulder.

"Sure." Charlie joked, completely unsure by what she had meant.

"What?" Elizabeth looked at him shocked.

"Huh?" Charlie said, playing as if he didn't hear her.

With the table set, Charlie lit the candles and welcomed everyone into dine. There was a savoury aroma in the air and beautifully crafted dishes of food lined the center of the table.

"This actually looks really good." Freddie said, unable to hide his surprise. They all settled around the table and Freddie took a moment to raise a glass. "To Elizabeth, we haven't eaten it yet, but it's already better than I expected."

"Is that a compliment?" Elizabeth asked.

"That's the closest thing that we can hope for from Freddie when it comes to Italian food." Alice assured her, and then raised her own glass. "And my kitchen is in one piece!"

Instead of raising his class, Lennie extended a hand, dishing a spoonful of the mashed potatoes onto his plate. When he reached to return the spoon, Lennie's hand bumped a candlestick.

After that the events escalated faster than anyone could handle. It played out like a tragic comedy scene, each moment worse than the one before. The candle dropped onto the table cloth which started a slow burn. Acting on instinct Freddie grabbed the nearest glass and threw it on the fire, but before Elizabeth could stop him, her small glass of vodka made the fire boom. Charlie reached for his, forgetting it was full of whisky.

"Charlie, no!" Elizabeth called out but she was too late, the table ignited further, spreading faster than they could handle. Elizabeth could hear the sound of cracking glass as the stemware and porcelain baking dishes began to crack.

"Nobody move!" Elizabeth yelled before she calmly walked out of the kitchen and up the stairs. Everyone stayed in the kitchen concerned, and watched her as she slowly excited.

When Elizabeth returned she had her watch in hand and dialed back to washaway the fire. While everyone moved slowly around her she crossed to the table and scooped out a piece of the lasagne, and then quickly popped it out of her mouth with a scowl on her face.

"Greaaat" she whispered in defeat. She contemplated going back farther to re-do the horrible tasting dish that sat on the table. "If I go back that far," she puffed out her cheeks, sighed and looked at Charlie, "I don't want to lose today."

Elizabeth slowly returned the time to minutes before the fire and returned to her position at the door.

"Nobody eats it." Elizabeth announced once the fire was erased. "I'm so sorry. It's so bad."

"How do you know? You didn't even try it." Charlie asked, and then he reached across the table with his fork towards the dish. Elizabeth quickly dove across the table, remembering to blow out the candles this time, and smacked the fork out of his hand.

"Trust me." Elizabeth begged them with her eyes. "Dinner's on me."

"What did you mix up?" Freddie whispered to her as they cleared the table.

"Salt." Elizabeth confessed, and then headed upstairs to return the watch while the others gathered their coats.

As she tucked the watch away, an annoying worry began to pick at Elizabeth's mind. *Did I do something wrong? I should've just redone it. I can't just pick and choose history, can I?*

Elizabeth stood with her back to the door, slipping the watch back into the drawer. "You have to be more careful. You don't know what this could be doing to the future." She retreated back to the bed, and nervously she picked at her fingernails and thought about the mirage old lady that told her someone would get hurt. Did she mean this? She grabbed her notebook to quickly jot down her feeling.

"Um, I would like to take you out to dinner. A proper dinner." Charlie's voice echoed out from the doorway and startled her. She was sitting cross legged on her bed scribbling rapidly, pouring her thoughts onto the page. "A dinner you don't have to cook. We could go to that italian place, or the diner with the great coffee." He paused and nervously played with the buttons on his shirt. "Just you and me."

"Charlie, are you asking me on a proper date?" Elizabeth joked and casually closed her notebook. Charlie's mouth did not smile at her joke, his lips held together in a tight line and he stood silent watching her every move. "Oh shit." Elizabeth whispered. "You're not."

In the future Elizabeth had dated a few people quite unsuccessfully. As Mary had often reminded her, she had a tendency to push others away. It wasn't because Elizabeth liked being alone, but because all of her romantic suitors left her feeling incomplete. But with Charlie he listened when she spoke, he challenged her sarcastic attitude, and never left her feeling like she wasn't enough, it was what Elizabeth needed. The sudden thought of him not feeling the same crushed her like a bug.

"I, uh, I think you deserve a meal where you don't have to cook. Maybe even something simple, like a picnic."

"A picnic is sandwiches Charlie, I can cook sandwiches."

"Can you though?" Charlie said, a small sarcastic smile breaking his face.

"Charlie Finley, did you just make a joke?" Elizabeth looked at him astounded.

"I know you're a strong independent woman who," he paused, "what do you always say?"

"Don't need no man." Elizabeth finished his sentence.

"Yes, but..." He lingered in the door frame unsure what to do. "If you do, maybe, I just thought that I could, maybe-"

"I would love to go to dinner with you, just the two of us." Elizabeth's words made a smile burst across his face.

"This next weekend? Sunday?" Charlie said, looking at the calendar beside the door.

"It's a date, Charlie." Elizabeth said, jokingly placing emphasis on his nickname.

"A proper date, Elizabeth." He planted a small and unexpected kiss on Elizabeth's forehead before the two of them slipped out the door, and headed out for dinner with their friends.

Chapter 7

The time began to slip by faster than a buttered bullet, and before Elizabeth knew it, a month had passed and it was October 21st. The weather had cooled, and leaves of oranges and reds blanketed the ground. That morning Elizabeth was making breakfast when she caught sight of the calendar.

"It's the 21st?" She was shocked after noticing Alice's red X's had almost filled the calendar. "I've been here a month? I am so sorry, I thought I'd be gone - " Her eyes were so wide it felt like they were going to pop out of her head.

"No apologies. I've really liked having you here." Alice chirped and walked past Elizabeth while she stared at the calendar.

"Why thank you, I am rather fond of being here as well." Elizabeth replied, squishing up her nose and smiling back at Alice before turning back to the calendar.

"What is going on? Why are you staring at the calendar like it is about to get up and run away?" Alice said, taking her coffee and sipping it at the table.

"Nothing really. It kind of just hit me how long I have been here." Elizabeth finally let her eyes drop from the calendar. "Honestly, I didn't think I would stay this long."

Elizabeth had thought that by now she'd have missed her life back in the future, but she didn't. And seeing all those days on the calendar overwhelmed her and caused her to start thinking that a month was easy so why not forever?

"Well, I am happy you stayed. It's nice to have another girl around." The two situated themselves at the table when a pair of feet began banging down the stairs.

"Were you feeling outnumbered Alice?" Charlie chuckled as he descended the stairs. "Alright, the upstairs sink is fixed. Anything else?" He crossed to the sink and began to wash the grease off his hands.

"Actually my dear, amazing, brother, my closet door squeaks and jams every time I open it. That's the last thing I promise." She asked, almost begging.

"Are you sure it isn't because it is overflowing with unworn shoes and clothes?" Elizabeth joked. "You should really throw some of that stuff out. I was in there the other day, and you have a box that says "Rarely Worn Underwear." I'm not judging, but honey you have a problem." She gazed at Alice over top of her coffee mug smirking.

"I just -" Alice was at a loss for words.

"Could admit you have a problem and stop being a hoarder." Elizabeth laughed.

"A what?" Charlie said. He always noticed when she used uncommon terms, but never really questioned her about them.

"A hoarder. Someone who can't throw anything out and keeps everything they have ever owned." Charlie let out an over dramatic gasp.

"Is there a cure?" He feigned concern.

"Yes, it's called -" she paused for dramatic effect, "a garbage can." The two caved into laughter.

"The next time you run out of clean underwear don't come complaining to me." Alice stood and marched out of the room.

"Happy one month of being here." Charlie said while he fixed himself a cup of coffee and took Alice's place at the table.

"How did you remember, I barely-" she shook her head in amazement. "I can't believe how fast the time went."

The two sat drinking their coffee and talking reminiscing about the day the papers took flight and she fainted into his arms. He told her about how much she had come out of her shell, and how well she has fit in since then. As they finished their coffee Charlie rose from his seat and scooped up their cups. In doing so he leaned towards her and made eye contact.

"I would like to restate Alice's comment, I'm really happy you decided to stay too." He lightly grazed her hand before turning to the sink and beginning to wash the dishes. When he touched her goosebumps shot through her body in a shivering wave. She watched him as he walked to the sink, her eyes distracted by his butt. Elizabeth shook her head to take herself out of her trance, stood and went back to looking at the calendar. Charlie snuck up behind her and rested his elbows on her shoulders.

"It's my birthday next Sunday." She sighed and Charles noticed a sad look on her face. "I'm not sad or anything, I just didn't expect to be spending my 24th birthday here."

"Have you told Alice?" He said, his voice getting giddy.

"No, why?" She turned and looked at him concerned.

"Alice loves birthdays, almost as much as she loves throwing birthday parties." Charlie raised his eyebrows with snarky joy.

"I don't want any fanfare for this. It's just a birthday." There was an excited, crazy look in Charlie's eyes as she spoke. "You're not telling her." Elizabeth panicked.

"Oh, I am." He headed towards the kitchen door. She ran and wrapped her arms around his waist trying to restrain him. He spun around, picked her up and placed her on the table. They stayed like that for a moment, eye to eye, him standing between her knees and his hands resting on her waist. Charlie's breathing stopped while Elizabeth's heart raced, not from the small bout of wrestling but from the look of intensity in his eyes. Her heart was pounding so loudly that she was sure he could hear it.

"Oh my!" Alice squeaked out at a whisper when she spotted them.

"Alright, so," He paused; staring into Elizabeth's eyes he completely forgot what Alice had asked.

"Closet." Alice chimed in from the edge of the kitchen, breaking up their moment.

"Yep." He said, taking off towards the stairs slipping on his way up two steps at a time.

"And after that could you paint the bannister?" She called after him.

"Ha! Nope!" He called from the top of the stairs.

"Worth a shot." She shrugged. "You know, since you've been here, my house has never been so well taken care of."

"Huh?" Elizabeth feigned naivety.

"Don't pretend like you don't know. My brother and I love each other, but I have a sneaking suspicion that I am not the reason he hangs around here all the time fixing things." She raised her eyebrows. Elizabeth tried her best to keep her smile under wraps, but it was quickly pushed away by doubt.

"I don't know." Elizabeth said nervously. "He used to be over here all the time to talk or he'd linger after dinner to listen to the radio, but now he's only here to fix things. I thought there was something there but now -"

"I think that's our fault." Alice cut Elizabeth off with her confession.

"Our?" Elizabeth asked.

"The night you cooked for us, Freddie, Lennie and I, may have poked fun at how much time the two of you were spending together. Jokingly calling him 'loverboy'."

"Oh." Elizabeth was defeated and confused. "I guess that's a relief, it wasn't me. But -" Elizabeth started to ramble through her confusion.

"It's clear you two are in love, you need to stop dancing around it and just be together already." Alice said definitively.

"Is it that easy?" Elizabeth asked, and Alice laughed at the naivety in Elizabeth's voice. But the confusion in her words was genuine.

"Have you never gone steady before?" Alice said leaning comfortably against the table, as if it was a regular evening and they were about to share some juicy gossip.

"Where I am from, you kind of just torment each other with your inability to properly communicate. Then we withhold our emotions, and act awkwardly around each other, too afraid to talk about our feelings, and mumble and stumble until something happens or nothing happens," Elizabeth explained as casually as possible.

"That's horrible." Alice sits with her mouth agape across the room.

"Oh it's the freakin' worst." Elizabeth confirmed exasperatedly and then began to ramble. "I'm a grown woman and I struggle saying my most basic feelings. But I don't know. Your brother drives me crazy, he just used my shoulders as an armrest. That's so annoying. How do you know if it's love when someone drives you absolutely crazy, but also when they put their hands on your waist it makes your heart want to leap out of your chest? He just makes me feel safe, and wanted and, well you all do but with Charlie-" Alice interjected Elizabeth's rant with a hug.

"Oh honey, you love him," Alice pulled back from the hug, keeping a hold of her arms. "Now please, you have to tell him, and put us all out of your awkward misery."

Charlie came bounding around the corner, and stopped when he saw them. "I didn't mean to interrupt ladies." He crossed across the kitchen and placed a kiss on each of their cheeks, "closet is fixed, but you do have a hoarding problem." He winked at Elizabeth. "And if you don't fix it Sis, I will send in Mum."

"Go home Charles." She turned him and pushed

him towards the door. His eye caught sight of the calendar on the way out. As Charlie was heading out the door, he quickly popped his head back in and called out, "Oh and by the way Elizabeth's birthday is on Sunday!" and slammed the door behind him.

"Strates Carnival!" Alice cheered. "The Strates carnival is coming to the pier next weekend! Don't argue Liz, it's happening!"

The afternoon before the carnival Elizabeth sat at home listening to the radio, she had been in her head since the incident with the fire, and was having a hard time finding her way out.

She walked past the bottom of the stairs and something caught her eye at the top. From where she stood she spotted Charlie standing in front of the dresser in Elizabeth's bedroom.

"Excuse me?" Elizabeth blurted out, turned on a dime and ran up the stairs two at a time. "What are you doing?" She tried to hide the panic in her voice as she slid into the room and right to his side.

"Nothing!" He responded, just as shocked and confused as she was. "I was fixing it." He had pulled the top drawer out of the dresser, neatly emptied its contents onto the bed and was fiddling with the drawer itself.

"Oh." Elizabeth panicked, praying silently that he hadn't touched the watch or journal. "Can I help?"

Elizabeth casually made her way to the bed and stood between him and her collection of future items.

"Nope. All done actually." He slid the drawer back into its place. "The wobbles are gone. See, smooth." He pulled the drawer in and out confidently demonstrating handy work.

Charlie crossed back to the bed and began to collect things while Elizabeth stood more confused than worried, she didn't remember a wobble in the drawer. Before Elizabeth had had a second to get out of her daze, Charlie had picked up her notebook. Elizabeth's heart stopped beating and her eyes bulged when Charlie quickly ruffled through the pages.

"I've got it." She snatched the book out of his hands. "This." She corrected trying to hide her panic. "I can put all of this away." She quickly tucked the book into the drawer. "I'm sure Alice has something else that needs fixing."

"Your book's almost full eh?" He let out a small chuckle. "You'll have to get a new one."

"And burn this one." Elizabeth whispered while she had her back turned to him.

When she turned back around the situation had only grown worse. Charlie stood closely behind her ready to hand her the rest of the things for the drawer, in one hand he had her dress and in the other the watch. His eyes were fixed on the watch, so he didn't notice Elizabeth's squeak of fear.

"This is beautiful." He handed her the dress, which she tossed over her shoulder carelessly. She reached a hand out for the watch.

He popped the front metal casing of it open to reveal the face of the watch. He gingerly ran his fingers around the glass admiring it. Not thinking he placed his hands on the dial and twirled it.

"No," Elizabeth screeched and grabbed his arm. They both stood watching the hands on the clock move forward and back, and forward and back, and finally resting at the original time.

"Sorry." Charlie said, placing his hand on hers that had rested on his arm. "Are you okay? You're acting strange. I mean when aren't you?" He tried to joke to break her grasp on him.

Elizabeth had gripped his arm so firmly her finger nails had left a mark, and her face had grown more pale than usual. Charlie gently closed the watch and handed it to her. "I'm sorry if I..." he paused to rub the place on his arm where her hand had been.

"It's an heirloom. I didn't want to -" Elizabeth managed to fumble out an excuse. She spotted the mark she left on his arm. "Sorry about that." She touched it gently and then nervously bit her lip.

"It's okay. No harm done." He placed his hand back on hers and held it there for a moment. They sat like that, silently hand in hand, for longer than would be considered normal.

"Hey, I'm not strange." Elizabeth said at last realizing he had poked fun at her.

"Well, I'll see you tomorrow." Charlie smiled.

"Tomorrow?"

"Carnival? Birthday carnival celebrations." He reminded her. He popped a kiss on her forehead and walked out of the bedroom.

Like a love struck teenager Elizabeth plopped back down onto the bed. When she landed on the bed the watch bounced out of her hand and onto her lap. She sighed in relief and tucked the watch into the pocket on her skirt. "Not letting you out of my sight ever again."

Saturday morning the five of them piled into Freddies car and set up the coast towards the famous Strates travelling carnival. As they drove Alice sat in the front fiddling with her camera. Every so often she would turn and try to snap a picture of Lennie, Elizabeth and Charlie in the back seat.

"Do you even know how to work that thing Ali?" Freddie jested.

"We will just have to see, won't we." She motioned for Elizabeth and Charlie to move closer together. He wrapped his arm around her and she rested her head on his shoulder. Before Alice could snap the picture, Lennie leaned in and planted a kiss on her cheek. Charlie swatted at him, pushing him back to his side of the car, but he left his arm around Elizabeth for the rest of the drive.

"Whooo! Carnival!" Elizabeth cheered when they came to a stop and finally got out of the car, Lennie and Freddie followed her lead.

"Have you ever been?" She asked, starting off towards the pier.

"Nope. First one." Lennie said, and looked at Freddie who nodded in agreement. "You?"

"Loads!" She was bouncing with excitement. "I go at least two or three times a sum-" she caught herself drifting into her 'future-speak' again.

Alice grabbed Charlie and pulled him back away from the group, she wrapped her arm in his as they walked.

"Charles. Brother. Charles." She struggled trying to find the words to calmly bring up the subject. "You have to hurry up and get her before someone else does."

She nodded towards Elizabeth as she spoke. Charlie rolled his eyes and attempted to shake her off, but she held on tight. "No, no, no. You are not getting out of this. I think we can agree that she is marvelous, strange yes, but marvelous. And the two of you have this unspoken thing but you're going to have to speak up." Charlie went to speak, but Alice gently tapped him on the arm to inform him she wasn't finished speaking yet.

"You have gone with a total of," she paused counting in her head, "two girls. Two girls six years ago. Clearly, you are no casanova, but she is perfect for you." He smirked. "You're shy, I understand that brother, but there is something about her. And I know you know it." She could see the agreement in his eyes, but the rest of his demeanor was still defensive.

"But, what if she is really only passing through? She could change her mind and leave. I finally somewhat have my life settled and I don't want someone who is passing through to ruin it." As he explained Alice saw the serious side of her brother that she had grown over these past few years. The side of him that always held him back.

"You lived through a war, your life has changed. Start fresh. Let someone shake up your new boring routine." He still seemed unconvinced.

Alice thought of how Elizabeth described her feelings for Charlie,

"Does she make you laugh?" He nodded.

"Does she make you mad?" He nodded.

"Does she make you want to be better?" He nodded. She looked at him with a huge grin filling her face.

"I'm not saying I know," her eyes grew big as she nodded, "but I know. All you have to do is something. Anything. How does Elizabeth say it, 'man up, and lock it down'." The two of them laughed and Charlie sighed, he knew she was right. He didn't want to admit it, but she was right. Charlie loosened himself from his sister's grasp and hurried forward to catch up with the others. He grabbed Elizabeth by hand and the two ran off in the direction of the rides.

The two worked their way through the carnival hand in hand. Every time they approached a ride, Elizabeth recounted stories of other carnivals she had been to and the dangerous rides she had been on, convincing Charlie that if she could handle that, he could handle this. If that failed, she would grab his hand with both of hers, and bat her eyelashes. Within a few hours she had managed to get him on every ride.

Between rides they would walk and talk about their lives, work, and family. As they neared the ferris wheel Charlie caught sight of someone at the end of the pier. The man was a few years older than they were and stood with an arrogance that Elizabeth did not like. Charlie grew rigid when he caught the eye of the narrow faced, black haired man. But before Elizabeth could ask what was going on Charlie had steered her back in the direction they came from, claiming he wanted to look for the others.

When they had found the others Alice was toting a large bear and at her side was Freddie, who was beaming and announcing to anyone who would listen that he won that bear for her. In turn Charlie cheered that he had been on every ride in the park, albeit with a little help.

He shrugged and wrapped his arm around Elizabeth. Alice raised her eyebrows in surprise, and shot a wink at Charlie as a reminder of how good she was for him. As they chatted they spotted Lennie standing amongst a group of younger girls. Elizabeth excused herself from her friends and marched over to the group and overheard the line Lennie was feeding the naive girls.

"We lost a lot of good men out there." He paused, wiping his eyes. Elizabeth had seen this routine often in 2012, a naive girl drawn in by a fake line accentuating the man's sensitive and emotional side. Lennie had stepped up his game this time, the addition of the tears was new. The girls asked questions about the front lines and if he had any scars, Lennie was answering faster and with more skill than a politician in a newsroom. Elizabeth couldn't help but chime in to push the conversation along.

"And where did you serve?" She called out. Clearly, with no forethought, he answered.

"The Cape." He knew his ship had sunk as soon as he said it.

"Were you on the USS Jacob Jones?" She knew Lennie was beginning to flounder and wanted to save him. Elizabeth spouted out some trivia she remembered from a highschool field trip.

"That was in '42, I didn't join until '43." Lennie spoke again without forethought. The girls scoffed and dispersed. Elizabeth came forward, wrapped her arm around Lennie and patted him sympathetically.

"You'll get 'em next time slugger." He scoffed at her encouragement. "Maybe you need to use a better line next time." He opened his mouth to object, but she stopped him. "Like, literally, anything but what you said. We'll work on it." She said through laughter as they reunited with the group.

When Charlie noticed the two coming back arms around each other, a spark of anger lit inside him. He quickly thought better of himself, jealousy was not something he liked to get wrapped up in. They chatted for a moment before there was a consensus of thirst. Charlie ran off with Alice and Freddie to find something to drink, and Lennie wandered off to another group of unsuspecting girls, leaving Elizabeth alone leaning against the pier railing. As soon as Charlie was out of range, the thin raven haired man from earlier slid up next to her. He leaned backwards, resting his elbows on the railing and introduced himself.

"I'm William, William Hanley. You must be new around here." Elizabeth watched him as he talked, he was exactly as arrogant as she thought he was the first time she caught a glimpse of him earlier. He went on to tell her that she had to be new because most girls around here swoon when they see him, and how taxing all the women flocking after him have been.

"Oh wow," she said sarcastically and politely, "that must be really difficult for you." He laughed jauntily. "Maybe if you didn't shove all of this," she gestured to all of him, "in people's faces you wouldn't have that problem."

"Oh, I like your attitude, making me work for it?" He stepped towards her, leaning in close. "That's alright, I am sure I can make you come around."

"Hey Char?" Freddie said to get his attention and pointed towards Elizabeth. Across the pier Charlie caught sight of William and Elizabeth. Charlie couldn't make out what they were saying but the spark of anger reignited and quickly burned like a bonfire inside him. He saw William attempt to wrap his arm around Elizabeth. She quickly sidestepped and caused him to stumble. Charlie began quickly walking towards them with Alice and Freddie jogging to keep up. William had moved in closer and closer to Elizabeth so that she was almost pinned between him and against the pier railing. Every step he took towards her, Charlie walked faster.

"Charles." Alice piped in, there was a concern in her eyes. "Don't do anything -" but before she could finish her sentence, he had taken off at a run.

"Oi!" Elizabeth said, pushing Willian off of her. "Douche, back the fu -" but before Elizabeth could fully get the words out of her mouth, a fist came flashing past her face colliding with William's nose. Freddie came in next and pulled Elizabeth out of harm's way, while Charlie and William's fists flew furiously. Freddie and Lennie attempted to stop it, but Alice held them back telling them to just let them tire themselves out. Elizabeth didn't understand what was going on, why wasn't anyone else as concerned as she was? She looked at Alice for help but she was wrapped tightly in Freddie's arms and the two had walked away.

Lennie took Elizabeth aside to explain the part of the situation she didn't fully understand.

"William and Alice used to go together, engaged even. He wasn't too good to her. They were together a long time, but when he started to lay his hands on her, she had to leave. He followed her for a while afterwards, but after we beat him within an inch of his life he let off." Elizabeth now completely understood why Alice had taken her in with no questions asked.

Charlie had William pinned against the pier railing. He looked up to see Elizabeth watching him with worry, and understanding. He lifted his fist one last time before knocking out William as it collided with his face.

There was a moment of shocked silence before Charlie turned back to Elizabeth. Blood poured down his face from his nose and the new opening across his cheek. His lips were split open and swelling. His left eye was already bruising and blood had pooled in the right one clouding over the beautiful brown she loved.

When she saw him clearly Elizabeth's heart ached like it was being pulled backwards through her chest. Time after time he had protected her, fainting, driving, crossing the street, catching her when falling, and now this. She wanted so badly to protect him this time, and suddenly the watch in her pocket felt noticeably heavy.

"I can." She exclaimed and shoved her hand into her jacket pocket. She felt the cool metal brush against her fingers. She fumbled for a moment before finding the circular at the top and firmly placing it between her thumb and forefinger. She locked eyes on the beaten and broken Charlie and began to spin the dial.

Suddenly the ferris wheel to the left halted and began to spin clockwise. In her peripherals she could see everyone slowly moving around her in reverse.

She moved back to her original position before she stopped reversing time. She caught sight of William moving towards her and instead of standing still she took off down the pier looking for someone she knew. But before she knew it, William found her again.

"No." She said as soon as he had approached. But it didn't stop him. She pushed him off of her and turned to walk away, but he grabbed her by the hand and pinned her against the pier railing, and then boom, Charlie.

"Son of a bitch!" She said taking her watch out and dialing back again.

She righted herself in her original position and started moving before William was even in sight. Sadly he found her again. No matter how hard she pushed, ran, maneuvered in another direction he always found her. On the seventh time back she tried a new tactic.

In the distance she spotted Lennie, striking out yet again. As she approached he slipped a flask from his pocket and took a long swig. When she reached him she extended a hand, grateful to see the flask. He handed it to her hesitantly, and she too took a long swig.

"Didn't take you for a drinker." He stared at her with his eyes wide.

"Depends on the occasion." She hesitated, she knew that she shouldn't drink because she needed to keep her wits about her, but she was grateful for the bite of alcohol to remind her she's in the real world. "Struck out again?" she nodded towards the girls across the way.

"Yes." He took the flask back and chugged the rest down. "You know, you should just give me a chance. It'd make my night!"

Elizabeth laughed. "Oh honey, that is never going to happen."

"Why not?" He took another drink.

"It's not you, it's me." Elizabeth giggled with her colloquialism, but when Lennie didn't laugh back she remembered it wasn't a common thing yet and she was lost in her futurisms again.

"What is that supposed to mean?" His tone was getting more and more aggressive. He leans in closer to her. "We'd be great together. You're alone and you need someone to take care of you. I know you say where you're from you don't need a man, but here you do, and I'm telling you that man is me." She wasn't sure if he was trying to sound romantic or pigheaded.

"No." She said again, rolling her eyes. "Not again. Please." Over Lennies shoulder she saw Charlie storming towards them.

"It's the least you could do." He grabbed her by the waist and forcefully pulled her towards him. He leaned in towards her lips, eyes closed. Elizabeth quickly took a step back as Charlie dove between them, this time his fists colliding with Lennie's cheek, taking him to the ground in one blow. Once Lennie was upright again, he and Charlie began to scream at each other.

Elizabeth didn't listen. Her thoughts were moving faster than the world around her. She turned and walked away from the arguing, she needed to hear herself think.

"Why can't I stop this? Why does he have to get hurt?" She demanded as she slowly put her fingers on the dial. Elizabeth was trying to pinpoint the exact moment she should stop to prevent all of this; but there wasn't one.

She watched Charlie and Lennie argue. There was no blood or no broken bones. She realized she had stopped it, he wasn't hurt this time. "I can leave it like this." She whispered. "He's fine." A relieved smile blossomed across her face, until she could hear them yelling about jealousy, selfishness, stabbing someone in the back, and their friendship being over.

"You're not doing this Elizabeth." She watched them yell at each other and she pulled the watch out of her pocket again and began to pace. "He's not hurt, but he would never be okay without Lennie in his life. But he deserves to be okay, no blood, no bruises." Elizabeth frantically moved back and forth across the pier. " No blood, no bruises, but no Lennie. I can't be the reason they aren't friends. Sure Lennie's a dick, but every group needs one."

With a sigh she returned to her original position and let the events replay as they were meant to.

Charlie had William pinned against the pier railing. He looked up to see Elizabeth watching him with worry, and understanding. He lifted his fist one last time, knocking out William as it collided with his face.

There was a moment of shocked silence before Charlie turned back to Elizabeth. Blood poured down his face from his nose and the new opening across his cheek. His lips were split open and swelling. His left eye was already bruising and blood had pooled in the right one clouding over the beautiful brown she loved.

"I'm sorry." He walked over to her, straightening his shirt and tie.

"You punched him." Elizabeth said, eyes wide and astonished. "Like, really punched him. Square in the face. Just, POW!" She couldn't form any other words short of the sound effects of William falling down onto the wood below.

She had seen this play out eight times now, and everytime he came to her rescue, before the cuts and blood, the only thing that left her wowed was his absolute drive to protect her.

Elizabeth stared blindly at the unconscious body on the dock. "Oh this is actually happening." She suddenly said surprised and slipped the watch back into her pocket, and looked at Charlie who was trying to wipe his hands clean of blood.

"Oh my god! Are you okay?!" She frantically rushed to his side, grabbing his hand. Alice motioned for the boys to follow her, leaving Charlie and Elizabeth alone.

"Ow!" He reacted to her squeezing. "I'm fine." He was clearly trying to hold the pain but in doing so also holding his breath.

"I'll just add this to the long list of times you've saved my ass." He chuckled and looked at her grateful eyes.

"I'm so sorry. There is just a history -" He bowed his head ashamed and leaned against the wooden pier railing.

"I know." She tore a piece of cloth from the bottom of her skirt and gently dabbed at a cut on his forehead. In her head she knew this was a cinematic cliche that she would've laughed at in the movies but she couldn't resist.

"Seeing him with you." He took in a sharp breath as she unskilledly poked at the blood, "I wasn't mad about what happened with Alice and him. I was jealous. I'm sorry, I shouldn't be jealous." He began to ramble, talking about how he doesn't want to be the jealous type, but the way she looks and the way she makes him feel took over.

Are you really going to be the damsel in distress cliche Elizabeth? The strong, independent, 2012 woman called out from the back of her mind. She took a moment and thought to herself, *it's 1945 and a handsome man just punched another guy in the face for me, my whole life is a cliche now.*

"You were jealous. So you punched him." She laughed lightly, a smile taking over her face.

"Not something I would suggest to others." He said, seeing the bruises starting to form on his knuckles.

"Right in the face." She re-lived it and punched her fist into her palm. Their eyes met and the look of sincerity in his eyes set her off.

"For me." She smiled before she grabbed him by the tie and pulled him in. Her lips planted on his and his arms wrapped around her, holding her tight to him. The kiss was too brief as he released her before pressing his hand to his lips and winced in pain.

"Oh my god. I am so so sorry!" She jumped up away from him, scared to make it worse.

"You're not the one who punched me in the face." He said laughing and taking her hand, pulling her back beside him.

"Well I did, I just gently punched your face with my face." Elizabeth began to joke uncomfortably.

"I blew it, didn't I?" Charlie said, but Elizabeth gave him a confused look. "The kiss. Alice wormed her way into my head and I - " She sat trying to think of a way to make it better, "Alice is an -"

Before she could call her an idiot, he had one hand behind her head, one wrapped around her waist lifting her up until their lips met.

"That's it. Right there." Alice said, snapping a picture of the two of them kissing in front of the lights of the ferris wheel. "That's love."

Lennie, Freddie and Alice stood across the way. Freddie stuck out his hand and Lennie placed a bill in it.

"Really? You bet on our friends?" Alice asked judgmentally. "And against them Lennie?"

"I didn't want to give up hope on Elizabeth and me." He shrugged.

"That was never going to happen." Alice laughed loudly and Lennie slumped off towards a pack of women on the other side of the ferris wheel. Alice then extended her hand toward Freddie.

"You disgust me." Freddie said, slipping the money into her hand and planting a kiss on her forehead.

The drive home was quiet. Freddie and Alice sat in front, hands intertwined. Lennie sat behind the driver, his head looking longingly out the window sad and defeated. Sat next to him were Elizabeth and Charlie, his arm draped over her shoulder and her head dozing against his chest.

It was nearing midnight when the car stopped in front of Alice and Elizabeth's house. Alice stretched and yawned before she gave Freddie a lingering kiss on the cheek and slowly dragged herself out of the car.

Elizabeth did the same, placing her lips on the only unbruised and battered place on Charlie's cheek.

"Good night boys!" She said to the others as she slipped out of the car and headed up the walkway, not noticing that Charlie filed out of the car behind her.

"I'm just going to see that they make it inside okay." He said as he shut the door.

"You have 5 minutes or you're walking home!" Lennie had jumped into the front seat and called at Charlie through the window.

"Hey!" He called before reaching out to grab Elizabeth's hand as she walked off infront of him.

"Yes, brother?" Alice turned. "Oh, not me." She quickly wheeled around and retreated into the house leaving Elizabeth and Charlie alone on the porch.

"Can I have a minute?" Charlie said and sat down on the front step, and gestured for her to sit down next to him. She dropped down next to him and he grabbed her hand gently.

"Um, Charlie. You're bleeding on me." She let out a gentle smile and pointed to the blood running off of his knuckles and on to her hand.

"Damn." he cursed and then slipped a handkerchief out of his pocket and dabbed at the blood.

Elizabeth quickly stood and raised a finger to indicate she'd be back in a minute, and then headed inside.

"Hey Alice, do you have any ice?" Elizabeth called out when she got inside. "Or medicinal tips? Charlie is sitting out there beaten like," she tried to think of something witty but came up short, "well like someone who kicked someone's ass tonight."

Elizabeth slipped into the kitchen she found Alice standing over the sink and Elizabeth was sure she heard a stifled sniffle. At the sound of her name the short bobbed head of hair slowly turned and gave her friend a small false smile. Elizabeth could clearly see a faded tear stream down the right of her face.

"Alice," Elizabeth hesitated, trying to find just the right words.

"You can ask about William. It's okay." Alice folded her arms uncomfortably across her waist.

"I'm not going to ask. It's not my business. But I am sorry you had to go through that."

"I always thought you knew, considering how you got to be here." Alice reminded Elizabeth and the two girls hugged each other tightly. Part of her always had guessed, but never truly knew what Alice went through, and it pushed Elizabeth to be a little more honest with her back story.

"I was running from something different, I think." Elizabeth knew that by comparison she hadn't gone through that many difficult things in her life, and running from an abusive husband wasn't Elizabeth's story and she had no right to pretend it was.

"I think it is the opposite. Now before you tell me I'm being 'cheesy,' whatever that means," Alice reached out and placed her hands firmly on Elizabeth's arms. "You know what, I'm not going to say it." She gave Elizabeth a cold cloth, bandages, disinfecting alcohol and a brief how-to-heal seminar, and then swivelled her around and pushed her towards the door.

"What? No, go get 'em tiger?" Elizabeth joked and stuck her tongue out at Alice.

"You're so very upright." Elizabeth said when she stepped back out onto the porch. Charlie turned on a dime to see her mimicking his proper posture.

"I don't think I could ever be that straight, it hurts my back." Elizabeth took her seat back beside him. "You got your ass beat tonight, you could relax, you know." Charlie let out a small sigh and tried to slouch unsuccessfully. Elizabeth placed the bundle of bandages between them, "I'm going to warn you I have no idea what I'm doing."

She took the cool wet cloth and wiped at the blood around his knuckles. She shook the bottle of alcohol onto the cloth and dabbed at the slowly bleeding hands, like Alice had shown her. Charlie flinched uncomfortably beneath her hand, but he didn't stop her. A silent moment passed as Elizabeth fumbled with the bandage trying to remember how Alice told her to wrap it.

"I should get Alice." Elizabeth said.

"No. You can do this." Charlie said, trying to instill confidence in her. She began to wrap his knuckles, she fumbled once or twice, unwrapping and re-wrapping as she went.

"I can do this, yes. But will it be right? Less yes. I just want to take care of you properly, and that means swallowing my pride." Elizabeth placed her hands on her knees to stand, but Charlie stopped her.

"I know medicine is not your gift. But this is." Charlie took the cloth out of her hand and left a perfectly wrapped rectangle in its place.

"That was smooth." A very impressed smile blossomed across her face before she quickly made work on the wrapping.

"I've been practicing." He said with a smug smile. "I wasn't fixing your drawer." Charlie clarified.

He leaned forward and placed his elbows on his knees. He nervously fiddled with the cloth, passing it from hand to hand. "I was going to give it to you on our picnic, but-"

"Oh fuck." Elizabeth cursed with her realization. "Our picnic. That was supposed to be today. A proper date. Fuck, shit, I'm so sorry." But her apologies were drowned out by Charlie's laughter.

"I love you Elizabeth, but that mouth surprises me." He laughed casually when he spoke, not hearing the words coming out of his mouth.

Not hesitating any more he placed his hand under Elizabeth's chin and pulled her lips to his. A shiver echoed through Elizabeth's body. She responded to his kiss by wrapping her arms around his neck and pulling him close to her.

This was their first private kiss, without the eyes of their friends or the random passersby at the carnival watching them, and neither of them wanted to let this moment pass.

Their lips moved easily together and with each touch the fire between them grew more intense. Her soft lips met the scars of the evening's battle on his, but neither of them hesitated. Elizabeth felt Charlie's tongue gently brush her lips asking, almost too politely, to move further, and before their lips met again Elizbeth's lips parted slightly and she felt the warmth of his breath meet hers. She pulled herself up onto Charlie's lap, moved one hand up into his hair and rested the other on his chest. He wrapped one arm around her back, running his hand over her, while the other held gently behind her head. Charlie's lips broke from hers for a moment before moving over her cheek and working their way to her neck. It was clear that their hands wanted to explore each other's bodies further but Charlie spoke before they could continue.

"Elizabeth -" Charlie said as he paused to catch his breath.

"Too much?" Elizabeth leaned back, resting her arms on his chest.

"God no." Charlie laughed, "It's just, I'm bleeding on you Elizabeth." Charlie said and he ran his fingers over the red stain on her neck and shirt.

"Damn." Elizabeth sighed.

"I should go," Charlie said, but neither of them moved, "and get cleaned up."

Disappointed but understanding Elizabeth nodded and stood. She crossed to the door, "I'm sure Alice is still awake, she can fix that up properly." She pointed at Charlie's wrist where her bandaging job hung loosely and ashamed.

"No. It's okay." Charlie stood one step down on the porch, slightly distancing himself from her. "I'll fix it when I get home."

"Oh. Okay." Elizabeth tried to hide her disappointment of his leaving but it was unsuccessful. "Well then I guess this is goodnight." She stood on the step above him so their eyes met. "Are you sure you don't want to stay? For a drink?" Elizabeth planted a baiting kiss on his lips.

"If I go through that door I don't think I'll be able to control myself." He whispered and gently tucked a loose strand of hair behind her ear.

Elizabeth quickly ran to the door, swung it open wide with a smash and gestured his way in, which caused them both to laugh. He held up a hand.

"I'm a gentleman, Elizabeth. A proper date first."
He winked, kissed her one last time before walking down
the steps.

"I both love and hate the fact that you're a
gentleman." Elizabeth called out to him.

"Me too!" He waved back and started his walk
home, smiling the entire way.

Chapter 8

After the fire that never was and the fight she couldn't reverse, Elizabeth became filled with more and more uncertainty about her staying in the 1940s. But everytime she looked at Charlie or heard him laugh in confusion at one of her jokes she pushed all of her fears away.

Shortly after the carnival the two set up their first proper date and Charlie promptly arrived on the doorstep at 11:00am the following Saturday.

"Hello brother." Alice said, swinging the door open. "Flowers? For me?" She laughed and tried to take the small bouquet of white daisies, and welcomed him into the house. As Elizabeth was slowly making her way down the stairs, she could see Charlie pushing Alice away.

"Don't be so nervous." Alice said before she left the room.

"You look beautiful." Charlie said when he spotted Elizabeth on the stairs.

"Why thank you." But before she could reach the bottom step, Charlie extended an arm, wrapped it around her waist and lifted her off the last step. She leaned against him and he slowly placed her on the ground.

"Ready to go?" Charlie said, taking a step towards the door, but not taking his eyes off of her.

"Oh hell ya." Elizabeth said with nervous excitement while she slipped on her shoes. He stood at the door watching her, and Elizabeth took a moment to take him in. He stood with his hands nervously resting in the pockets of his grey pants, but the rest of him was far from nervous. The top buttons of his white button up shirt sat slightly open casually showing the white t-shirt he wore underneath. His hair had slightly grown out from its militarily short cut but a few untamed strands hung loosely in the front, that Elizabeth longed to run her hands through.

"Am I overdressed?" She questioned when she caught sight of her high waisted black skirt, white button shirt and black jacket. Before Charlie could answer Elizabeth tossed off her jacket, slightly unbuttoned the bottom of her shirt and tied it into a knot, and tore off her skirt to reveal a pair of denim jeans below. Charlie looked at her in shock, "what, I wanted to be prepared. An all terrain outfit, ready for any date senario."

"I think you're beautiful, regardless." Charlie said, and took her by the hand and led her towards the door.

"You make sure you get her back before curfew, 9pm mister." Alice called out before she shut the door.

Elizabeth and Charlie laughed as they walked down the pathway. Elizabeth turned to go down the sidewalk when Charlie pulled her in the opposite direction and opened a car door for her.

"Where are we going?" Elizabeth asked once Charlie was in the car with her. "Ooh, a picnic eh? Trying to prove me wrong?" She said when Charlie had pointed to the basket nestled in the small back seat.

"Maybe a little, we're headed over to the Rotary." He announced with pride.

"Wait, the Rotary, that's not that far at all. Why are we driving there? We could just walk." Elizabeth asked, confused.

"You'll see." Charlie said and winked at her. With his eyes locked onto the road, his right hand reached across the seat to grab hers. Even though it was their first date, the way he reached over to hold her hand was effortless, it was like he had always done it and she had always been there on the receiving end.

When they arrived at the park Charlie quickly jumped out of the car, ran around to the passengers side to open the door, but Elizabeth was already one foot out.

"Sorry." Elizabeth said when she saw the look of disappointment crossed his face. She quickly slipped back down into the seat and shut the door. Charlie bowed his head in thanks and re-opened the door for her.

"Why thank you sir," Elizabeth said, and extended her hand to him to help her out of the car. Charlie quickly scooped the basket out of the back seat and headed out towards the park, not letting go of her hand.

He led her down the pathway through the park. "Where do you think would be a good place to settle in?" He asked with a strange tone in this voice.

Elizabeth looked around and then a little way down the path she saw a perfect picturesque picnic scene layed out in front of them.

Underneath a large old willow sat a red and white blanket. At the center of the blanket was another bouquet of white daisies. To protect the blanket from the wind, in each corner of the blanket sat a book holding it down to ensure it wouldn't blow away. Beside the daisies sat a smaller basket, matching the one Charlie held in his hand, and a tiny unlit candle.

A laugh sputtered out of her lips while she watched Charlie feighn looking for a place to sit.

"Well, this just looks perfect." He said when they reached the red and white blanket.

"It really does. How convenient we got here before anyone else could beat us to it." Elizabeth joked.

"That's why we had to drive. I didn't want the birds or strangers beating us to it." Charlie confessed.

Charlie put down the larger basket next to the other one on the blanket. The two then took a seat at top of the blanket, in a position where they could lean back against the tree.

Charlie opened the smaller basket and began to pull out cutlery and plates. Wanting to be helpful, Elizabeth opened the large basket and began to pull out food; wrapped sandwiches, containers of salads, plates of fruit, and a small collection of cookies (with a note from Alice).

"You don't need to do that." Charlie quickly stopped in his tracks to help her, taking the cookies out of Elizabeth's hands, trying to hide the note from Alice.

"I understand that you want to take care of me Charlie, share the responsibility and all," Charlie listened hesitantly. He had always been caring; taking care of Alice when they were kids, being most the leader of his squad at the base, and the overly doting partner. Once Elizabeth had given him the go ahead, that side of him had taken over.

"Don't get me wrong, all of this, I love it. But honestly, you helped me down the stairs and out of the car - two things I can do safely like 90% of the time. I can take care of myself too. I'm not a piece of glass that is going to shatter, let me help." She stated firmly and extend her hand to take back the plate.

Charlie handed her back the cookies and slipped the 'good luck' note from Alice away in his pocket.

Charlie scooped some matches out of the basket and reached for the candle between them. Without thinking Elizabeth quickly shot out her hand and covered the top of the candle.

"Mmm, better not." She blurted out casually, she didn't have the watch with her and an open flame made her uneasy. Charlie looked at her confused, "Open flame, windy day," Elizabeth gestured to the very dry grass around them. *"History of fire's ruining a perfectly good meal."* Elizabeth finished her thought to herself. Charlie nodded and tucked the candle and matches away in the basket.

The two dished out food, and they spent the entire afternoon snacking and relaxing in the sunlight. All the food that Charlie had brought was perfect. The sandwiches were full but not messy, the salads were creamy but not dripping, and the collection of fruit was balanced and not overly sweet. It was clear to Elizabeth that he had taken the time to make sure everything was thought out, and it made her heart soar that

"This is delicious Charlie." Elizabeth said through a mouth full of food. "Thank you."

"Was I right?" Charlie asked, and raised his eyebrows in a sassy manner.

"Is that the polite way of saying, 'I told you so'?" Elizabeth giggled. "Yes Charles, you were right. You told me so. This trumps my lasagne and I couldn't cook this. My compliments to the chef." Elizabeth leaned across the blanket and gave him a small peck on the cheek. Charlie's face turned a rosy pink and he dipped his head in thanks. "But hey, everything else that night, other than that lasagna, was probably delicious." Elizabeth defended herself.

"I hate to remind you darlin' that everything other than the lasagne was made by me." He said with a reminding wink.

Trying to get more comfortable, Elizabeth stretched and swiveled until she was laying on the blanket with her head in Charlie's lap. Charlie draped one arm across her stomach and the other was still snacking on fruit.

The two continued to munch on grapes and pineapple while they discussed their time together so far. They laughed about the day he pulled her out of traffic, they argued over the best artists on the radio, and they reminisced about Charlie's goofy faces during the rides at the carnival, all while dancing around the topic of the fight at the end of the evening.

A calmness washed over Elizabeth while she looked up at Charlie's face. She had been on multiple first dates before this and her nervous butterflies would make her uncomfortable, jittery, and overall a bad companion. But with Charlie, talking to him was easy, they clicked; they hadn't known each other for long but somehow they understood the nuances in their facial expressions and the changes in the tones of their voices.

"Tell me a story Charlie." Elizabeth asked and she reached up to gently tossle his hair. Not thinking, he reached out and grabbed one of the books holding down the blanket.

"Not from the book." She giggled and took it from his hand. "About you. We've talked alot about what we've done together, but I want to know more about who you are, from *before* I came around."

Charlie hummed and hawed and casually ran his fingers through Elizabeth's hair.

"Tell me a story about a major injury." Elizabeth encouraged him to continue story telling.

Charlie told her story of how he broke his arm. Lennie and Freddie had dared Charlie to chase Alice and her friends down the street and into the lake near their house.

"The problem was, I didn't account for the fact that the girls were smarter than I was." Charlie helped Elizabeth off of his lap and once she was sitting up he flipped his left arm over to reveal two large scars running down the backside of his forearm. "Instead of the lake, they led me towards the small cliffside. They weren't expecting me to tumble down it."

Elizabeth couldn't help but laugh at the thought.

"My mom didn't let me see Freddie or Lennie for a whole month. She was certain that they would kill me one day." Charlie chuckled, "yet here we are, all still alive."

"It's your turn." Charlie said once he had finished.

"My turn?" Elizabeth looked around and feigned confusion.

"Broken bone story. Everyone has one." Charlie said. "I'll tell you mine if you tell me yours."

"I think you mean, I'll show you mine if you show me yours." Elizabeth gave a saucy wink, and tried to joke and dance around the subject. Elizabeth was nervous to share, not because she feared altering the future, but she feared sharing her life would change Charlie's opinion of her.

"Broken bone story. Go." Charlie laughed. He leaned back onto the blanket and rolled on to his side and waited for her to speak.

"In highschool I cracked my pelvis. Giving someone a piggyback ride." Elizabeth sighed, everyone else she knew had such exciting broken bone stories and hers was just simply bad luck.

"That's your only broken bone story?" Charlie asked and Elizabeth nodded. "With the frequency at which you stumble into traffic, faint, and cause fights, I thought there would be more."

"Oh I have a ton of bruises, sprains, and tears stories, but not a lot of broken bones." Elizabeth reassured him.

The two laid on the blanket sharing childhood stories until the sun hung low above the horizon.

They told each other stories about their driving mishaps; how Charlie's dad taught him to fix the car after Charlie had driven it dry, and Elizabeth's had to direct traffic around her car while she was stalled at a stop sign for a full 5 minutes.

They laughed about mishaps and failures in school; Elizabeth about her utter failure of cursive writing, and Charlie needing to retake the second grade because he couldn't add without the help of counting on someone else's fingers.

And they shared descriptions of their favorite places; Charlie's being the lake behind his parents house where they would pretend to fish. Elizabeth's was a viewpoint at a roadside turnout about 20 minutes outside of town.

"It's the best, how you can see the entirety of the city and the water surrounding it, and how if you were there at just the right time you could see tonnes of boats sailing at sunset." Elizabeth finished describing. "You just have to go when there isn't a bunch of people crowding it up and talking."

"I'd like to go there one day." He said after Elizabeth finished describing it.

"Charles Finley you're so proper, even picnicking you're proper." Elizabeth said when she caught sight of the neatly piled plates and fruit stems that he had organized while she was speaking. "I just can't imagine you running over a cliff, or pushing a car 12 blocks because it was out of gas, or unable to count without someone's toes."

"I think it was the war that changed me. The training, and," Charlie suddenly confessed and then trailed off silently for a moment.

"You don't have to talk about the war." Elizabeth said when Charlie clammed up.

"No, it's okay." He said. "We were never in any real danger. Enlisted late, stayed at the base, war was never really on the horizon for us."

Elizabeth watched him as he spoke; his facial expression, body language and tone of voice was different. Something stern washed over him. This was something Elizabeth couldn't understand, this time she didn't have a story to tell, she didn't live through the war, or any war for that matter.

"I learned a lot, it definitely changed how I live my life. My place has never been so clean, and I have never been so attentive to detail and structure ever. It worked for me. But I don't think it hit as hard for Freddie and Lennie. They'd just spend their time laughing and joking around the base." Charlie explained. "There was this fear that hung over everything. It always felt like if you took one step out of line or made any small mistake people would die. A lot of people. I saw a lot of flags come home, and a lot of broken families. I didn't want to lose anyone or hurt anyone like that."

"So I guess yeah, before I was someone, and now I'm someone else. It's probably too hard to understand." Charlie said and rolled onto his back to look up at the sky.

"No, no, I understand." Elizabeth said. Charlie's words resonated with her in a way she didn't expect.

Elizabeth sat back up and began to ruffle through the picnic baskets. "Water?" She looked at Charlie after her search was unsuccessful.

"Damn. I forgot something to drink!" Charlie exclaimed and dropped his head back in frustration. "I'm so sorry Liz."

"Where are you going?" Elizabeth asked and watched him as he began to stand up.

"I'm going to go get drinks. There's a corner store. I'll be right back." He kissed her on the forehead and took off.

Elizabeth settled back in with her back against the tree. Elizabeth pondered what Charlie had said, *I was someone, am I someone else now?*

In all of the stories she told Charlie it was just her. Alone in her car, alone at school, and alone at the lookout. The way Charlie spoke about not losing anyone hit home with her, not because she left everyone in her life behind, but because she didn't feel the same way about it. But now, she couldn't imagine not taking Charlie or Alice to the lookout with her, or getting stuck in traffic without Freddie and Lennie in the car to help her out.

"I am someone else now." She whispered to herself and a smile slowly appeared on her face.

"Excuse me miss." A familiar voice said and drew Elizabeth's attention away from her thinking. "What is a beautiful girl doing all alone on a fine day like this?" Lennie said when Elizabeth had looked up at him.

"I'll have you know I'm on a date." Elizabeth said.

"Uh, did you forget something?" Lennie asked with a flirtatious tone in his voice.

"Yeah actually, drinks," Elizabeth chuckled, shooting down the opportunity he was trying to create.

"I mean, did you forget to invite me?" Lennie chuckled and sat down on the blanket next to her.

"Aw damn." Elizabeth said and snapped her fingers.

Lennie made himself comfortable, and began to sift through the picnic basket searching for a container.

"What are you looking for?" Elizabeth asked.

"If you're here on a date, that means Charlie is here, which means there should be," he paused for dramatic effect, "ah yes, strawberries."

"For someone with such a thick head you are quite the detective." Elizabeth sarcastically congratulated him.

Lennie made quick work of the wrappings around the strawberries and he popped one into his mouth.

"So let me guess, you're out on the prowl yourself?" Elizabeth asked and looked around. Lennie grabbed another strawberry off of the plate and held it out to her, trying to feed it to her. Elizabeth rolled her eyes and let it play out.

"I don't need to be on the prowl." He scooched up closer to her. "When the girl I want is right here."Lennie puckered his lips and moved in closer.

Charlie came back across the hill at a quick pace, but he slowed down to a casual stroll when he came close.

"Lennie, stop." Elizabeth said, "nope, no thanks, not interested." She put her hand on Lennie's face and shoved him away. "I'm not above smacking you."

"Why? I'm a catch, you've said so yourself." Lennie reminded her of the many times she had tried setting him up with other girls.

"Yes, a catch for so many other people, but not for me." Elizabeth clarified.

"Why him?" Lennie's voice was filled with disappointment.

Every bone in Charlie's body wanted to intervene, but as he stepped closer he heard Elizabeth speaking.

"It's gonna sound lame but, we're from completely different times but we still have things in common, and he laughs at my jokes no matter how bad or confusing. He just gets it. It's weird because I don't know if I should or not, but like permanence is my problem." Elizabeth felt relief venting to Lennie, she knew he wasn't going to listen enough to understand what she was saying.

"I know a lot of men like you Lennie, shallow, arrogant, clearly not listening to me while I speak." Elizabeth explained while she watched Lennie's eyes wander off in the direction of a passerby. "And Charlie is none of those things."

"Come on. Give me a chance." Lennie said once he had refocused his attention. He leaned in towards her again.

Elizabeth quickly pulled her hand back and then promptly swung it forward, and slapped Lennie across the face. "I warned you." She said when he looked at her with surprise. "I want to be your friend Lennie. But you need to get your head out of your ass."

Charlie had watched the scene play out between them and he was filled with pride.

"You are definitely not a piece of glass Elizabeth." Charlie said, making his presence known to them.

"Walk me home Charlie?" Elizabeth said and extended her hand to him.

After they had packed up their things and started walking home Charlie spoke,

"Hey Liz, I just wanted to let you know that," he hesitated, unsure of his words, "I am in this with you. 100 percent."

Elizabeth didn't know what to say. She wanted to confess her feelings too, but she didn't know what they were. She cared for him, but part of her always wondered just *how* permanent her being here was, and she couldn't stand the idea of breaking his heart. Instead of using words, she wrapped her hand tightly around his and kissed him on the cheek.

On their walk home they crossed paths with the library, and with every step closer to the building their pace slowed down. Both of them knew they wanted to go in.

"Do you want to go in?" Elizabeth said at last, breaking their slow walking.

"Do you?" Charlie asked, not answering the question.

"They won't let me take anything else out." Elizabeth sighed in shame. "I keep taking things and forgetting to bring them back. It's a curse."

Charlie took a step away from the library, but he was tugged backward by Elizabeth planted firmly on the sidewalk still holding his hand.

"But if we go home, this date is over. And I'm not ready for that yet." Elizabeth confessed, saying what they both were feeling.

"Well should we just go look around." Charlie asked, but before Elizabeth could answer he had already started heading up the path. Elizabeth understood, being in the library would let them be alone, without the eyes of nosy people watching.

They made their way to the back of the library and as they moved through the shelves they collected books they wanted to discuss, share or brag about.

She stood leaning against the shelf, one foot on the floor the other resting up on an empty shelf. Charlie leaned next to her, eyes transfixed on the page in front of him.

"What are you doing?" Charlie asked when he realized Elizabeth's eyes were not on her book.

"Just looking at you." She said, making Charlie blush. "Like really looking." Her words made him a little self conscious. "Do you know you have a tiny little speckle of grey hairs on the side of your head?" She reached her hand up and gently ran her hands through them. Charlie's hand reached up nervously, and he let out a goofy nervous face. "You also do this squinting thing, when you're listening or reading something and you need to pay attention." Elizabeth squished up her face trying to mimic Charlie's thinking face.

"I think I could fall in love with you, Elizabeth Whitley." Charlie blurted out while he watched her squishing up her face to make fun of him. "If you'd let me."

"I think I could." Elizabeth allowed herself to confess, and blush covered his face.

Charlie gently placed his book back on the shelf and scanned the area nearby for others. Not wanting to let the moment pass, he quickly slipped one hand behind Elizabeth's back and cradled her head with the other. Elizabth barely had time to realize what was happening before his lips met hers. The book in Elizabeth's hands dropped with a thud when her arms draped themselves over Charlie's shoulders. The spark had ignited between them once more, both of them eager to pick up where they had left off after the carnival.

When she returned his kiss, she felt his tongue on her lips. Elizabeth stood up onto her tip-toes making their faces level, but she faltered backward after a few seconds. Charlie ran his hands down her back, firmly gripping her backside, before lifting her up and placing her on the shelf.

"Much better." Elizabeth thanked him before she pulled his lips back to hers. Their kisses were electric, sending waves of goosebumps through their bodies with every touch. Elizabeth's body moved on instinct and she lifted her legs and wrapped them around Charlie's waist. Charlie's kisses moved from her lips to her neck.

"Excuse me!" A voice called out from the end of the shelf. "What are you doing?"

Filled with embarrassment Elizabeth dropped her legs from around Charlie's waist and he helped her down off of the shelf. The two collected their books and placed them on the returns cart before bowing their heads in shame and walking towards the front counter. They stood at the check out desk, heads down, hands at their sides, averting their eyes like kids in trouble at the principal's office.

"Out! Now!" The librarian exclaimed and pointed towards the door. Elizabeth began to ask about extending her overdue books. "Keep the books Miss Whitley. Just don't come back."

Elizabeth and Charlie fell into a fit of laughter once they were safely outside the library.

"Damn." Charlie suddenly exclaimed and looked back at the door. "Picnic baskets."

"Oh!" Elizabeth said when she remembered them sitting on the window sill at the end of the aisle. "They are gone forever now." Elizabeth nodded, because they both knew that they could not go back through those doors.

"Actually, Alice's picnic baskets." Charlie clarified. "We have to go back. She'll kill me."

"It was really lovely getting to know you," Elizabeth laughed and planted a kiss on his cheek, "you're pretty much dead either way."

"Or you could tell Alice." Charlie began to negotiate.

"What am I going to tell Alice, sorry we lost your picnic baskets because I got caught making out with your brother in the library, and now I may never return." Elizabeth stated the facts and they both let out a blush filled giggle.

Charlie and Elizabeth made their way home, rehearsing exactly what they would say to Alice.

"You will say the baskets are gone. I will offer to go with her to get it back." Charlie said, solidifying their plan. "And hopefully she won't ask why we can't do it."

"And if she does ask, we will rock - paper - scissors for who has to explain." Elizabeth extended her hand to him and they shook on it. Charlie kept his grip on her hand and pulled her in for a kiss before wrapping his arm around her and continuing on their way.

Once they had reached Alice and Elizabeth's house Charlie stopped at the doorstep.

"Want to come in, or should I bring Alice out here?" Elizabeth said with her hand on the door knob. "You don't have to work tomorrow, it's not that late, plus even if you do stay a little late you can just drive home."

"Damn." Charlie said and dropped his head in embarrassment.

"A triple damn day, what did you forget?" Elizabeth said, recounting the water and the baskets.

"I forgot the car." Charlie said remembering his car at the park.

"Well I'll walk back with you." She quickly jumped back down off the step. "Then you can drive me home and we can do this all over again."

Chapter 9

Before Elizabeth knew it, two more months had flown past, the trees had moved from the sepia tones of fall to barron skeletons dusted with snow.

Elizabeth woke up Christmas morning to the sound of rain on her window. She looked to the bedside table that held her watch and for a moment she thought of people and what they were doing right now in 2012. Was it Christmas there too? She wondered about all of the things she had likely missed; birthdays, Easter, her drunk friends eating green until they puke for St. Patrick's Day. Elizabeth realized that she really only ever saw her family or friends on major holidays, but when she did it was always a joyous affair. Her grandfather would tell the Easter story and make them all watch the Ten Commandments movie, or her sister freaking out over her mother-in-law for age inappropriate gifts for the boys. For a moment a small part of her heart felt jealous that she was missing out on those things. She looked again at the watch and realized she could go back at any moment and it would be as if she never missed a beat.

Elizabeth knew the longer she stayed here the harder it would be to return home to that life. She would be a different person, 'older and hopefully wiser', she told herself. Everyday as happy as she was in 1945, there was a small sliver of guilt in her heart that she was here, unsure if she'd ever see them again.

She struggled to remember the date she left and how long it had been since she was there. The sound of

Alice in the kitchen broke her out of her mathematical trance. Elizabeth gave up on trying to remember, got dressed, and headed downstairs.

Over the last week, the house had been completely transformed to celebrate Christmas. The stair rail was wrapped with green garland and every room smelled strongly of cinnamon. Across the mantle of the fireplace sat five stockings, each embroidered with their names in gold, a christmas gift from Lennie who stated that "we are a family, and we will have Christmas together, it is only appropriate." Since their 'chat' in the park, Lennie had changed into the secret big softy he had always been, and he no longer pretended to be the tough soldier around his friends.

In the corner of the sitting room was a large evergreen tree covered in tinsel, lights, and large brightly coloured balls. A large smile bloomed across Elizabeth's freckled face when she saw it as she came down the stairs. Last night the five of them came together to decorate it. Lennie was right, she thought, they are a family now with holiday traditions and everything.

"Merry Christmas!!" Alice screeched, running across the kitchen to embrace Elizabeth.

"Merry Christmas!" Elizabeth squeaked out in return. Still trying to wake up, Elizabeth puttered around the kitchen, scooped up two cups of coffee, placed a candy cane in each and then sat them at the table.

"What's the plan for today?" She knew Alice always had a plan and she would burst if she didn't explain it. Alice jogged out of the kitchen and upstairs calling out her plan as she moved through the house.

"First, when the boys get here presents, of course. Second, carol -"

"I'm not caroling!" Charlie called from the hall. Elizabeth stood but before she could reach him he slid up behind her.

"Merry Christmas." He cheered, wrapping his arms around her, revealing the flowers he had in one hand, and a wrapped box in the other. He kissed her on the cheek and pulled her close to him.

"Ugh." Alice said re-entering the kitchen. "You're here. You two never should've gotten together, I have had zero privacy since. You're always here, it sickens me." She laughed and wished him Merry Christmas with a kiss on the cheek. Out of the corner of her eye Elizabeth spotted someone.

"Hypocrite!" She called out as Freddie descended the stairs, "at least mine goes home sometimes!" The girls laughed as Charlie demanded to know why Freddie was allowed to stay over and he wasn't. Alice went on to point out how she is his sister and that would be weird. Elizabeth quickly redirected Alice's thoughts to the plans for the day.

"Yes, you are caroling. It's tradition." Elizabeth said sternly.

"We've never caroled." He let her go and walked over to pile the gifts he had brought under the tree.

"It's a new tradition starting now." The two kissed when Charlie sighed in agreement. Alice clapped joyfully and continued with her list.

"After caroling we will walk to Mom and Dad's for dinner." Alice said, pouring two more mugs of coffee for the boys.

"I'm nervous." Elizabeth said sitting and anxiously stirred her coffee with her candy cane.

"Why?" Charlie tapped her with his foot under the table.

"I'm meeting your guy's parents." She took a deep breath. "What if they think I'm not good enough for you Alice?" Elizabeth laughed and winked at Charlie.

A few minutes later Lennie arrived, arms piled high with presents. They took their coffee and retired to the sitting room, all gathering on the floor around the tree. Elizabeth had filled all the stockings with sweets and socks, or as her mother had always called them the 'necessities.' They sat around opening gifts and discussing the various books, records, and clothing they were given.

"This one is for Alice." Elizabeth announced and pulled a large, decorative wrapped box out from behind the tree and slid it across the floor to Alice. On the box was written "Often Worn Underwear" Charlie chuckled upon seeing it, and Alice shot a look of daggers at Elizabeth followed by a stream of laughter. Inside the box was freshly bought underwear as well as a Nat King Cole record.

The next gifts under the tree were two long narrow boxes. Elizabeth and Alice opened them at the same time. Inside each box was a fragile silver chain, with a matching dangling heart. The boys exchanged looks of confusion and worry, while the girls met eyes and began laughing. It was not as if the two had planned this, but Charlie had asked Alice to pick out something she thought Elizabeth would like, not knowing Freddie had done the exact same.

"Clearly we both just have excellent taste." Elizabeth giggled before wrapping her arms around Charlie's neck and kissing him in thanks. Their kiss lingered uncomfortably long for everyone else in the room. They had yet to continue their moment from the evening of the carnival, and with every kiss it was like slowly lifting the lid of the box they had closed that night.

The last gift under the tree was a paper thin, delicately wrapped square. Freddie picked it up and passed it to Alice, who passed it to Lennie, who passed it to Charlie and at last to Elizabeth. They all watched her closely as she gently opened it.

Tucked inside the wrapping was a picture of a chestnut bookcase. Excitement bloomed across her face.

"It is at my place." A shocked silence blanketed the room, his words sounded like an invitation. "I'll bring it over later." Charlie said quickly calming the situation. "You need a place to store all of these books." Charlie gestured around to the piles at Elizabeth's feet.

"Not to mention the stacks on stacks in your room." Alice reminded her. "You should really return them to the library now that you have a collection of your own."

"I'm pretty sure I should just keep them at this point." Elizabeth shot a cheeky look at Charlie. "Seeing as I'm not allowed back there."

"Banned from a government building, alright!" Lennie said enthusiastically, and gave her a high five. It took a moment for Elizabeth to remember that no one really knew the reason for her banishment.

"Are you rewarding me for this?" Elizabeth said, but still returned the gesture.

"Now that you've gone full geek." He gestured to Charlie. "You're losing your cool."

"Excuse me, I am plenty cool." Elizabeth said before reminding him of the girl she had set him up with the previous weekend. "I schmoozed her for you, I cried, literal tears, of your praises. I said you saved my life. I was drowning, in shark infested waters, and you rescued me, shirtless, rippling muscles and all." Lennie gave her another high-five and conceded. Once he was out of ear shot, Charlie questioned her.

"Did you really say all that stuff? Rippling muscles?" He asked in both jealousy and misbelief.

"No. I was honest with her. I told her he was a naval officer, fought in the war, and just a sweet guy." She stumbled over the last part, remembering the Lennie that tried to force himself upon her, though she rewrote time and that version of him never existed; the thought of it still lingered in her mind. "But honestly, I think she would've believed the rippling muscles story. She's was very pretty, but dumb as a bag of rocks."

"Just Lennie's type." Charlie confirmed.

"Right, she could be the one." Elizabeth laughed. "Thank you for my bookcase." Elizabeth said before placing a kiss on his cheek.

"It's about time you got some furniture for that old room upstairs." Charlie said and Elizabeth's face dropped. Once again overwhelmed by the thoughts of 2012. "Hey, you okay?"

"Huh - yeah, I'm fine." Elizabeth said, trying to shake the feeling. Charlie sat in silence, knowing she had more to say, she always had more to say. "Up until now everything I've had here wasn't really mine. Outside of my birthday notebook and the clothes on my back, everything else here was borrowed. Now I have all of this stuff that is mine. It feels so very permanent. It's nice." Charlie kissed her on the forehead and held her close. There was more Elizabeth wanted to say, but she wouldn't.

They all paid thanks to each other, and hung around the sitting room for the rest of the day. Charlie and Freddie did their best to keep Alice occupied in hopes to distract her from the thought of caroling. Sadly for them, when the clock hit four Alice jumped out of her chair and began demanding they all get dressed to go.

Shortly after their carolling journey started Elizabeth quickly figured why they had never gone carolling before, they weren't good. They were only three houses down the street when they realized that they will actually have to practice next year before they go. Alice quickly admitted defeat, between Freddie not knowing the lyrics and Lennie's lack of rhythm she called it a day. She decided that the Finley house would be the fourth, and final stop, on their caroling world tour.

The cold was biting as they walked through town. Charlie and Elizabeth walked arm in arm holding each other close to stay warm. Ahead of them Freddie and Alice were doing the same. Charlie cleared his throat in the protective older brother way he usually does, causing the two to separate slightly.

"Oi," Elizabeth sighed. "Leave them be." She looked to Charlie waiting for a rebuttal.

"But -" Charlie began but she cut him off.

which was perfectly cleaned and organized. *How very military of him*, she thought. She bet his bed was properly made with hotel corners and everything.

"I really need to step up my cleaning game." She whispered. She thought back to the shambles she had left her apartment back home, there were forsure her breakfast dishes in the sink "soaking" she always told herself when she was too lazy to clean them.

"What no place for guests." Elizabeth joked when she sat down at the lone chair at the table.

"I spend most of my time at the base." Charlie explained. With that Elizabeth stood up and moved on with the tour.

"Plus I've never really wanted anyone here." He confessed and followed as she poked her head into the spotless bathroom. "Until now." He continued speaking slowly as she casually approached the bedroom. "Until you."

She had her hand on the door knob to the bedroom when she turned back to him, "well that makes me feel pretty special."

"You are pretty special." He grabbed her hand and led her back to the sitting room.

He let her roam a moment, so she could snoop freely, but as she approached the shelf of photo albums, full of embarrassing memories that his mother had given him, he grabbed her by the hand and attempted to pull her down onto the couch next to him. But Elizabeth stepped quickly out of reach and flicked on the radio.

"So, go about your evening as if I wasn't here." She sat down next to him and she spun and draped her legs across his. He ran his hands up and down her calves in his lap, watching her as she continued to gaze around. "I'm serious. What would you be doing if I wasn't here."

"I wouldn't be here. I'd be at Alice's with you. Or I'd be on the phone with you." He joked.

"Well, I'm here. What do you want to do with me?" Elizabeth heard what she said as she said it, she didn't mean for it to sound so sexual, but she saw Charlie's face go flush. She couldn't resist pushing it further and seeing just how red his face could go. "I mean I'm yours all night, we can do that later." She winked and his face went from mild sunburn to boiled lobster. The redder the shades of his face, the more nervous she became. Elizabeth was sure that this wasn't either of their first times, but she knew it would be different this time. More passionate? More gentle? More something, and she had begun to worry about disappointing the both of them.

"Seriously, it's a Tuesday night, what are you doing?" She asked to change the subject.

"I would be reading a book, or going for a stroll," while he spoke, Elizabeth leaned back on the couch to reach the pile of books sitting on the end table. She grabbed one for herself and handed one to Charlie.

It wasn't long before she was lost in the words on the page and she was relieved that the sexual overtone of the evening had subsided for a moment. Slowly she felt eyes lingering on her.

She peered at Charlie over the pages of the book. "Yes? Can I help you?"

"I'm just looking at you." He had dropped the book entirely, not even pretending to read. "Really looking at you."

"Why are you so hard on them?"

"But, she's my sister, and he's, well he's," He trailed off trying to think of a negative descriptor for his friend.

"Literally one of the nicest and most loyal people you know?" She said bluntly. "And, I'm her best friend, so logically, if she acted the way you did, you wouldn't be allowed to be with me." She raised her eyebrows knowing she had won him over.

"I'm sure it's the other way around, you wouldn't be allowed to be with me." He wrapped his arm around her.

"Whatever you say darlin'." She patted him sarcastically on the arm and went back to leaning on his shoulder.

"Fine." He sighed and loudly announced, "You two have my blessing." Alice rolled her eyes, and called out that she didn't need his permission but thank you anyways. As Freddie wrapped his arm around her tighter he casually shot Charlie and thumbs up in thank you over Alice's shoulder.

When they reached the Finley household, they all tumbled in from the cold and were greeted with a chorus of Merry Christmases and hugs. Helen Finley was a spitting image of her daughter, looks and attitude. She welcomed Elizabeth in with open arms, telling her how nice and grateful she was for Elizabeth putting up with her two crazy children with no complaining.

"Well not no complaining." Elizabeth clarified as Mrs. Finley let her out of her arms, giving her to the arms of John. John's face was round like his daughters but his eyes were Charlies, the deep brown stared into her before he pulled her into a hug.

"Welcome to the family," as he let her go he turned to Charlie and, not so subtly, gave him the okay symbol with a wink. Helen ushered everyone into the sitting room, fitting them with drinks and announcing that dinner would be ready in thirty minutes or so.

Elizabeth wandered around the room looking at the pictures that hung on the walls with Charlie hanging close behind trying his best to hide any that were embarrassing. Noticing his mother in the kitchen alone Charlie quickly gave Elizabeth a kiss on the cheek and slipped into the kitchen. Before the door closed she caught sight of him asking his mother a question and then he pointed to his ring finger with a large smile building across both his and his mother's faces.

Charlie and Elizabeth had been seeing each other for months now. Due to the 1940's of it all they had taken it slowly, not that Elizabeth was complaining. Ever since she had arrived the cloud of uncertainty floated above her. No matter how happy she was, the thought of staying or not staying had always stopped her from doing important things; purchasing items, moving up in her career, and committing to her feelings for Charlie. Seeing Charlie thinking about the future for the two of them spurred that feeling once more.

Elizabeth gasped and turned around to find Alice. When she did she frantically waved Alice over, mouthing "Here. Now."

"I need you to go in there." She pointed to the kitchen. "And tell me what they are talking about."

"Liz. I thought we talked about this. I'm not comfortable nosing into my brother's business." Alice sighed.

"Don't lie to me." Elizabeth shook her head and Alice cracked a smile.

"Charlie called your mom in there. Pointed at me and then." Elizabeth mimicked Charlie's gesture and pointed to her ring finger. Alice's eyes bulged.

"I'm on it." Alice nodded.

"Thank you!" Elizabeth sighed with a grin.

Alice quickly and casually snuck her way into the kitchen and joined her family. She shot a look back at Elizabeth, stuck her tongue out and then shut the door.

"Damn it!" Elizabeth slumped back into the sitting room and plopped down on the couch next to Mr. Finley. Freddie had started up the radio and went to fetch Alice. Mr. Finley looked at Elizabeth and extended his arm. Despite his age, the quick pace of the jazz had him flinging her around the room.

"I see where Charlie gets it." She said smiling as their dance came to an end. He bowed and she curtsied. Before he could take her hand for another round, Charlie came sliding in, grabbing her hand, dipping her and planting a kiss on her lips. The two slowly moved around the room singing along with Nat King Cole and his rendition of "Unforgettable" until Helen emerged from the kitchen asking everyone to follow her to the dining room.

As they ate dinner, Elizabeth told the Finley's about her teaching at the elementary school and tried her best to answer any questions they asked about her past and family. Someone had clearly told them how she appeared out of nowhere and not to ask too many questions about it. But thankfully when the questions became too personal Alice or Charlie would redirect the conversation.

After dinner they each lay relaxed in their chairs, too full to go on, when Freddie entered the room looking very nervous. In his hand was a small, wrapped, perfectly square box. He fumbled with it between his hands as he approached her.

"Hey Al, I found this in my jacket pocket. I must've forgotten it this morning during gifts." He placed it down on the table in front of her and took his seat next to her, shaking nervously as he did. As she opened he spoke.

"Alice, I've known I've wanted this for a long time. While we were stationed I thought about you everyday. What it would be like to come home to you, what it would be like if I couldn't. I didn't want to live in a world where coming home to you wasn't an option. I still don't." She had stopped unwrapping the box and was sitting completely still listening to him talk. Tears had begun to form in his eyes.

"Then on the way here your brother gave me his blessing, so I thought I better do this now before he changes his mind." He chuckled, breaking the tension, and took the box out of her hand and got down on one knee. She gasped as he opened the box, and to no one's surprise she said yes. Everyone in the room cheered and clapped.

The congratulations fizzled out and the night was coming to an end. The five of them gathered their coats and headed out the door. They walked down the street,

which was perfectly cleaned and organized. *How very military of him*, she thought. She bet his bed was properly made with hotel corners and everything.

"I really need to step up my cleaning game." She whispered. She thought back to the shambles she had left her apartment back home, there were forsure her breakfast dishes in the sink "soaking" she always told herself when she was too lazy to clean them.

"What no place for guests." Elizabeth joked when she sat down at the lone chair at the table.

"I spend most of my time at the base." Charlie explained. With that Elizabeth stood up and moved on with the tour.

"Plus I've never really wanted anyone here." He confessed and followed as she poked her head into the spotless bathroom. "Until now." He continued speaking slowly as she casually approached the bedroom. "Until you."

She had her hand on the door knob to the bedroom when she turned back to him, "well that makes me feel pretty special."

"You are pretty special." He grabbed her hand and led her back to the sitting room.

He let her roam a moment, so she could snoop freely, but as she approached the shelf of photo albums, full of embarrassing memories that his mother had given him, he grabbed her by the hand and attempted to pull her down onto the couch next to him. But Elizabeth stepped quickly out of reach and flicked on the radio.

"So, go about your evening as if I wasn't here." She sat down next to him and she spun and draped her legs across his. He ran his hands up and down her calves

in his lap, watching her as she continued to gaze around. "I'm serious. What would you be doing if I wasn't here."

"I wouldn't be here. I'd be at Alice's with you. Or I'd be on the phone with you." He joked.

"Well, I'm here. What do you want to do with me?" Elizabeth heard what she said as she said it, she didn't mean for it to sound so sexual, but she saw Charlie's face go flush. She couldn't resist pushing it further and seeing just how red his face could go. "I mean I'm yours all night, we can do that later." She winked and his face went from mild sunburn to boiled lobster. The redder the shades of his face, the more nervous she became. Elizabeth was sure that this wasn't either of their first times, but she knew it would be different this time. More passionate? More gentle? More something, and she had begun to worry about disappointing the both of them.

"Seriously, it's a Tuesday night, what are you doing?" She asked to change the subject.

"I would be reading a book, or going for a stroll," while he spoke, Elizabeth leaned back on the couch to reach the pile of books sitting on the end table. She grabbed one for herself and handed one to Charlie.

It wasn't long before she was lost in the words on the page and she was relieved that the sexual overtone of the evening had subsided for a moment. Slowly she felt eyes lingering on her.

She peered at Charlie over the pages of the book. "Yes? Can I help you?"

"I'm just looking at you." He had dropped the book entirely, not even pretending to read. "Really looking at you."

"I'm cute right!" Elizabeth chuckled and went back to her book. She felt the book fall from his hands, she peeked at him again and he was simply watching her read.

"Tell me a story, Elizabeth." Charlie said, mimicking their picnic in the park. Elizabeth began to read aloud from *The Murder on The Orient Express.*

"I've read that one. You're right, his mustache is glorious. Tell me a story about you?" Charlie said again, but the joking tone was more subdued.

"Oh I have lots of stories, none of which you'd understand." Elizabeth let the mystery hang in the air. "I was someone and now I'm someone else." She played along with their picnic escapade. "But I like who I am a lot more now. With you." She added, being completely honest with herself now.

They stayed like that for a moment, silently staring at each other. His hands had begun to run up and down her legs again, slowly working their way up her body. Elizabeth scooched further up into his lap so her hands were within reach of his arms. She let the book fall to the floor and she ran her fingers up his arms and rested on his shoulders. His hand had done the same, he now had one firm hand gently cradling her face, with his thumb gently rubbing over her bottom lip, and his other rested on the nape of her back.

"I love you Elizabeth." Charlie said almost breathlessly.

"I love you too Charlie." Elizabeth said, filled with relief that he said it first. This was the first moment they had said those words to each other without subtext or joke. It was honest and true.

They both knew that if they opened the lid of that box, this time there would be no stopping like the night of the carnival.

"Are you sure you want to do this?" He asked her.

"With every part of me." She confirmed. "What about you?"

"I'm yours Elizabeth, every part of me." With that the talking was over.

Charlie wrapped his hand around to the back of Elizabeth's neck and pulled her lips to meet his.

Their motions were hungry as they devoured each other's lips. Every touch was a spark, and everywhere his hands ran they left a line of goosebumps in their tracks, causing Elizabeth's entire body to shiver with the anticipation of what was to come.

Elizabeth readjusted herself, swinging her legs from their draped position so they were straddled over his. Her hands held his face tight to hers until their tongues found each other again. Charlie's hands left her neck and slowly traced their way down her back and to her thighs where they rested, except for his thumbs that had begun to deeply knead and massage the inner edge of her thighs. As he moved his thumbs Elizabeth's skirt slowly lifted higher and higher. Elizabeth moved her hips in time with his massaging, and with every movement she could feel him growing harder against her.

Elizabeth moved her hands to the top of Charlie's shirt and began to unbutton it. As she moved down the shirt, she let her finger graze the exposed skin underneath. A shiver ran through Elizabeth when Charlie's hands moved back up her body, lifting her shirt slightly as he went. His hands moved between the fabrics of her shirt and bra, and he ran his fingers across her breasts. He cradled them in his hands and traced her nipples with his thumbs. Elizabeth lifted her arms giving him permission to remove her shirt. She quickly finished removing his shirt so she could feel his skin on hers.

His lips left hers and she let out a small sigh of disappointment. His kisses traced their way from her mouth, across her cheek and down her neck. Elizabeth tossed her head back in pleasure as he kissed and nibbled on her skin. His lips reached the fabric of her bra and she felt his hands begin to fumble with the clasp.

"Help." He whispered and dropped his head onto her shoulder embarrassed. Elizabeth made quick work of her bra. The second the fabric was off her skin, his hands took its place, holding her breasts, admiring the shape and texture of her skin.

"You're so beautiful." He said looking up at her.

"Charlie." Elizabeth gasped when his lips found one of her erect nipples. Every flick of his tongue on her body caused her hips to gyrate against his. He noticed how his mouth caused her movements and he moved his tongue faster, moving back and forth from nipple to nipple, stopping to kiss her neck as he went. As his lips moved to her neck, she ran her hands up into his hair, cradling his head, she pulled his mouth off of her for a second.

"Bedroom?" She asked.

"Bedroom." He confirmed with a nod. She slid off of his lap, and they both stood. Elizabeth watched as Charlie took a moment to straighten his stiffness in his pants. Unable to resist herself, Elizabeth reached out and stroked him through the fabric of his pants, returning her lips to his. She ran her palm up and down his shaft, causing him to let out an uncontrolled moan. She could feel his erection twitching at her touch.

Her forwardness egged Charlie onwards. He scooped her, wrapped her legs around his waist and carried her down the hall towards the bedroom.

He lowered her gently onto the bed and lifted himself over top of her. Gently he ran his hands down her body, slipping her skirt and underwear off as his hands moved to her feet, stopping to kiss the different parts of her body as he moved.

Their lips found each other once more, but Elizabeth's hands made quick work of the belt and buttons on his pants, slipping her hands into his underwear and taking him into her hands once more. He kissed her shoulders and massaged her breasts as she stroked him. With every movement Charlie moaned into her neck where his head rested. She wanted to take him into her mouth, to see how far she could push him, but she needed more.

She pulled his face up to meet hers, and wrapped her legs around him nervously, and he hovered over her a moment waiting for permission to go further. Elizabeth nodded, and Charlie ran his hand down her back and lifted her hips to meet his. Their lips touched for a brief moment before he entered her and she let out a pleasure filled gasp. They lay like that, feeling every touch of the other's body against their own. Charlie held her with one hand on her back and one cradling her head, passion filling his gaze. Elizabeth wrapped her arms around him, holding their bodies close together while she adjusted to the feeling of him inside her. The two moved together, their bodies intertwined until they were both overcome with pleasure and exhaustion.

"I love you Charles Finley." Elizabeth said as their bodies parted.

"I love you Elizabeth Whitley." Charlie whispered into her ear as he stroked her hair and spooned her. "Every part of you." He kissed her on the shoulder before falling asleep.

Once Charlie had fallen asleep Elizabeth slipped out of bed and crept out of the bedroom and down the hall. The speech that she had given herself on the doorstep was no longer in effect.

"So very permanent." She picked at her fingernails as she paced around the living room. "This could be permanent, if I want it to be." She walked over to the chair, thought better of herself, turned around and paced away. "Should it be? Can it be?" She rushed back to coat and opened the pocket a crack, just enough to peek in. She couldn't see much, but a small metallic shimmer like that of a hinge on a box.

Unable to stop herself, Elizabeth reached into the pocket and felt a soft fabric square. She let out a quiet gasp and pulled it out. She held it in her hand, staring at it. She cracked the box open and caught a gleam of the beautiful diamonds set in a twisted white gold band.

"Fuck." She slammed the box closed.

Chapter 10

When Bea showed up to pick up her kids she was prepared for a mutiny. She entered her father's room to see the three of them caught up in laughter. Charlotte lay on the bed and Grant sprawled across the couch looking at old pictures in photo albums. Bea crossed the room, giving her father a kiss on the forehead and looking at the photos over Charlotte's shoulder.

"Grandpa Charles was telling us the story about Uncle Fred and the bear at the carnival," Charlotte explained, pointing to the picture of the huge bear fully encompassing Alice in the picture.

"And he told us about the horrible pick up lines Uncle Lennie used to get girls." Grant said, flashing a picture of Lennie decked out in his Naval uniform. "And how Gran always used to put him in his place every time he used it." The kids put the pictures back into the albums and Bea put the albums back into the bedside table drawer. They gathered their things and Bea thanked her father for taking care of them.

"We actually had a really good time with gramps today." Grant said high-fiving him as they said goodbye. Charlotte kissed her grandfather on the cheek and the three headed out the door.

"Maybe you will have to come back again soon, how about -" Grant cut her off.

"It was a good day, but not that good." Bea wrapped her arms around her kids and kissed each of them on the forehead as they walked down the hall.

"It couldn't have taken all day to wind those clocks. What did you do for the rest of the day?" Bea questioned as they exited Charles' wing of the nursing home and into the lobby.

"He told us stories about him and Gran. It was really cute, he still loves her even though she is gone." Charlotte's emotions got the better of her and tears built in her eyes.

"Grandpa beat a man to a pulp for Gran before they were even dating." Grant cheered about the tough genes he had inherited.

"Real romantic." Bea said, hardly listening while she washed her hands with the mandatory nursing home hand sanitizer as the kids put on their coats.

"Did you know that Grandpa was going to propose to her with his mother's ring at Christmas, but chickened out because Uncle Fred proposed to Auntie Alice instead and he knew that Auntie would've killed him if he had stolen her thunder." Charlotte laughed but Bea interjected.

"No he didn't." She paused looking at her kids confused and concerned. "Mom and Dad married after great grandma had passed away, he bought a ring from a pawn shop. I know because dad always said it was because his father didn't want to part with her ring after she was gone."

The three of them stopped at the door, watching a woman struggle with the code on the keypad trying to get in. Bea quickly opened the door letting her in, and shooed her kids out to the car.

"I am just going to talk to the nurse for a moment." Bea said, throwing her son the keys. She turned around and rushed towards the nearest nurse.

"My father needs to see a doctor." Physically she was calm but she was talking frantically, "He is making up stories. Something is wrong, he has always had an amazing memory." She began to ramble about how her mother forgot things with ALS, and how there was a history of dementia in the family, trying to find any way to make the nurse feel as panicked as she did.

The nurse stood calmly in front of her nodding. She picked up a pad of paper and began writing down what Bea was saying.

"Is there anything we can do Nurse," she paused reading the name tag, "Liza." Liza stood in silence writing. After a minute she stopped and looked up at Bea.

"Okay, ALS, Dementia, stories. Anything else?" She had her pencil poised at the ready to continue writing.

"Clocks?" Bea said angrily, as if it was something that should've been obvious. Liza excused herself for a moment and Bea stood impatiently tapping her foot. Liza had stepped aside to give a woman directions to a room down the hall. She came back to a frustrated Bea's side and continued to reassure her that her father was on the right medication.

"We will see if we can have a doctor come in on Monday and look him over. Does Monday work for you?" Bea nodded. "Okay, I'll call today and when it is all arranged I'll call you and let you know when to come in." Bea let out an exasperated sigh, but knowing that was the most she was going to get from them, she turned and left the building.

Moments later there was a knock on Mister Finley's door.

Chapter 11

Mister Finley called out to welcome his new visitor into the room. They entered the room slowly and found him stationed in his chair facing the wall of clocks. He was so fiercely focused on the hands ticking in the Eastern Time Zone that he didn't bother to turn and see who it was.

"I am not sure if I should feel insulted or confused that you have no pictures of us in here." As her voice broke the silence, the hands on the clocks hit 1:28, matching the large broken clock in the middle of the collection. Charles swiveled in his chair so quickly that it almost tipped over as he stood up.

"Elizabeth." He tumbled back into his chair having lost his balance without his cane.

She stood across the room looking at the pictures by the bed. "Either you propose to me and I say no. Or you don't propose at all." She mumbled under her breath and then turned and flashed him a gentle smile. "Hi Charles." He gestured for her to sit on the couch across from him.

"So which is it? Am I confused, or offended?" He reached out and touched her face.

"My Elizabeth." He sighed and gently rubbed her cheek. The breath caught in her throat. As she looked into his eyes she could see the man she left behind and a pain grew in her chest, an ache to be back in 1945 with her Charlie.

Elizabeth stood again trying to shake the ache away, and walked around the room looking at the clocks hanging on the wall.

"Can I get you something to drink? Eat? You can sit in my chair if you'd like." He said trying his best to make her comfortable.

"You don't have to take care of me Charles." Elizabeth chuckled.

"It was my job once, you did promise you'd let me be responsible for you part-time, and a soldier never leaves his post." He smiles. He sat remembering times that she hadn't even experienced yet, it made her uncomfortable.

"You were waiting for me." She changed the subject and turned to him as the realization hit her. "How did you know?"

"Why, you told me." He stood and shuffled to his bedside table. "When you left, you wrote a letter to try to explain everything." He pulled an aged piece of paper out of the bottom of the drawer. "I never really believed it, until I saw you on the street that day." They both returned to their seats and he handed her the letter.

"You know, I've seen you. Walking around town." He said smiling. She thought back on her life trying to remember the moment he was talking about. "I introduced myself, but you didn't know who I was." He sighed. "It was okay though. I think that was when I finally believed you. That you were living in the before, and I was living in the after."

He sounded so content with living in the after, living life without her. The pain in Elizabeth's chest grew, she stood looking at the letter in her hands so he wouldn't see the pain in her eyes.

"I can't read this." She said, handing it back. "It is like a cardinal rule of time travel." Charles began to laugh. "What? Doc Brown says it's dangerous to know your own future. How would I know if my choices are my choices or not?"

"Yet he still read the letter that Marty gave him in 1955." He said, extending the letter to her again. "I have watched a lot of time travel movies after that letter. Trying to figure it all out."

"Maybe later." She took the letter, folded it and placed it in her coat pocket.

"I have to ask. Where are you from?" Charles looked up at her, a sweet curiosity in his eyes. "Wait, when are you from?"

"December 25th, 1945." As she spoke, shock crossed his face.

"Oh, that night. That can't be right. You don't leave for -" she raised a hand to stop him, not wanting to know too much of her future.

"I found the ring in your coat pocket. I freaked out, and when you went to bed I snuck off and came back." She felt ashamed, but also strangely relieved. Knowing that tomorrow in 1945, she will be back there again with *her* Charlie. He beamed with confusion. Elizabeth stuttered trying to explain her thinking that led her back here. "I didn't - I couldn't. I didn't know what would be the right decision. If I was supposed to stay there or if I belonged here. I wanted to know where I was meant to be." She finished firmly. Charles wanted to say how she belonged back then, with him, but he stopped himself, not wanting to sway her to stay.

"How do you do it?" Curiosity was gleaming in his eyes. Elizabeth pulled the watch out of her pocket, opened it, and held it carefully in her hands.

"The first time, it was a fluke. I spun the dial when I was fidgeting, I didn't think anything of it." She continued to recount her incident with Alice and the changed the outcome of that dinner. "As far as I can tell, it's the person holding the watch and anything they have with them. And it only goes through time, not space." He nodded, trying his best to follow along.

"This was the first time I've touched it since -" she trailed off for a moment, not wanting to explain the fire or the watch's failures from the carnival." I wanted to see if anything had changed since I left, to help me make my decision. I tried my best to be precise, she pointed at the date dial. Sadly I overshot it by a couple of weeks." His head was reeling. Elizabeth sighed. "You must think I'm insane."

"No, I think you are a wonder." He reached out to touch the watch, but Elizabeth snapped it shut quickly when Nurse Liza popped her head into the room.

"Oh, sorry for interrupting. But visiting hours will be over in 15 minutes." She gave Elizabeth an empathetic look and shut the door on her way out. Elizabeth stood and scooped up her coat.

"Stay." Charles pleaded, She opened her mouth in protest, "Or at least, come back tomorrow, we can swap more stories then." He reached out and grabbed her hand. "Please." Elizabeth looked at him in his aged, watery eyes, and the pain began to grow again. She wanted to find out what happened, what reason there was for saying no, and most of all, she wanted to know if her staying in 1945 would be a better choice.

Elizabeth pulled her jacket tight around her to protect herself from the cold as she made her way back to her apartment. As she walked she looked around; nothing had changed since she first left, but still everything seemed different. The cars and people zipped past her without any recognition. She couldn't quite put her finger on it; It was as if she was looking through a foggy window. After living in the 1940s, life here seemed arduous. People were less friendly, everything moved too quickly, and felt too complicated.

Would she miss 1945 if she left? Would it miss her? Does 2012 even need her?

"I need some time to think." She said to herself. She looked at the watch in her hand and started to laugh. "Lucky I've got plenty of that." She shoved the watch back into her jacket pocket.

She stood in her hallway fumbling with her keys, nervous about what she would find on the other side of her door. She didn't know what she expected; letters piled under the door, a full voicemail, cartons of milk with her face on it, dust and cobwebs covering the furniture. She opened the door and walked in eyes closed. When she opened her eyes and felt very disappointed to see nothing. Nothing had changed. No cobwebs, no mail, no messages, only a slight layer of dust sat on her shelves.

Elizabeth took off her coat and paced around the room, her mind flying. No one was concerned about her being gone, or at least they didn't show any concern. The only people who had contacted her were email ads from ebay and pinterest, and one note from her professors reminding her of a meeting when school was back in session. As she stewed over her friends and family's sheer lack of caring, she brewed a pot of tea and sat on the couch.

She wrapped herself up in a blanket and flipped through the channels on tv. She thought about how much she had missed television, the never ending crime shows and the Friends reruns that were on every channel. As she sat she thought more and more of how she wished she could share this with Alice and Charlie. She turned off the tv and paced around the room again. She stopped at the bookshelf and stooped to the bottom shelf. She ran her fingers across her stack of records looking for an old Etta James record. When the music filled the room, she closed her eyes and let herself forget for a moment, when she turned around she half expected to see Charlie sweeping up behind her to spin her around the room and disappointment washed over her.

Her mind wandered to thoughts of her friends, curious to know where they were now. She had found Charlie by simply knocking on the door of his old house and asking about him. Lucky for her, everyone knows everyone in the Cape, and sent her to the nursing home.

But what about Alice and Freddie, and Lennie? What had become of them? She eyed her laptop across the room. She chewed on her lip while she contemplated. Had she run into them on the streets of the Cape before, like with Charlie, back when she was living in the before?

She opened her laptop and began a search for Leonard Knox. The first result was from a local newspaper, the obituaries.

"Nope." She slammed her laptop closed. "I don't want to know." She cleaned up her things and headed to bed.

Before she fell asleep she thought of Charlie, laying in his bed in 1945, completely unaware that she was a lifetime away. The pain came back in her chest, and the tears built up in her eyes and she fell asleep.

Chapter 12

When she arrived the next day, Charles greeted her at the door with two cups of coffee and he had photo albums lying across the table.

"I thought you might be curious," he walked over to the table, and pointed to the stacks of photos "Hopefully, this will help. And I'm prepared to answer any and all questions you have of me." He settled into his chair looking as if he was about to be swarmed by a news room. He motioned to the chair for her to sit and nodded giving his approval to begin asking questions.

She grabbed the book closest to her and began flipping through the pictures, these ones were fresh in her memory.

"You've kept all of these?" She ran her fingers over the photographs from the 1945 carnival.

"Alice had them. She tried to take them after you left, to help me move on. But I hid them. I didn't want to forget. This one is my favorite." He pointed to the two of them in front of the ferris wheel. When their eyes met they saw a mutual longing in each other. Both missing the past, and wishing they could be in that moment again.

They flipped two through the pictures. Freddie and Lennie posing on the pier, Elizabeth and his father dancing at Christmas, and Elizabeth and Alice posing with their matching necklaces. Elizabeth slipped her hand into her shirt and pulled out the glistening silver chain and heart.

"It's like new." Charles spun it between his fingers.

"Well it is only a day old." She smiled. "Thank you again by the way. I love it." She tucked it back into her shirt. She turned the page and gasped.

"Oh, look at Alice." She swooned at the sight of Freddie and Alice's wedding photograph. Alice and Freddie stood in the middle, Charlie on his right and her mother on the left.

"Yes, married August 1947." He explained while Elizabeth lifted the photo to her face to examine it. "Didn't feel right without you there." The two sat in solemn silence for a moment. Elizabeth wondered what else she had missed out on, and how things would've been different if she had stayed. She threw Doc Brown to the wayside.

"When did you propose?" She asked, closing the album in her lap. He hesitated to answer. "Oh shit, wait, did you not propose?" He then let out a laugh.

"Of course I proposed. I would've been stupid not to." He leaned back in his chair, and closed his eyes tightly, trying his best to recall the moment. "It was May 8th, 1946. The Andrews Sisters were in New York." A smile bloomed on his face, but faded too quickly. "But you said no." He finished with a heartbroken sigh. Watching the emotions flicker on Charles' face unlocked the cage on the pain she was feeling last night. Elizabeth knew she should stop asking questions, but she wanted to know how much time she had left with Charlie.

"When did I leave?" She asked while she fidgeted with pages of the album.

"The very next day." He said quietly. They then sat through a painful silence. Elizabeth picked up another album. This one was filled with a collection of more modern photos. Elizabeth could see the gradual aging of Charles and Alice. She was happy to see that the two had stayed close, photos of them spending summers on the beach, attending concerts, and following the Christmas tradition of tree decorating and early morning presents.

"Were they happy?" She said and broke the silence at last.

"Have you looked them up?" Charles wasn't sure how much she knew and didn't want to be the bearer of bad news.

"I started, but I ended up with an article I didn't want to read." She bowed her head, tears forming in the corner of her eyes.

"Yes." He said reaching over and taking her hand. "Lennie in 2002, cancer. Alice in 2009 and Freddie shortly after." He paused, taking in a deep breath. "But yes, they were happy." His smile comforted her.

As her eyes travelled through the pictures, her heart began to ache. Photos of Charles and Alice, changed to Charles and a woman who she did not know. Their wedding, together celebrating birthdays and anniversaries, and slowly she could see his family grow through pictures from vacations and holidays.

Elizabeth couldn't wait any longer, she kept seeing picture after picture of Charles and a tall woman with a delicate face. Jealousy had bubbled up inside her.

"You're married." She pointed to the woman in the picture. "And kids." She let out a gentle sigh. He knew she had been avoiding the subject, as had he.

It had taken Charles many years to move on from Elizabeth, and he was unsure if now was an appropriate time for her to know about Peg. He had told Peg about Elizabeth after they had gotten married, though he only ever said that she was simply an old friend of Alice's.

"Peg." He cleared his throat, unsure to go on. Elizabeth nodded for him to continue. "We met at the dance hall in June 1951, and married a few months later."

"Well, congratulations," was all Elizabeth could muster. She ran her fingers over the three kids in the photo. He pointed to the tallest, brown eyed boy.

"That's Theodore, my oldest. He is clerking for a judge in New York." Charles beamed with pride as he told her. "Freddie," Charles caught sight of Elizabeth's smile. "Yes, and they are very much one in the same." He pointed to a smaller boy with blonde hair and deep brown eyes. "He is running around somewhere in Europe. Writes home every so often."

"That's my youngest, Bea." Elizabeth looked closely at the picture, she had long dark wavy hair, blue eyes, and a thin face. "Short for Elizabeth." Elizabeth shut her eyes tight, accidentally letting the tears roll down her face. She quickly dried them hoping Charles could notice. He caught her hand before she could finish, and wiped them away himself.

"I'm so sorry." She said sniffling. "I'm jealous."

"Well, crying is a much better way to deal with jealousy, than say," he pulled a tissue out of the box from his bedside table.

"Punching a man square in the face." She took the tissue and blew her nose.

"Pow." He whispered with a chuckle. "Elizabeth, please listen." She sat at his bedside. He reached out for her hand. "I am 91 years old. I have lived sixty-one years without you. My life has been wonderful. I've lived through a war, gone on adventures, travelled, lost friends and family, fell in love, had kids, watched them grow up, and now my kids have had kids."

As he spoke, a wave washed over her. She started to realize how much she missed, or will miss. "My life has been full. But I can't honestly say that I haven't thought about you." He placed his free hand over top of hers, holding both of her hands tight. "Ever since that day, the day I saw you lost in the - " he fumbled for his words.

"The paper tornado?" she laughed through the tears building in her eyes.

"Yes, but the paper's weren't the tornado. You were. You spun in and changed my life. There have not been any moments where I haven't thought about how much I wish I could've shared it with you." The tears began to stream down her cheeks.

"My Elizabeth. You taught me to enjoy my life. I have lived every moment to the fullest because I didn't know if they were going to disappear the way you did." He reached out and wiped them from her face, resting his hand on her face as if he had done it every day of his life. "Don't feel sad that you left, never regret the moments we had together, because I don't. Not one. I love every part of them." He paused repeating what had become their mantra to each other, and an idea flickered in his mind.

"I have lived my life. But, I have always wondered how it would've played out with you." He took a deep breath trying to muster the words. "Marry me Elizabeth." He paused trying to understand the concern and confusion that flashed across her face. "When you go back. Say yes."

Chapter 13

Elizabeth woke up the next morning feeling nauseous. She had spent the entire night tossing and turning trying to decide what would be the right choice. After she rolled out of bed, she marched into the living room and pulled out the Pros and Cons list she had made last night before she went to bed.

2012

Pros	Cons
No worries about Butterflies	No Charlie.
	No Alice
Less worrying about my accidental future speak.	No Freddie
	No Lennie
	No Charlie
TV, Smart Phones	
	Will I regret it if I leave?
INTERNET	Family
	Clothes (Hella uncomfortable)
Family	
Time has already proved that I leave 1945	*Will things change if I go back and stay?*

Her main reasons for going back were the people; she genuinely missed them. She felt strange, why should it matter this time? She hadn't taken any friends or family into consideration when she decided to stay in 1945. She thought back to the fight with her sister. Was she really that selfish? Had it distanced her from everyone so much that there was no one left? It was obvious to her now, she had disappeared for weeks and no one had worried enough to take the time to check up on her.

But when Elizabeth looked into her kitchen and saw the empty chairs around the blue wooden dining room table and she felt a tug at her heart. She had never sat at it, not once, it was a piling place for jackets, mail, and old grocery bags. Now she longed for it to be the coffee stained, brown, square table covered in newspapers and flowers, surrounded by dinner guests.

Elizabeth began to pace studying her pros and cons list, hoping that she would look at it and just know what was the right thing to do. She paced past her bookcase and came to a sudden stop. She ran her fingers over the stack of records and sighed. She wanted nothing more than to turn around and find Freddie and Lennie arguing on the couch, Alice fussing in the kitchen and Charlie sitting on the counter pestering her.

"I'll go," she decided, "and stay only until the proposal and then leave. I get to be with Charlie a little longer at least. Plus I'll keep the future on track by leaving just as I was told I did." She dashed to the closet and pulled out her suitcase. She jogged around the apartment grabbing any clothes, books, and records she wanted to take back with her.

Despite their lack of concern, she called her mother and texted her friends, just to let them know she was alive. She made excuses for her being away, and said she was going to be travelling for a few more weeks until the school year had started, just in case she overshot her return again.

Elizabeth stopped into the nursing home one last time before she headed back to her life in 1945. She entered the room to find Charles asleep. She went to his bedside and planted a kiss on his forehead. She had wanted to thank him for everything he had shown her, and apologize for how melancholy their reunion was.

She saw the photo albums spread across the table. If she was going to be faithful to the timeline she needed a way to be sure that nothing would change. Quickly she flipped through them and gently pulled out the picture of Alice and Freddie's wedding, and one of Charles' family pictures labeled 2002. She tucked them away gently in her coat pocket.

She returned to Charles' bedside and whispered to him, "I'll consider it." She kissed him one last time on the cheek and headed out the door.

She slowly walked through town, taking in all of the high tech sights and sounds before she bid it farewell, for who knew how long. When she reached Charles' house, she felt a kind of excitement, the kind you feel when you are going on a big adventure for the first time. But she also had an overwhelming feeling of comfort, like the kind you feel when you're coming home from a long trip.

She had a firm grip on her suitcase and stared at the watch closely as she turned the dial. She needed to be precise this time to be sure no one would know that she left, there would be no way to explain her disappearance.

As the date turned to December 25th, 1945, Elizabeth stopped to look around. The sun had just begun to rise and as she looked around she noticed that all of the houses on the street had seemed to shrink, meanwhile it was like all of the cars had expanded. A smile grew across her face as she walked towards Charlie's house. She crept up the steps and moved slowly and quietly into the house. She slipped her coat and suitcase into the hall closet, and headed into the kitchen to make breakfast.

Moments later Charlie came gliding into the kitchen with a smile beaming from his face. He walked over to Elizabeth and pulled her close, planting a soft kiss on her cheek, and with that Elizabeth felt relaxed from head to toe.

"Good morning darling." He said before he kissed her again. He was practically waltzing around the kitchen while he made coffee and eggs.

"What has gotten you in such a marvelous mood this morning?" She cocked her eyebrows. She watched him watch her and her heart felt full.

"I am just happy to wake up and have you here. It is something I could get used to." His voice was sincere and tentative. He said nothing else but nervously grabbed two cups from the cupboard and placed them at the table. His hands shook as he poured the coffee, quietly awaiting her response.

"Well you better get used to it. I'm not going anywhere." She reassured him. He dashed from the table, over to her side, grabbed her shoulders and turned her towards him.

"I love you Elizabeth." He said, staring directly into her eyes. She could feel his hands shaking on her shoulders.

"Wait, this isn't because we -" She sighed.

"No!" He cut her off. "I mean, yes, but no." He kissed her on the forehead and went back to staring into her eyes. "I love you, truly, wholly, love you."

"I love you too Charlie." He grabbed her face in both of his hands, and kissed her with everything he had. Their lips fit perfectly together and they moved together easily. They stood in the kitchen a moment, arms around each other, forehead to forehead before Charlie gave her a final kiss and walked away.

Something felt different now that she was back. It wasn't the lack of technology or the general kindness of people in this time. Knowing that she was only here now on borrowed time she felt a greater appreciation for every moment and promised herself that she wouldn't let any of them go to waste.

"Well, now that we've settled that." She dished out the eggs onto two plates. "I guess I should be moving in."

"Huh?" Charlie sat jaw hanging open like a door with a loose hinge.

"Alice and Freddie are getting married," she had begun thinking out loud, trying to reason with him about why she should be here. "It would be weird if I stayed with them. Plus I like being here, and most of my things are already here."

Charlie looked at her completely bewildered. "What?"

"I'm serious. What all do I own? This necklace, these clothes, and that stunning, but surprisingly heavy, bookcase. All of which is already here. And like 10 other things. So I was thinking you could just have both the bookcase and myself here. If you'll have us?"

Charlie jumped up off his chair and began to run around the house making room for her yelling as he went from room to room.

"I will clear out a few drawers, make some room in the closet. We could rearrange the furniture if you like. I'm sure I could find a truck to move the things from Alice's and-"

"Doesn't your dad have one? A truck? I'm sure he would let us borrow it." She called out from the kitchen. Suddenly Charlie paused in his tracks and cursed under his breath. "Yes Charles?" Elizabeth said, popping her head into the hall.

"Mom and Dad are rather," he let out a great sigh, "conservative. And after last night we kind of put the kibosh on the conservative part of our relationship." He said with a wink.

"Shit!" She cursed her future forgetfulness. "It's frowned upon, isn't it? The sex before marriage and the whole unwed living together thing?" Elizabeth said with a serious tone and a nervous quiver in her voice.

In 2012, it wasn't uncommon for a woman to sleep with a man she had been dating. Heck it wasn't uncommon for a woman to sleep with a man she had just met. "I don't want to do anything to offend anyone, especially your parents." She sighed defeated and went back to sit at the table. "But I also don't want to waste any of the time I have left here." She said with a whisper.

"It isn't frowned upon. More so it isn't the traditional way." He nervously ran a hand through his hair thinking.

"Where I'm from, there's the traditional way," she gestured, weighing the options in her hands. "And literally any other way, because we are grown-ass adults and we do what we want."

"I want to be where you're from." He joked.

"One day." She winked. "But until then I guess you'll want me to stay at Alice's."

"No!" He said firmly as he made up his mind. "I want this. Screw tradition. I'm not letting you get away." Elizabeth's eyes grew wide. Charlie had always been level headed and by the book, only giving in to her whims on rare occasions. "I love it when you curse, you know. It's something surprising, I guess. You have this nice, sweet, look on your face, and you curse so casually, it knocks me off my game." With her cup in hand she walked over to him.

"To being grown-ass adults." She cheers-ed and raised her cup to him, took a sip and kissed him. Before she could be seated Charlie had his hands around her waist, and was lifting her onto the table.

"To being grown-ass adults" Their lips met and sparks flew.

Her hands wound themselves into his hair, and he grabbed her by the thighs and pulled her to the edge of the table. Elizabeth quickly wrapped her legs around his hips and pulled him tightly to her. His hands ran up her body gently grazing over her breasts as they made their way to her hair. Her hands ran down his chest making quick work of unbuttoning his shirt. The lower she went, she could feel him growing stiff against her. He reached for the base of her shirt and began running his hands up her bare back to find the clasp of her bra. Elizabeth's hands quickly unlooped his belt and moved for the button of his pants. When a loud knock from the door echoed through the room, followed by the sound of footsteps.

"Really!" She threw her head back to the sky cussing out whichever god was tormenting them.

"No!" He sighed resting his head on her shoulder.

"Charlie? Elizabeth?" Alice's voice rang out from the entrance way. The two had just enough time to part themselves, readjust their clothes and clammer into their respective seats before Alice entered the room. She caught them slightly out of breath and flustered.

"What is going on?" Alice said when she barged into the kitchen.

"We were about to start celebrating!" Elizabeth responded coldly and raised her eyebrows.

"Liz is going to be moving in!" Charlie walked over to Alice and gave her a hug. "I'm sorry that I'm stealing your roommate."

"This is so unlike you Charlie. I told you she was good for you." She whispered into his ear as they hugged. "Well you are going to have to move without her for today."

Elizabeth gave her a confused look as Alice crossed the kitchen to her. "Because I need my Maid of Honor to go dress shopping with me." Alice was bubbling with excitement as she said it. "Freddie is driving the car over now, and then you and I are going to drive into the city!"

Freddie showed up moments later and was less than pleased to hear that they would be spending their day moving Elizabeth's things.

"Luckily, I don't own that much stuff. It shouldn't take you all day." She kissed Charlie on the cheek before climbing into the car. "It's all clothes, books and records. And I want to steal the dresser from my room at Alice's." She looked to Alice who nodded in approval. "Oh but you will need to ask your dad if you can borrow his truck for that one."

"HA!" Alice blurted out. "I'm sorry." She said opening the driver's side door. "I am so sorry that I'm going to miss you telling mom and dad you are moving in with an unmarried woman."

Charlie let out an exasperated sigh and looked at Alice as if he was about to plead for her to stay and help him break the news to their parents. Alice continued to laugh, shut her door and the two pulled away onto the street.

It took Alice and Elizabeth about an hour to get into New York. When they arrived Alice parked the car and pulled out a map. She had circled all of the dress shops in a five mile radius.

"It will be in one of the 15 shops, I know it!" She pulled her purse up over her shoulder and began to head down the street with a determined look in her eyes.

Five shops and thirty dresses later Alice had a firm idea on everything she didn't want in a dress.

"No long sleeves, no no train, no abundance of lace." She listed her no's as they headed into a nearby cafe for a break. Elizabeth took a piece of paper out of her purse and began writing.

"So you want short sleeves, a long train, a little bit of lace, the fancy buttons down the back, and a long veil." Elizabeth said as she recalled the picture of Alice's wedding. Alice paid for their coffees and hooked arms with Elizabeth.

"I'm so lucky I have you." Alice said, giving her a squeeze.

"Well it's your wedding, you're allowed to be a nut job. When it's my wedding I'll get to torture you." Elizabeth spoke without thinking and then sadness suddenly washed over her. It wasn't completely untrue. She would get married one day, but it wouldn't be in the 1940s, Alice won't be in the wedding and she will not be marrying Charlie. A lump of disappointment formed in her throat and she quickly swallowed trying to make it go away.

"Why did you and Freddie wait so long to get married?" She asked Alice, quickly trying to change the subject.

"After William I was tentative. Then I met Fred, and then the war came. I wasn't ready to be a widow." She spoke and looked at her map trying to figure where their next location was.

"But you aren't getting married until August of 47. You are clearly organized enough to plan a wedding in a week." Elizabeth chimed in. "Why wait so long?"

"Huh?" Alice was confused and then Elizabeth realized she had slipped into her future-speak again.

"Oh. I could have sworn you mentioned a date, last night, when we were walking home." Elizabeth fumbled and Alice shook her head. "Weird. I must've dreamt it." She waved her hand as if to wave away the nonsense idea.

"Maybe you're right though. I think I want to wait because I don't want to stop working." Elizabeth's face showed zero understanding. "Once I'm married I won't be allowed to work." Her face was still blank. "I think they call it the Marriage Bar. As a nurse I make fair money, and so when I get married the doctor will be forced to let me go. Same goes for if you marry Charles. The school will probably have to let you go. "

"What!" Elizabeth stopped dead in her tracks. "I'm sorry but that's a load of shit!" Two elderly women across the street gasped as Elizabeth cursed. "Sorry." She waved to the women. She moved closer to Alice and spoke again quieter. "That is a load of shit."

Alice laughed at Elizabeth's candor. "I know you aren't one for the traditional way, but that's how it is."

"But it's wrong. Where I am from women work, they have careers and families. And if you try to fire a woman for those reasons you get sued. Hard." Alice stood silent, intrigued and listening. Elizabeth never realized how passionate she was about women's rights before. It wasn't something she was overly concerned about in 2012, because it was something she already had. Living in the backwards way of 1945 made her realize how hard all of those women had to fight for what they deserved.

"Women had to fight for a long time for this, but they got it eventually. That isn't to say it is perfectly fair, we get the shaft when it comes to equal pay." She sighed.

"That place sounds amazing. Why did you ever leave?" Alice said in ah and wonder.

"Charlie, you, Freddie, and Lennie." Elizabeth said with a melancholy smile on her face.

"I think you have it in the wrong order. It should be Me, Charlie, Freddie and Lennie." Alice giggled.

"You're right. Priorities Elizabeth." She jokingly smacked herself on the forehead.

The girls continued their wandering through the city, talking about the plans for the wedding.

By the time they had climbed into the car to go home, they had chosen their venue, the bridesmaids dresses, the music for the first dance, and what they would eat at the reception. They didn't manage to find Alice the short sleeve, laceless, button up the back dress she was looking for, but they decided they weren't destined to find it so they had a reason to come back into the city for another shopping day.

They arrived home late that night. When she reached the house Charlie was already in bed, reading, waiting for her to come home. She entered the house and he called out a hello of welcome telling her to hurry up and come to bed. But before she headed to bed she stopped at the hall closet. She breathed a sigh of relief when she saw that her suitcase and coat had not been touched. She slipped her hand into the coat pocket and pulled out her two pictures from 2012.

"Good," she sighed. Nothing had changed. Elizabeth still wasn't in the photo at Alice's wedding and Charlie's family was still intact. She gently placed them on top in the suitcase and closed it firmly. She took her suitcase down the hall to the bedroom and tucked it under her side of the bed.

Chapter 14

Months had passed since she had returned from 2012, and Charlie had still not brought out the ring, and every night before she went to sleep Elizabeth breathed a sigh of relief that it hadn't. But as relieved as she was, every calendar she saw was a ticking time bomb, constantly reminding her that her time here was brief. Elizabeth knew that when he proposed it would be her time to leave.

By the time the flowers of spring had blossomed, Elizabeth had completely forgotten she was living on borrowed time. Between work, planning Alice's wedding and living with Charlie, life was constantly on the move and she didn't have time to stew over sad things of the future. Nevertheless, She still embraced and appreciated every moment.

Charlie swooped into the room and covered her eyes.

"Guess who?" He asked.

"It better be Charlie Finley, because if it is not, whoever you are is about to get a massive ass kicking." She laughed. He removed his hands to reveal he was holding five tickets. Written across them in big black letters was

The Andrews Sisters
New York City, New York
May 8th, 1946

Elizabeth jumped for joy when she read them. She turned and gave Charlie a huge hug and snatched the tickets from his hand and headed to the door.

"Where are you going?" He called.

"I'm going to tell Alice! She is going to freak out." She replied, trying to throw on her shoes.

"Wait for me!" He chased after her as she headed out the door.

The next day Elizabeth and Alice stood in Alice's bathroom preparing for their night of music.

"Have you ever gone to something like this?" Alice asked, curling her hair.

"No." She said surprised. Elizabeth tried to think of a 2012 equivalent for how exciting this concert would be. The only comparison she could make was the hype that came with attending a Beyonce concert.

"What?" Alice dramatically gasped in disbelief.

"Despite what you believe about where I am from, there are some things I have never done before." She said sarcastically.

"Oh speaking of that! One day this week I'm going to have all the girls from work and the book club come over and I want you to tell them about the place you're from." Alice seemed pleased with this idea but Elizabeth felt fear flare up in her.

"What? Why?" Elizabeth questioned with panic. "I can't."

"I want you to tell them about the place where women have families and work. How women make decent money for the same work as men." Alice spoke, ignoring Elizabeth's protests. "It's all very brilliant. And I want them to see that it can happen. Maybe we can start something. Mary had a great job as a teacher, but when Neil proposed she had to stay goodbye to it. Broke her heart."

Alice continued to talk about her friends and what they had given up to be wives, and how infuriating it was and Elizabeth couldn't help but agree with her. It would be amazing to be at the start of a revolution but it also made her nervous. She wanted to see a change but didn't want to step on too many butterflies while she was here.

"12 women in the Cape aren't going to start a revolution Alice." Elizabeth said, and tried to defuse the situation.

"I think I have 15." Alice bragged, "But I know. We still have to try." Alice nodded, looking at herself in the mirror determined.

An hour later the five of them filed into Freddie's car and sped their way up the highway to New York City. While they drove they all laughed, joked and blasted the radio. The boys graciously allowed Alice and Elizabeth to sing along with every song at the top of their lungs, regardless of if they knew the words or not. The car was noisier than all, except for Charlie. He sat still and quiet, hands in his pockets the entire drive up, only chiming in when he was directly addressed.

The sound of The Andrews Sisters filled the hall as their group entered. Without missing a beat Charlie grabbed Elizabeth by the hand and flung her onto the dance floor, with Freddie and Alice following suit, sending Lennie off to find a table.

Everytime a song would slowly wind down, Elizabeth would edge towards exiting the dance floor, and before she could get a toe off the floor a new song would strike up causing Charlie to sweep her back to the center of the room once more. Elizabeth knew he had the stamina for dancing, but this was something else, like he was avoiding slowing down.

"Charlie!" Elizabeth said, she held his hand firmly and dragged him off of the dance floor. The time passed too quickly and before they knew it the evening was dying down.

"I need a break. Must. Find. Sustenance." She pleaded with him as the Andrews Sisters took a break while their guests took a break at their tables.

As the two of them worked back to their seats Lennie sat at their booth looking dejected. Elizabeth slid in next to him and said. "Struck out again?"

"How did you know?" Lennie slumped over the table, sadly sipping his drink. She gave him a look encouraging him to straighten up and try again.

"I will find you a girl. One second." Elizabeth slid out of their booth and walked from their table. She casually looked around the crowded space and then headed to the group of women that Lennie had been eyeing up all night. When she reached their table she introduced herself and pointed to Lennie.

"Lennie Knox. He is one of the sweetest men you will ever know. He plays a tough soldier, but don't believe him for a second. When you talk, he is genuinely interested, and not too bad on the eyes." As Elizabeth talked she could tell the girls weren't buying it. "Let's be honest ladies. Time is short and Lennie is one of the last handsome and genuinely kind men that you have a chance with, at least for tonight." The honesty of her words clearly struck a chord with the women and their tone changed.

Elizabeth whistled and waved Lennie over. He grabbed Charlie by the arms, looked him directly in the eyes and said, "never let her go." Then he took off towards the swarm of women waiting for him. As their paths crossed he mouthed thank you and they exchanged a casual high-five in passing.

When she reached the table Charlie looked at her, eyes wide with wonder.

"What?" Elizabeth asked.

"You must have magic powers to make that happen." He joked pointing at Lennie leading a girl to the dance floor.

"He is a good guy, the girls around here are too stupid to give him a shot. I just simply nudged them in his direction." Elizabeth sighed happily. Charlie gave her a peck on the cheek and headed to the bar to get another round, to celebrate the moment.

When he reached the bar he looked back at her. While the barman made their drinks, Charlie fiddled with a small fabric box in his hands.

"Whoa. Big night eh?" He chuckled, placing the two glasses on the counter in front of Charlie slightly startling him. Charlie reached into his pocket to pay and the man waved him off. "On the house, friend. Good luck." He winked.

"Fingers crossed." He took a deep breath, put the box back in his pocket, grabbed the drinks and made his way back to her.

Across the dance floor Elizabeth sat at their table alone, watching Charlie make his way back across the room. As he crossed from the bar, he was panicked, sweaty and nervous. Watching him that way reminded him of how Freddie looked before he proposed to Alice. Suddenly, Elizabeth felt faint.

"This is it!" She screamed in a whisper. Her eyes grew large and frantically darted around the room, as the memory of old Charles came rushing back to her.

"It was May 8th, 1946. The Andrews Sisters were in New York...But you said no." his voice echoed in her ears.

"No, no, no, no!" Elizabeth looked around the room and panicked. "It's too soon. I don't want to leave." Her heart was racing, her breath was short and her tears began to well up in her eyes. "I haven't had enough time yet. This isn't fair!"

Elizabeth watched Charlie cross the dance floor trying to memorize every part of him. As he walked A little old woman grabbed him by the arm and pulled him to her. She was holding Charlie firmly by the hand, desperately pleading with him about something. Charlie was polite as always. He stood and heard her out, shook her hand and walked away. Elizabeth was grateful to the woman for slowing him down, giving her more time to process the situation and prepare herself for the heartbreak she was about to cause.

Charlie broke out of the old woman's grasp and walked towards Elizabeth. He straightened his tie and nervously ran his hand through his hair. When he reached the table, she had her back to him trying to keep her composure. He took her hand and spun her to face him.

"Elizabeth." He held his hand to her face. "My Elizabeth. I never expected you. You were a whirlwind. A tornado every day since you showed up. You spun in and changed my life. You have taught me to live everyday to its fullest and never let a moment go to waste. Throw conservatism, caution and tradition to the wind. I know you aren't one for the traditionally traditional, but I hope you'll do this one traditional thing with me." He bent down onto one knee and outstretched his arm with a box in his hand.

"I am done living my life alone, I want to live the rest of it with you. I want to share my life with you, it's yours, every part of it." He opened the box and there it was. The white gold band twisted almost a full circle, except for where it met the square diamond at its center.

The sound of her own heartbeat flooded her ears blocking out the rest of the room. The ring in the box stared at Elizabeth, tormenting her. Her memories of Charles in 2012 ran through her mind, the way he pleaded with her, and the hurt that was in his eyes when he talked about their time together.

She thought of the pictures in the suitcase under the bed, how she had promised to follow time's plan, to say no and go back.

She looked down to Charlie, tears had begun to swell in his chocolate brown eyes. "*I can change things.*" She thought. "*I can make things right - better. Charlie and I don't deserve to feel pain. We can grow old together. Those can be our kids in the picture.*" Thoughts were flying rapidly through her mind. She took a deep breath.

"Yes." She said blankly.

"What?" Charlie looked up at her, waiting to hear it again.

"Yes." This time a smile grew across her face. Charlie stood up, wrapped his arms around her and lifted her to his lips. He held her there a moment, forehead to forehead. Things are going to be different now. She kissed him and thought of all of the possibilities for their future.

"One more time." He said.

"Yes."

Chapter 15

Two days after their engagement Elizabeth woke up squished between Charlie and the diamond ring on her finger. She watched the diamonds sparkle in the sunlight as she moved her hand.

Ever since she had said yes, she was waiting for the other shoe to drop, for something to happen that would show her she had messed up. But lightning hadn't struck her, she hadn't started to fade away, and the pictures hadn't changed. Elizabeth breathed a sigh of relief.

She began to close her eyes, hoping to drift back off to sleep, when her eyes caught the sight of the clock.

"Wake up Charlie!" Elizabeth said with a scream and smacked him until he groaned awake. "It's 10:30, I was supposed to be at Alice's for that bookclub thing!"

"When?" He said groggily.

"Now!" She jumped out of bed and began rushing around the house dressing and throwing clothes at Charlie. And within minutes they were in the car speeding across town.

When they arrived she walked into the kitchen left hand first, flaunting the heavy weight upon it. Alice laughed at the sight of her hand dangling in the doorway.

"I get it, you're engaged!" she called out before pulling her into the kitchen.

"Yes I know you know, but I want the whole world to know." Elizabeth laughed, staring at her hand. "I'm sorry I am so late." Alice snickered. "What?"

"The ladies aren't arriving until 11. I fibbed a little to be sure you'd be here on time. I know what it is like to be newly engaged." She shot her a wink. Charlie entered behind his fiance and gave her a hug.

"If you don't get it together Alice, Liz and I might beat you to the wedding punch." He winked. "Alright darling. I will see you when you've finished." He tipped his hat to Alice and headed out the door.

The ladies slowly arrived and Alice made them comfortable with drinks and snacks until it was time to begin.

"Alright, have you thought about what you're going to say?" Alice said when she pulled Elizabeth into the kitchen.

"What *I* am going to say?" Elizabeth said, confused. "It's bookclub Alice, I just come here for snacks and to pretend like I've read the book. I don't intend to say anything."

Alice looked at her baffled. "All of these people came here to hear you speak. About where you're from." Alice spoke in short choppy sentences trying to trigger Elizabeth's memory. "I told you about it. The night of the Andrews Sisters. Revolution. Changing the future? Ring any bells?"

It did suddenly occur to Elizabeth that Alice had told her. But in the whirlwind of the engagement and Elizabeth's constant fear of tempting fate she had completely forgotten.

"Alice, I can't." Elizabeth thought about old Charlie and how much she had already risked changing the future by staying. She wasn't sure what her saying yes had done, she was sure she shouldn't push it any farther. "I've already changed things enough. I can't do this."

"Changed things? What?" Alice waved her hands. "I'll just have to do it myself. I've heard you talk about it enough."

There were 15 ladies in total, all sitting in a semicircle watching Alice. Elizabeth stood to the side of the room, in her head she was chanting, *'No future-speak. Bite your tongue.'*

Alice began to explain how life worked where Elizabeth was from. She told the women about working whatever job they wanted, through marriage, equality, maternity leave, paternity leave (which received a lot of laughter to her surprise), and *almost* equal pay. But most of them listened with eyes wide in disbelief. While Alice spoke Elizabeth realized that her 'no future-speak' mantra had really failed her, she had spoken a lot already about the future and how all the feminist optimism had rubbed off on Alice.

Elizabeth felt a spark of pride for bringing this about, even if it was a horrible, possible future destroying accident. She thought about when Alice said they'd change the future, maybe she should.

"I've said yes. I've committed to staying. I did that for me. Maybe I do this for everyone else, as an 'I'm leaving the future behind' present." Elizabeth told herself as she watched the women in the room watching Alice unblinkingly. *"Why shouldn't I make the world a better place for women?"* Her brain spiraled off on a tangent, *"Maybe I am meant to? Maybe this really is where it starts and I am creating the future I am from?"* The thoughts started to sound ridiculous, so she

refocused. *"There is nothing wrong with female empowerment and independence coming a few decades early. The only thing stopping us was men -"*

"Nonsense," said a woman in a large purple hat from her seat in the back corner. An uproar of chatter overtook the room while the ladies discussed what they could or could not accomplish. The woman in the purple hat stood again, "Everything is finally going back to normal after the war. Don't ruin it with all these ideas. The people who want these changes are just women who may never marry." She spat her words at Elizabeth.

Elizabeth uncrossed her arms and casually swept back her hair making a show of her new engagement ring.

The purple- hatted woman gritted her teeth and continued, "the system works perfectly fine, my husband is home, I make him dinner and keep his home, raise his kids and I am completely happy, who are you to take this from me."

"But it doesn't work!" Elizabeth said, finally unable to stop herself. "You're completely happy cooking your husband dinner, in *his* home, with his children, where he goes out to work at *his* job, and makes *his* money." Elizabeth began to rant emphasising every 'his' in her sentence. "What if all that could be yours. *Your* house, *your* kids, *your* job, *your* money. Not everyone can cook." Elizabeth heard a distinct laugh slip from Alice's lips. "But some could be damn good teachers, nurses, business owners, leaders. But you want to drop all of that opportunity to what -"

"And what are we going to do?" She interjected. "15 housewives have no say."

"If they can do it there, why can't we do it here?" Alice stepped back in, taking control of the room again. "If we want a change we are going to have to fight for it. And we better start fighting soon."

"If you aren't with us, you may as well leave. There's the door." Elizabeth was completely frustrated. The woman in the purple hat, along with two other women, stood and exited the house. "Yeah. Go on and run back to your husbands." Elizabeth called out, the women laughed and began circling around Alice to debate their plans.

Within the next few hours the women had made plans to create flyers and attend all public political gatherings to bring up their point until they are heard. Feeling successful and each having a job to complete they went on their way.

When Elizabeth arrived home she found Charlie sitting on the couch reading the paper.

"Dear, have you heard about this?" He waved her over to the paper. The headline read, **Estonia Girls Blow Up Soviet Memorial.** "You'd think that the war is over, but every day people are still fighting."

"This astounds me, the world can and will come back from this war, but honestly people will never stop fighting. Hell, even where I'm from, people have to fight for their basic human rights strictly because it offends someone else's religion." She huffs beginning to tidying the living room.

"You always speak so highly about where you're from. What's going on?" He folds the paper into his lap, preparing to listen as she plops down on the couch next to him.

"It is all this stuff with Alice." She sighed. "Being here at the start of this change, it makes me realize how backwards everything is. And you'd hope that years from now we would have moved forward and people would be more understanding and welcoming, but it isn't, some people want to crush development and stay in a backwards, unequal society."

"I think you're more meant for Alice's cause than you thought you were. Maybe you're the change the future needs." He kissed her on the cheek. "I have some errands to do before the shops close. Love you." He scooped up his hat and headed out the door.

Elizabeth went about her day, marking student's work and tidying up the house. As happy as she was in 1946 a thought kept blinking her in mind, "maybe you're the change the future needs." Elizabeth shook her head in an attempt to shake the thought away, but it had opened the door to so many questions. She had talked herself into speaking up at the meeting, she had told herself that it was a gift to the future, but maybe it wasn't a change for the good. Elizabeth remembered learning about the suffragettes in school, and the persecution they went through.

Was what I did today wrong? Were the women of the Cape not supposed to start fighting? Did I change the future for better, or for worse? The uncertainty tore through her stomach, like a dog gnawing on a chew toy.

She thought of the suitcase that lay under their bed, and right now it held her peace of mind. She could look and know if things had changed drastically. She stood from her seat in the sitting room and walked to the bedroom. She stopped herself and shook her head.

"Don't be paranoid. Everything is fine." She walked away to tidy the house and distract herself. She walked past the bedroom multiple times and spied the suitcase under the bed. It was as if it was calling her to open it and check on the future. After her fourth pass of the bedroom door she broke.

"I have to know." She opened the suitcase and pulled out the pictures she had taken from Charles. Her hands shook as she turned them over.

Alice stood in her short sleeve, laceless dress in the center of the photo, Freddie at her side and Charlie on his right, exactly how the picture was before. Only now instead of her mother by her side it was Elizabeth. It was exactly like she had pictured, the four of them side by side, *"just like it should be"* Elizabeth thought.

She flipped to the second picture and her heart dropped into her stomach. It was wrong; not at all like Elizabeth had hoped. She had expected Charles' 2002 family to have been replaced by their future family. Charlie, Elizabeth, and three rounded faced, glasses wearing kids with dark brown hair and eyes. But instead all that sat in front of her was a photo of a middle aged Elizabeth, completely alone.

She stood in disbelief, her mind racing, and then suddenly she felt sick. She ran out of the room into the bathroom. She ran and dropped herself face first over the toilet. She slowly lifted herself from the toilet and slid onto the floor. She stared at the picture and every glance made her feel sick all over again.

"No." She flipped it over in her hands, as if she was expecting to see it had changed. "This doesn't make sense. Where is Charlie? Where is our family?" She stared at the picture, willing it to change.

"What have I done?" At last she stood, rinsed her mouth and wiped her tears. Throwing caution to the wind she did the only thing she thought sensible. She dashed to their bedroom and threw open the top drawer. She pulled out the watch, put on her coat, and slipped the photos in her pocket. She stopped in the sitting room and left a note for Charlie saying she was headed out to do some "running around for the cause," in case she didn't make it back within a few hours.

She stood on the street in front of the house, and held the watch firmly in her hand. She watched life move forward around her in a blur.

As the date rolled to January 1st, 2012 she stopped turning the dial and was hit with a downpour of rain. She quickly looked around and nothing had changed since the last time she had been here. Charlie's house was standing exactly where she had left it. She quickly hailed a taxi and went to the nursing home to check on him.

She ran through the halls to Charles' room. When she reached his room there was a person sitting in the chair near the window, but it wasn't Charles. She turned confused and looked at the plaque on the door, she sighed when her concerns were realized. She walked down the hall towards the nurses station but was tapped on the shoulder before she reached it.

"Are you Elizabeth?" A nurse asked her as she turned around. "Someone said you would be stopping by and I was to give you this." He fished a small white envelope out of his pocket and handed it to her with an apologetic look on his face.

Elizabeth read the note and bolted through the door, catching her cab before it had left. She recognized the address instantly and hoped beyond hope that it was wrong. She spent the entire cab ride convincing herself that the geography had changed, or she had read the address wrong and prayed that she would find Charlie sitting waiting on the porch of a house when she arrived. When the taxi turned from Cherry Street to Parkside Elizabeth knew that her prayers went unanswered.

St. Mary's Cemetery was by no means a large place; Elizabeth didn't have to wander long before she spotted his name on a headstone in an empty space near a collection of large fir trees.

As she approached the headstone the words became clearer.

Charles John Finley
1920 - 1951
Beloved Son, Brother and Husband

Elizabeth dropped to her knees and reached out to run her fingers over the words, thinking that if she couldn't touch them they wouldn't be real.

"No. This isn't right." She said as her hand touched the cold, damp, rock of the headstone. "It - it doesn't make any sense. He was supposed to be alive now. We were supposed to have this time." Her breath was shallow and her stomach felt like it was twisting side of her. "What did I do wrong? How am I going to fix this? I have to fix this."

She sat on the sodden ground thinking through all of her actions since she went back to 1945. She had done a lot of things in the five months that she had been back. Including forgetting about the possibility of affecting the future. She cursed herself for being so careless with the butterflies.

"What was the damn butterfly?" she kept asking herself.

"You said yes, dummy." A voice spoke behind her. Elizabeth jumped up startled, completely unaware that someone had been there this whole time.

"What?" Elizabeth turned to see a short, blonde haired woman, holding an umbrella some five feet behind her. "Who are you?" But the question didn't need answering after she saw her. It was Charles' nurse from the nursing home from the first time she came back.

"You said yes. That was the butterfly." Liza said, walking towards her.

"That doesn't make sense." Elizabeth shook her head and turned back to the grave. "He lived his whole life before. So clearly he didn't get sick, or go to war again, or -" She was running out of ideas. "There is no explanation for this."

"Yes, there is." Liza outstretched the umbrella so it was covering them both from the torrential downpour around them. "You said yes dummy, now shut up and listen. You stepped on that butterfly, and everything that was supposed to happen *because* of that butterfly didn't." Elizabeth didn't want to admit that Liza was right, she didn't want to be the one responsible for this. She looked at the headstone again, closed her eyes tight, hoping that when she opened them she would wake up in 1946 and everything would be fine.

"That's not going to work." She sighed. "I'm Liza." She said, extending her hand as an introduction.

"I know. I remember you. Wait, how do you know all of this? About butterflies?" Elizabeth quickly realized that if Charles was dead then they would've never met. "Who are you?"

"I'm Liza." The short-haired woman said again.

"No shit I know that," Elizabeth spoke, growing more and more defensive.

"It's short for Elizabeth stupid." The realization hit Elizabeth like an out of control car. She understood what she was trying to say, but she was struggling to believe it. She looked up at her analyzing her face. Elizabeth shook her head denying it.

"I woke up a few mornings ago with a ring on my finger and a lifetime of Charlie memories that I didn't have the day before." She fidgeted with the diamond on her finger. "And I thought to myself, when I changed history, where did I go first?" She lifted her hands pointing to the headstone. The more she spoke the less Elizabeth understood. "I'll explain. Come on, let's get you somewhere dry." She extended her hand and helped Elizabeth up from the wet ground.

The two climbed into Liza's car and she began to drive. Elizabeth sat feeling completely empty. Inside her head she wasn't thinking, she was so overwhelmed, that everything inside her was completely blank. She sat, stone still while the tears ran down her face.

Liza drove quickly, winding through the streets back into the Cape. It suddenly occurred to Elizabeth that, despite what Liza wanted her to believe, she had climbed into the car with a complete stranger. She watched her from the passenger seat, trying to figure if what she said at the graveyard was true. Liza had a round face, small nose and blue eyes, those features Elizabeth recognized as her own. Her hair was blonde, a look that Elizabeth swore she'd never do outside of highschool, but as Elizabeth looked closely she spied the dark brown roots that were beginning to peek through.

"Where are we going?" Elizabeth said at last, breaking the silence.

"Coffee." She replied, keeping her eyes on the road.

When they arrived Liza grabbed a shoebox and a blanket from the back of the car and the two headed inside. She sat the box, blanket, and Elizabeth down at a table and went to the counter.

Elizabeth sat at the table wiping the tears and makeup running down her face, trying to make herself more presentable for the public around her. For the first time, she had calmed down enough to realize she was sopping wet and she began to shiver. She reached for the blanket on Liza's chair. As she did she caught sight of the shoebox underneath it. She lifted both the box and blanket off of the chair. She placed the box on the table and wrapped the blanket around herself.

The box read: **DO NOT OPEN UNTIL ALONE.** Elizabeth chewed on her lip pondering opening it. *"I have literally ruined everything today, how much worse could it get?"* She thought before popping the lid off and sitting on the opposite side of the table. She peered in the box to see a large collection of black and white pictures, newspaper clippings, and letters.

When she came back Liza saw the box lid sitting off of the box.

"Really?" She lifted it and pointed at the label on it.

"Sorry." Elizabeth shrugged. "Couldn't wait."

"I know." Liza smiled. "It was a bit of time travel humor. We are the same person, so technically if we go through it together-"

"We will still technically be alone." Elizabeth snickered and appreciated the joke for lightening the mood.

"It is really our sense of humour." Liza placed the coffee on the table.

Elizabeth opened the lid on her cup, dropped in the stir stick, cream and two sugar cubes. She looked down into the coffee cup and stirred waiting for the sugar to dissolve. When it had, she tapped the stick on the rim of the cup twice, licked it off, and lifted the cup to her face and inhaled.

As she did this, Liza did the exact same thing at the exact same time, making it look almost as if there was a mirror between them. Both of them sniffed and let out a satisfied sigh after the ritual was complete. Others in the coffee shop were looking at them thinking they were some kind of almost identical twin performance piece.

"What's going on?" Elizabeth looked around feeling concerned, like maybe the two of them shouldn't be in the same place at the same time.

"It happens when we get together. Our mannerisms are identical so people tend to think we are a circus act." She waved off those who were watching. Elizabeth sat staring at the woman across from her. "You're waiting for me to prove that we are the same person." She stewed for a moment. "Think of a number between 1 and 10." Elizabeth cocked an eyebrow and nodded. Liza raised her hand and counted down, 3-2-1.

"Two." They said in unison.

"See that's not fair, I always pick two. Unless -" Elizabeth began and Liza cut her off finishing her sentence.

"Unless money is involved and then you pick seven because it seems more likely." Elizabeth's jaw fell open, and Liza nodded. "Believe me now?"

"I guess. I have travelled through time for christ sake. Nowadays pretty much anything seems possible." Elizabeth said and Liza let out a snicker.

"Are we safe to be here? Like this?" Elizabeth asked, suddenly becoming concerned and inspected her body and hands.

"What do you mean?" She giggled.

"I mean, one of us isn't going to disappear, implode, or have a mental breakdown." Liza grabbed Elizabeth's hands and placed them back on the table.

"Well I didn't when I was you, so I think we are going to be okay." She gave her a reassuring wink. "It's good to see that you've come around to the idea that you are me."

"Or are you me?" Elizabeth jested.

"I came first honey, you're me." Liza leaned back in her chair and crossed her legs.

"Yes Mam'." Elizabeth sarcastically retorted but was honestly taken aback by the sass. "Man, I get mean when I grow up."

"Not mean. Just cynical." The two sat silently for a moment. "Alright let's get down to business." She pulled the box away from Elizabeth and closer to herself. She began to rummage through the papers looking for something. She pulled out a large photo and handed it to Elizabeth.

The second her eyes hit the photo, she was swept up by feelings of unabashed joy. The massive smile on her face was only matched by the ones on the faces in the photo. Charlie and Elizabeth filled the frame of the photo. He had his arms wrapped around her waist, and had her dipped halfway to the ground and was planting a kiss on her lips. Charlie had on a strikingly black tuxedo and bow tie, while white lace flowed around her body and down onto the floor. Hanging from her left hand was a bouquet of white daisies.

"We get married?" Elizabeth asked, running her hands over the photograph.

"No, I *got* married." Liza snappily retorted. "None of this has happened for you yet, and well, none of this even happened for me really."

Elizabeth shot her head up confused. Liza handed her more photographs from that day. The two of them dancing their first dance, wedding party photos, Elizabeth dancing with Charlie's father, Elizabeth and Alice singing karaoke as the night is winding down.

"It was me, but it wasn't me. That's me in the photo and I have memories from that day. But it all feels foggy." She chewed her lip trying to think of a good analogy. "It's like deja vu. I remember it, I feel it, but I didn't live it."

"You feel it?" She flipped to a photo of Charlie and his mother dancing.

"I look at the pictures and I feel happy. I think about Charlie and I feel crushed and sad. I didn't get to experience it, but I feel every single ounce of it." She took a sip from her coffee trying to fight back any emotions she was feeling. "It's kind of our punishment for meddling with time."

"Awful things happen to wizards who meddle with time, Harry." The two of them said at the same time before settling into a brief chuckle.

"How long did he and I get together? Sorry, not me - you. How long did the two of you have together?" Elizabeth asked, looking at a photo of Charlie holding her in his arms outside his house. She paused thinking back.

"5 years. 46 - 50. He passed away in early 51." She fished through the box and handed her the newspaper clipping of his obituary.

"That's it?" She asked in disbelief, she pushed away the square paper without reading it. "How? What happened?"

"One day, doing errands around town, he wasn't paying attention and neither was the woman driving the car." Liza said all of these things so easily. Elizabeth's hand flew to her mouth in shock. It felt as if someone had punched her in the stomach knocking all of the air out of her.

"How are you handling this so well? Your husband is dead." She said, gasping, trying to deepen her shallow breaths.

"I'm sorry." Liza reached out and grabbed Elizabeth's hand trying to comfort her. "I keep forgetting how fresh everything is for you." She contemplated for a moment, scooped everything up and waved for Elizabeth to do the same. "Come with me." They clambered back into the car and drove for only a few blocks, stopping outside the Cape city hall.

When they stopped Liza reached across the car, opened the glove box and snatched something out. She then reached and opened the passenger door.

"Okay. Out." She said, waved her hands, and shooed Elizabeth out of the car.

They stood on the sidewalk and Liza took hold of Elizabeth's hand. Out of her pocket she pulled the rusted gold pocket watch, a twin to the one resting in Elizabeth's own pocket.

"Hell if you had just shown me that, we wouldn't have had to go through all the number-guessing nonsense." Elizabeth shook her head.

"Damn." Liza laughed. "I guess so. Remember that when it's your turn, okay."

Before Elizabeth could ask her to explain what she meant by 'your turn', Liza had begun to spin the dial and the world was changing around them. When they had stopped, Elizabeth couldn't quite put her finger on where they were. It seemed familiar, but before Elizabeth could ask, Liza grabbed her by the arm and dragged her over behind a tree.

"We have to stay right here." She said pushing Elizabeth in front of her so she could see the street. "No moving, no speaking." Elizabeth nodded in agreement.

The two stood tucked behind the tree watching, Elizabeth having no idea what she was watching for.

Time slowly passed and nothing had happened. Elizabeth turned to Liza, opened her mouth to speak, but Liza put a finger over her lips and pointed out to the road. Elizabeth's heart skipped a beat when she saw him. Charlie, her Charlie. *"Well, sort of,"* she thought, *"he looks older."* Her eyes exploded wide and her head snapped around to Liza.

"Are you fucking crazy, I don't want to see -" Elizabeth screamed in protest but Liza grabbed Elizabeth's face and turned it towards the road.

Charlie stood slightly back from the street corner allowing a steady stream of cars to flow past him. Elizabeth recognized this habit. He was always too polite to let someone stop for him. He waited with his head in his paper casually watching over the top of the words for when the cars had fizzled out and he could cross. At last the line of traffic had faded. He folded his paper, tucked it neatly under his arm and stepped out into the street.

Elizabeth could feel a scream building in her chest, trying to crawl up and burst out of her throat. Her muscles tensed and flexed, she tried to move, tried to run out onto the street and catch him. She looked down to see Liza's arms wrapped so tightly around her that moving was impossible.

"No. Watch." Liza loudly whispered into Elizabeth's ear while she held her in a vice grip. Elizabeth lifted her head just in time to see the car fly through the intersection. His body went completely limp, flopping like a rag doll against the hood of the car and then landing against the pavement a few feet away from where they stood.

The driver of the car swerved towards the side of the road, slamming on their breaks directly in front of their hiding place by the tree. The driver burst out of the car, and for a split second the girls caught sight of the delicately thin-faced woman with bright blue eyes and lengthy straight brown hair, before she was in the street standing over Charlie's body.

Elizabeth burst out of Liza's arms and ran to the woman yelling, "what did you do?"

But before Elizabeth laid eyes on Charlie's body, Liza said, "That's enough." She grabbed Elizabeth by the wrist and dialled the watch forward in her hand.

"Why?" Elizabeth called out in shock when they settled back in 2012. Her shock wasn't from witnessing the accident, but in shock from the fact that she was brought there in the first place. "For what god forsaken reason did you think that would be a good idea?!"

"That was Peggy." She responded calmly.

"Who the fuck is Peggy?" Elizabeth said looking at Liza like she was a lunatic.

"His wife." She said matter of factly.

"Why does it matter?" Elizabeth shook her head in wonder. She took a moment and tried to remember the woman from the picture before it had changed, but with everything that had happened in the last ten minutes she was feeling faint.

"*She* is the butterfly." She sat down on the curb. She looked to Elizabeth and patted the empty spot beside her encouraging her to sit down. After she sat Liza gave her a moment to wipe her tears and catch her breath.

"Alright." She said when Elizabeth was at last seated next to her. "I - I mean - you," she stuttered, "fine. *We* marry Charlie. We have been happily married for five years. But that means, he never met Peggy. And on that day she is the one driving. She's flustered and angry because her husband didn't fix the leak in the roof, causing it to collapse and they lost their kitchen. Which meant Peggy had to drive and pick up food from the diner across town every day." She paused and took a deep breath before continuing on.

"In the proper 1951, he is the one driving that car, not Peg. They live in Charlie's house with a well tended roof. It doesn't leak or collapse. They drive to the diner that day just for fun. No one gets hurt, and Charlie and Peg go on to live a long and happy life together." Elizabeth listened but in disbelief.

Elizabeth sat for a long time trying to calm all of her sadness and anger. "How in the damn hell did you figure that?" She said once she had finished fully processing the story.

"Beth and myself took a long time, jumping around, watching the timelines, observing their lives to finally track down the butterfly." Liza nodded eyes wide remembering the hours and days of jumping around in time until they had finally tracked it back.

"Beth?" Elizabeth questioned.

"Beth, the Elizabeth that came before me."

"Wait, how many of us are there?" Elizabeth asked, both completely fascinated and confused.

"To the best of my knowledge, " she paused and began counting on her fingers, "you are the fifth."

"So you're saying I go back, say no, and go on living my life. Become this cynical woman, who is, honestly, a little bit of a masochist apparently." She waves her hands to indicate the experience she just put herself through. "Going through the motions like nothing happened until this moment where I come back to teach myself a lesson." She shook her head sternly. "I'm sorry but no. I can't do that." Elizabeth's eyes met with her older self. "I will not just forget everything that happened." She stood. "I will not forget Charlie. And the fact that you did, makes me seriously wonder just how much we really are alike." She crossed her arms and began walking away up the street towards the car.

"I didn't forget." Liza called out to her, and took off after Elizabeth down the street. "None of us ever forget." When she reached Elizabeth she grabbed her by the arm and spun her around.

"I feel the pain of leaving him every single day, and don't you dare say that I don't." Up until now Liza had always been so calm and level headed about everything that seeing the anger filling her face was surprising to Elizabeth.

"Sometimes it is a twinge when I remember the way he would wrap his arms around me. And when I remember the heartbreak in his eyes when I said no and walked away it is as if someone has pulled my heart out of my chest." Elizabeth didn't know how to respond, so she stayed silent. "I worked at that old folks home part-time, just so I could be sure he was okay. I watched him mourn his wife, watched his kids come into visit, knowing that we could never have that." It took Liza's outburst to remind Elizabeth of where they met, and the choice Liza made. "The pain never stops. But you have to learn to push it away. If you spend every single day stewing over what happened, good or bad, you'll never be able to live."

The two walked in silence until they reached the car. Liza walked around to the driver's side and looked to Elizabeth, knowing that she needed to say something.

"But I don't want to live without Charlie." She looked at Liza through watery eyes. Liza said nothing, simply nodded and climbed into the car.

Chapter 16

The car came to a stop in the driveway of a small, one story yellow house, with a large bay window that faced out onto the street. When Elizabeth stepped out of the car she became overwhelmed by a feeling of familiarity. She let her eyes wander around the neighborhood until they landed on the house next door. There sat the beige one story house that she had become very accustomed to, Charlie's house.

"Wait. You live here?" Elizabeth said, pointing to the house next door as if Liza was unaware of the proximity to Charlie's home.

"Technically in this timeline I live there." She pointed to Charlie's house. "He left it to me after he passed, and I never have the heart to sell it." She sighed and looked at it as she walked towards the yellow house. "Don't worry, you won't find another one of us in there. She travels a lot." Liza paused, feeling the need to confirm. "Space - not time." She let out a little snicker. "Time travel speak, you never really get used to it." She fumbled her keys out of her pocket and led Elizabeth into the house.

"We buy it after we come back, always. It is one of those things that is set in stone in every timeline." She explained after they entered the house and tossed their coats on the chair in the hall.

Elizabeth moved from room to room taking in the atmosphere of her future home. It was a nice house, small but not cramped, stylish but not over the top. Her eyes popped when she reached the light grey living room. Wall to wall bookcases covered two of the four walls. She scanned the shelves impressed, the collection was piled high featuring books, movies, records, music, and video games from every decade. The inside center wall held a tv, speakers and various artwork collected through the times.

After staring in wonder at the shelf after shelf of collectibles, Elizabeth turned to face the window. It took up the majority of the last wall in the room, leaving small panels on either side that dorned even more artwork. In front of the window was a wooden bench with large, fluffy, black cushions laying across it.

"Why this house?" She asked and took a seat. She leaned against the window frame and threw her feet up on the bench.

"To keep an eye on who comes next." Liza went on to explain that there was a sudden and deafening silence when someone travels into your own timeline. "I hear it and from the living room window I can see *you* coming and going. That's how I knew where to find you when you arrived."

Elizabeth gazed out of the time-watching window while Liza ran down the hall and into the kitchen. As she shuffled around the house she filled the awkward silence that was building between them.

"I know you don't want to live without him. Or any of them for that matter." When she came back she was carrying glasses of water and a stack of papers.

"But -" Elizabeth said optimistically, encouraging her to finish her sentence.

"No buts, it is true." Liza said firmly, and joined Elizabeth on the window bench. "It is not an easy choice." Elizabeth scoffed at Liza's attempt at comfort.

"It's not like it is my choice really." Elizabeth sighed and rolled her eyes.

"It's your choice Elizabeth. Right now you're thinking it isn't but it is." Liza's face was stern and serious. "When I was there, I said yes too. I have literally lived through this conversation, and yes everything is exactly as weird as you think it is." Elizabeth laughed realizing that they really did share a brain.

"Right now you are thinking about Harry Potter and how time is just a loop." Liza said, and Elizabeth looked at her astonished. "We are the same person, and I know how you think."

"Well, clearly time is a loop." Elizabeth quickly moved her hands between the two of them, gesturing to the obviousness of the situation.

"No it's not." Liza grabbed Elizabeth's hands and knocked them down into her lap. "Now, shut up and listen!"

"Fine." She sighed, angrily leaning back against the wall and crossing her arms.

"I said yes, but Beth before me, she didn't. She said no, left a note for Charlie, and came back and no one was the wiser." Elizabeth furrowed her brow confused. Liza continued trying to explain what had happened but they both knew that using words wasn't working. She grabbed a piece of paper and began to draw.

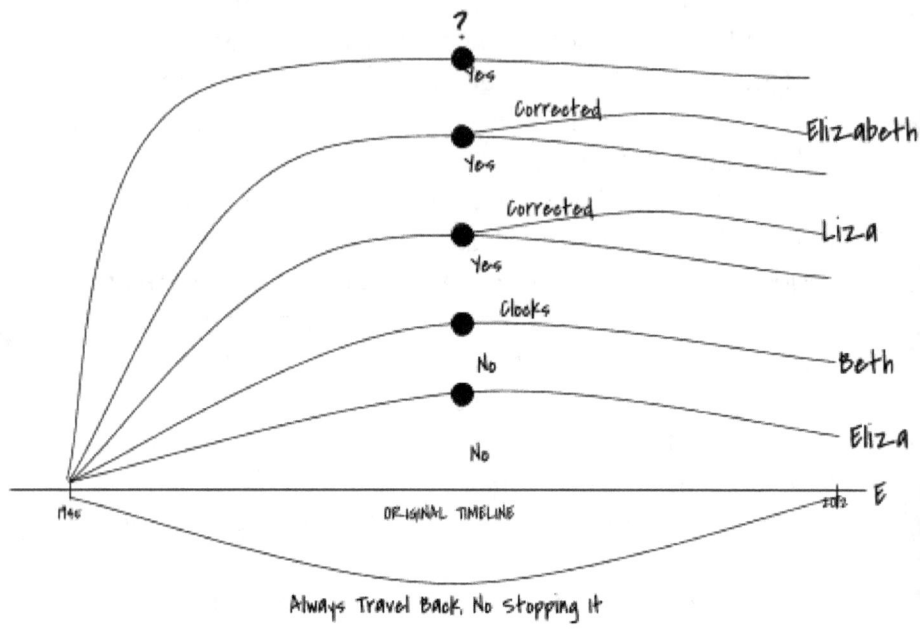

Always Travel Back, No Stopping It

"Well there are things that don't change, aren't there?" Elizabeth said, noticing the note at the bottom of the page.

"Yes, two things are fixed by time." Liza pointed to the note under the diagram. "We always go back, there is no controlling it." Liza saw a question bubbling in Elizabeth's mind. "The first Elizabeth, E, she tried to stop it. She tried to block the others from going back the first three times after her. She failed every time. There is no stopping it." Elizabeth nodded to reassure Liza that she was listening and understanding. She vaguely gestured with her hand encouraging Liza to continue.

"And buying this house. It can't be another house, it has to be this one." Liza looked around the house. "Not like that's a bad thing." Elizabeth nodded in agreement.

"There is a third," Liza continued, "but it is more of a tradition, than a point set in time."

"The letter to Charlie?" Elizabeth guessed. Liza put her finger to her nose letting her know that she was spot on with her understanding.

"Good, I don't need to explain that one then." Liza laid back on the bench relaxed.

"Do you ever think about not telling him we'll come see him?" Elizabeth asked almost at a whisper.

"No." Liza lost her relaxed demeanor and sat up confused. "How else would he know to expect us?"

"Is it right to make him wait though?" This thought had been bouncing around in the back of Elizabeth's mind since she saw Charles in 2012. Liza said nothing in return, waiting for Elizabeth to continue. "I know it's horrible to say, but would he be happier if he didn't know?" Liza leaned back against the window frame, arms crossed and brow furrowed contemplating Elizabeth's words.

"He said he lived a happy life, but if he is always waiting, is that really living?" Elizabeth paused trying to think of another way to phrase it. "Is he better off without us?"

The girls sat in silence, they didn't need to speak out loud. After all they did share the same brain, they were going through the same thought process, thinking of the ramifications if he didn't know to wait. After ten minutes of silence Liza spoke.

"We make our own choices. Everyone of us has changed something. Eliza was the first one to leave him with the time she'd be back, Beth was the first one to say yes, I was the first one to leave my pocket watch with him." Elizabeth squinted in confusion at mention of the pocket watch. It never occurred to her how she got it. She opened her mouth to ask, but Liza raised her hand to silence her.

"You could change things too. You could not leave the note. Hell, you could say yes and live out your life there with him until he passes. It's your choice."

"But -?" Elizabeth egged her on again.

"But," Liza said with a smile. "You need to make the choice that you think is best."

"What is best?" Elizabeth sighed.

"Oh no," Liza turned and walked back to Elizabeth. "I am not answering that question. I know how indecisive we are. I tried to get Beth to tell me the right decision too."

"But -" Elizabeth tried to explain her reason but Liza interjected.

"This is a decision you have to live with for the rest of your life. You have to be the one to make it." With that she walked out of the room, signaling that their conversation was over.

That evening Liza helped Elizabeth prepare her for the trip back, warning her that when she arrived she would need to be exact, to the precise the second she crossed into her past timeline.

"Wait -" She called out from the bathroom where she was changing back into her 1940's clothes. "I crossed into your time stream now." She stuck her head out into the hallway looking for Liza. "How are we both here?"

"It is like the only kind thing Time does for us." Liza came out of the bedroom carrying a pencil and paper, and a smile across her face. "It only works when you move backwards. Think of it like writing with a pencil. When you work forward it writes, when you want to work in reverse, it erases." Liz used the pencil in her hand to solidify her example. "Time knows that you want to fix it, and it helps out." Elizabeth nodded, pleased and appreciated by Time's helping hand.

After she was dressed, Elizabeth went back into the living room and plopped down on the window seat. Liza followed suit a few moments later and stopped in the doorway when she saw her sitting there 1940's head to toe.

Sadness washed over Liza like a wave on the beach. She longed to be in that position, travelling back, being with Charlie again, getting to gossip with Alice, and harass the boys.

"What's wrong?" Elizabeth said when she caught sight of Liza crying in the entryway.

"You'll understand when it's your turn to be a mentor." She wiped the tears from her eyes and sat across from Elizabeth on the bench. "Made up your mind yet?"

"Nope." Elizabeth let her head fall in shame. "Had you when you were me?"

"I had, actually." She said, which made Elizabeth even more confused.

"How?" Elizabeth was exhausted from thought. Liza tried to remember her reasons for her actions when she was there.

"When you decided to stay in 1945 the first time, why did you do it?" Liza thought of the questions she used to help her make her decision.

"I felt like I didn't really have a reason to go back. I wanted the adventure. I wanted to see Charlie again. I didn't want to be here." Elizabeth quickly stated.

"And what about when you said yes?" Liza questioned again.

"I wanted to spend more time with Charlie. I wanted more time there." She said quickly again.

"You might want to take a little more time in your decision making this time. Pros and Cons lists work great for one person, but - " she trailed off, either unable or not wanting to complete her thought. A strange silence fell across the two of them, like for a moment the sound had been muted on the TV. She walked to the door, scooped up their coats and tossed Elizabeth's to her. "Time to go."

They stood in the doorway before they left the house, both girls looked at eachother and took a deep breath. Both of them felt nervous and unsure of what their futures held.

Liza drove the long drive into New York City, to the old dance hall from 1946. After they arrived, the two girls stood on the curb saying goodbye.

"Thanks." Elizabeth said feeling sad emotions bubbling up in her. "For everything."

"No crying." Liza said firmly wagging her finger in Elizabeth's face. She quickly wrapped her arms around her former self and squeezed her tight.

"You have to make the decision, you have to be the one to change it. You can." Liza whispered almost desperately as she held her close. She let her go, turned and walked away to the car, not looking back. Elizabeth stood on the curb, eyes distraught, and more confused about her decision than ever before.

Chapter 17

When she arrived in the crisp cold air of 1946 Elizabeth could hear the sound of the Andrews Sisters bouncing inside the dance hall. She quickly jogged into the hall and looked around, just in time to see Charlie leave the table to get some champagne to celebrate. She looked back to the table in time to see herself fading. Elizabeth looked down to her hand and there it was, glistening and mocking her as it hugged her finger.

"Damn, too late." She thought reaching back into her pocket to dial back further. She stopped reaching for the watch when she caught sight of Alice and Freddie on the dance floor. She casually moved across the floor until she had reached them.

"May I cut in?" She said, looking at Freddie. He turned to face her and extended his hand to her, only to have Elizabeth grab Alice by the hand and whisk her off the floor, leaving him alone and with a dramatic look of shock on his face.

She led Alice to an empty table nearby and pushed her down onto it. Alice grabbed her hand, pointed to the ring and began to squeal.

"Not important right now." Elizabeth took it off and put it into her pocket.

"You have to listen to what I'm going to say. It isn't going to make sense but you need to listen." Alice sat wide eyed and still, with a nervous look on her face.

"You know, when you guys took me in, I know you thought I was running from something. But I wasn't. It

221

was a total accident that I am here. I found a watch, and accidentally travelled back in time." Alice leaned backwards, put off by the mention of time travel. "I didn't know it at the time but you were right. I think I was running towards something, something that I didn't know I needed or wanted. I landed here and I am forever grateful I did." She leaned down and gave Alice a big hug. "You aren't going to remember any of this in a moment, because I'm going to go back and make things right. But I wanted you to know how grateful I am for you Alice. You made me so much better, stronger, than I ever thought I could be." She kissed her on the cheek and walked away. "Change the world Alice."

Elizabeth made her way to the table her previous self faded from. She took the ring off and pocket watch out of her pocket and placed them on the table. She watched as everyone moved backwards around her as she spun the dial. When she stopped she looked and the ring on the table was gone. She spied Charlie across the hall back at the bar looking nervous and sweaty. She stood, taking deep breaths trying to confirm her decision. She watched the old lady grab him by the arm and with that Elizabeth turned around. She still had no idea what she was going to say when he reached her.

"I need more time." She whispered to herself and looked down at the watch in her hand and laughed. She spun time back again.

"If I stay, he dies. If I go, I will lose him." She took a deep breath in. Every thought sucked a breath from her body. "If I leave he moves on. If I stay we are happy, at least for a little while." She exhaled. "I want-" inhale, "I want -" exhale. Charlie was beginning his pursuit again.

Elizabeth held the watch in her hand fidgeting with panic. This time she didn't spin the dial as her hands worried. Instead she rested her thumb on the top of the dial and clicked it up and down quickly.

Suddenly it appeared as if everyone was moving in pieces, like they were moving and flickering in the glow of a strobe light. Elizabeth had become so distracted by the strange movement of the people she managed to calm her thoughts. Her calm reprieve was brief. Once the people had stopped flickering her panic set in again, and she retired to her nervous clicking the top of the watch. Her eyes fluttered as the people did as well.

She stopped clicking the watch again, and looked around, everyone stopped, stuck in their active dancing position. She clicked the watch again and watched everyone spring back to life.

"Damn!" she screeched excitedly, and looked around the room. She clicked it again. Everyone was completely still, frozen. She looked at the watch. "The hell?!" She was shocked and confused. She clicked it again and they sprung back into motion.

"Oh shit!" She exclaimed with a gasp of surprise and laughter. She stood, and even though she had her back to him she could feel him getting closer and closer.

He grabbed her by the hand and turned her around. With that Elizabeth was swept up in a cloud of deja vu.

"Elizabeth." He held his hand to her face. "My Elizabeth. I never expected you. You were a whirlwind. A tornado every day since you showed up. You spun in and changed my life. You have taught me to live everyday to its fullest and never let a moment go to waste. Throw conservatism, caution and tradition to the wind. I know you aren't one for the traditionally traditional, but I hope you'll do this one traditional thing with me...." He bent down onto one knee and outstretched his arm with a box in his hand.

She knew he was speaking but she couldn't hear him, her heartbeat in her ears was deafening. She was beginning to feel faint, still unsure of the words that would come out of her mouth.

She slipped the watch behind her back and clicked the top. Charlie froze and everything fell silent. She stood as still as those around her, her mind racing. Charlie's frozen face looked up at her, eyes hopeful and wide.

"My Charlie." She reached out and touched his face. "Tell me what to do." She begged, dropping to her knees in front of him. She gently held his face in her hands and rotated it down to face her. "What do I -" she paused when she saw his eyes again. The deep chocolate brown eyes sat fixated on her, but this time she didn't see her Charlie in them, she saw old Charlie, sitting in his chair reminiscing about their lives together, longing for her to change his life.

Her memories with him echoed in her brain, ringing out louder than any words Liza had said to her. At that moment she knew what she wanted.

"I want to stay here with you." She said and kissed him on the forehead. "More than I have ever wanted anything in my life." She stood up, "but it isn't right." She walked back to her position at the table. "You deserve more than that, you deserve the truth," she lifted the watch, her thumb hovering over top of the button. "A lifetime's worth." The button clicked and everyone sprung back to life.

Chapter 18

Thinking quickly she grabbed Charlie by the hand. She lifted him to his feet and led him, running and confused, through the building until they were outside the back of the hall and in the alleyway.

"Elizabeth, Liz." He panted trying to keep up with her. "Slow down." When she finally came to a stop, he grabbed her by the shoulders and held her still in front of him. "What is wrong?"

"No." She said sternly and closed her eyes tight, afraid to open them and see any type of pain on his face.

"Huh?" His response was almost a whisper, but the sadness in his voice echoed deep into her heart, forcing her eyes open to meet his. They stood there for a long moment, eyes locked on one another, searching for answers in the pain they saw mirrored on the other's face.

"I can't." She whispered. He shook his head in confusion. "It's not that I don't want to. Please believe me, if I had any other choice." She tried her best to keep her voice steady so she could explain, but the tears ran in a steady stream down her face.

"I'm not from here Charlie." She said exasperatedly.

"I know that." He nodded, reminding her, his voice thick with a comforting tone.

"No. You don't." She sighed, breaking out of his grasp.

"Then tell me. Please." He stood firmly planted. "If you are going to walk away from me, you're going to have to put up one hell of an argument." He raised his eyebrows, egging her on, as he always did when they were fighting or competing for something.

"You better buckle up then buddy." She took a deep breath, and gestured for him to get comfortable. He took a defensive stance, up right and hands in his pockets, not moving. Elizabeth popped her hip to the side and crossed her arms, telling him she wasn't starting until he was at ease. Finally he let him settle himself leaning against the wall comfortably, his hands still in his pockets.

"Okay." Thankfully the sound of the street drowned out her story to the passersby. She told him about the watch, travelling here and meeting him, travelling back again, "no wait, forwards, no back, no forward, it's all very complicated," she paused her story to interject with confusion. She told him about seeing him, old him, saying yes, and the butterflies. By the time she reached the end of the story she was emotionally exhausted.

"You will live this full life. You will travel, have a family, kids, grandkids." She rambled on. He lifted himself off the wall, thinking it was his turn to speak, but she continued over top of him. "I've been there, I've seen it." She said firmly. "I love you Charlie, but I refuse to take all of that away from you."

She finished her spiel, leaned against the wall, and slowly slid down until she was sitting on the ground. He stood above her, silent, thinking through everything she had told him.

"Prove it." He said at last.

"What?" She looked up at him in disbelief. She said, extending a hand to him. "You don't think I'm crazy, a liar, a lunatic?" He shook his head and helped her to her feet.

"You are crazy. But I still love ya." He nodded. "So, prove it."

"All of that and you simply want me to prove it." She looked at him in disbelief and he nodded again. "Okay." She chewed her lip. "How?"

He stood contemplating the possibilities, and then suddenly doing the only thing she could think of, Elizabeth clicked the watch. As time froze she walked down the alley way until she was a far enough distance away to hopefully give him his proof. She clicked the watch. Charlie furiously looked around trying to figure where she had gone.

"You ran there." He called her when he finally spotted her. She clicked the watch again, and slowly took her time walking back towards him.

"You know me. I wouldn't run even if there was a fire," she retorted once she was back at his side. Her sudden reappearance made him jump.

"You have to do something else. Something futuristic." He said, crossing his arms, challenging her further.

Elizabeth looked around her, to take in the sights and sounds of the alley. A yellow cab flew past on the road to their right, a police car on their left, and then three loud drunk men came bursting out of the dance hall door arm in arm reciting Boogie Woogie Bugle Boy and then proceeding to whistle in her direction. She stood still a moment, closing her eyes tightly, and silently reciting cab, police, drunks, whistle, trying to drill those things into her brain. He stood watching her as she did so.

"You may be crazy," he said again with a shrug and a smile, "but I still love ya."

She quickly stuck her tongue out at him as she always did when they would bicker, completely forgetting the overwhelming sadness from moments prior. She pulled the watch out of her pocket, waved it in his face and spun the dial back until those three events had passed.

"Something futuristic," Charlie said again.

"Now pay attention. Yellow taxi," she pointed to the right, "police car," then pointed to the left, "drunken douchebags," and lastly she pointed to the door as the three men tumble out.

"Well they are drunk, but -" Charlie began.

"Wait for it." She interjected, and nodded as the men whistle and call out.

"Hey, sweetheart, want to finish this dance at my place?" They began to walk towards them.

"Oh keep walking." She flipped them off and watched them stagger down the alley towards the street. She turned back to Charlie, "See, douche bags." She then crossed her arms, popped her hip and raised her eyebrows as if to say, 'what else ya got.'

Charlie looked impressed by her proof but only for a brief moment. His look of wonder quickly faded to shock and then disappointment. Elizabeth watched, confused until she made the connection he did moments earlier.

"So I -" He slowly stuttered, and raised his eyes to the sky. "I die."

"No." She shut him down firmly. She took him by the hand, squeezing it tightly so he would look back at her. She placed her hand on his face in the same comforting way he always did to her. "I won't let you."

"I just don't understand." He shook his head in disappointment, but the strange thing was he did understand. He had always expected her story to be something unexpecting, but never expected anything like what she had described; but he did not doubt her, not for one second.

"It's the butterfly. I said yes, it changed everything in your future." Elizabeth began her explanation again, trying to simplify it for him. He waved his hands telling her to stop.

"I understand that. Stuff happened, the future changed." He raised his head from it's hanging position. "But how can you be so sure? You changed it once, can't we just change it again?"

Elizabeth loved how hopeful and determined he sounded. She wanted to agree. She didn't want to believe that she was given this power just to have it wasted on heartbreak.

"I don't think that's how it works." She solemnly shook her head and sighed.

"Then you stay and I die." He said working through the options. "Or I live, without you." He sighed. Even though she wasn't looking at him she could hear the smirk building on his face. "I guess I will die then. And I will live a happy man every moment up until then because you'll be here."

"Don't joke like that." She snapped at his words, her face sad and serious.

"Well, you've put me in a difficult situation Liz." He kissed her on the forehead. "I don't know what to do." He said with a sigh, full of defeat.

The two sat in the alleyway, his arms wrapped around her as she apologized through her sobs. They stayed like that for a long time. The music began to slow down and people began slowly meandering out of the hall.

"Don't marry me then." He had rested his chin on the top of her head, and gently rubbed his hands up and down her back. "That's fine." She looked up at him through her puffy, tear swollen eyes.

"Okay." She said lifting herself out of his arms and wiping her eyes. "Okay." She said again with a nod. She was relieved that he had come to her side and agreed that it would be best for her to leave. But at the same time she was disappointed, not wanting to go.

"But stay." He spoke surely, firmly. With the tone of voice ensuring her that there was no changing his mind.

"But -" He raised his hand to her lips to stop her from arguing.

"As far as I can tell, it's us getting married that is the problem. Then we don't. Simple as that." Elizabeth listened to him as he tried to convince the both of them that this was the most logical decision. "We will keep a steady track of the future, be aware of any changes you cause. And if anything happens, we will figure it out, together." He lifted her face so their lips met.

"And you're totally okay and accepting of all of this?" She said finally realizing how easy he was taking all of it in. He looked at her and nodded.

"You've trained me for this Elizabeth." He smirked, thinking of all of the times they were lost in the library together, the nights they would spend listening to sci-fi radio. "You were unexpected, untraditional. I neve expected this, but it'll never stop me from loving you."

Chapter 19

The first moment they were alone after he found out, Charlie began rattling off question after question about her life, wanting to be filled in on every little bit of Elizabeth he could. She quickly shut him down, hearing the words of Doc Brown in her mind, "Having information about the future can be extremely dangerous!" Regardless, he put up a fight, stating it wasn't that he wanted to know about his future, or the future in general, he just wanted to know more about her.

She couldn't argue with him there, they had been together for almost two years and he had been very patient with the little information she had given him. Before he found out the truth, she was nervous that he wouldn't embrace her strange origin story, but now she was unbelievably relieved that he wanted to know more. But Elizabeth remained cautious, only telling him in bits and pieces every night. And every night after she finished telling him a future story, he would make her promise that one day, after they had defeated the issue of his passing, she would take him to the future so he could enjoy it properly before he aged his way there.

That first night, as they sat wrapped up in each other, they had changed. Not a miniscule change, but a world bending change.

Charlie lived every day, never regretting the choice he made in asking her to stay. He saw his life anew knowing about her secret and this whole other life and world she came from. He wanted to learn more about her and dig deeper to her mysterious side she had always kept bubbled up. His eyes had been opened and he saw the world differently, bigger somehow, as if there was more than just the Cape.

While Elizabeth lived every day more relieved that she had someone to share her secret with; someone else who could hear the ticking of the clock of her time there running down. There was a new comfort she felt in his arms, knowing now that she didn't have to hold anything back from him anymore.

After their decision was set Elizabeth and Charlie easily slipped back into the routine of their lives. They had decided to stay tight-lipped about Elizabeth's 'futurism,' keeping everyone out of the secret, except for the two of them. They wanted to live as if nothing was different. But much to their disappointment things were different.

They didn't want to admit it to each other but they both felt the rushing wave of their lives. Time was ticking by too fast, the fuse of their time together was burning too quickly for them to comprehend, and every moment they had together felt too brief.

The next few years flew past faster than Elizabeth and Charlie would've liked. In their memories, those years are but a haze of rare important moments strung together. Elizabeth had changed things for them, and their system ensured that she would get to stick around for longer, but it by no means meant that they would get to live out their lives together forever.

*****

The spring of 1946 quickly turned to summer and summer began to fade into the fall, keeping the secret became less and less important but harder and harder to deal with as the time passed. Not due to a slip of the tongue or a future altering accident, but the longer she stayed, the more tedious the issues that came about.

Getting her driver's licence, health care, teaching certification, it was one thing after another that piled up that she couldn't accomplish. There was no paper evidence of her existence at this time, she had tried filling out paperwork with her real social security number and people scoffed thinking they were fake. The only proof was her physically being there, which wasn't enough for the United States government.

Elizabeth was becoming frustrated with her inability to be a proper member of this society. She and Charlie turned to their friends and family for help. The overall consensus was that it was about time they got married and that they had put it off for long enough.

"Maybe it has been long enough." He said hopeful and he slid the ring out of its hiding place in the bedroom, but Elizabeth sighed.

"I love how much you believe in this." She kissed him on the cheek, still unsure of how successful this would be.

"No big ceremony. Just you, me and if it doesn't work. We'll go back and undo it." He said putting an end to the whole thing with a kiss on the forehead. The two grabbed their things and headed to the courthouse to sign the papers to be legally wed.

"Alice is going to be so mad." Elizabeth said as they sat in the waiting room. Elizabeth had begun to fidget nervously. She played with her ring, her bracelet, her earrings. She was beyond excited to be finally marrying Charlie, doing what no Elizabeth had come before her had done, but she worried about the repercussions this would have.

"Because we beat her to the altar?" Charlie said, and took Elizabeth's hand to stop her from picking at her fingernails.

" No, because I'm not even wearing white, Alice would riot at our lack of tradition and planning." The two giggled at the truth.

"Should we call them?" Charlie asked, starting to question their choice.

"Finley and Whitley." A voice called out, to bring their attention back to the moment.

"I just need identification from you both." The clerk behind the counter said.

"Identification?" Charlie said casually, but he gave Elizabeth's hand a nervous and reassuring squeeze.

"Yes. Driver's license, birth certificate," the clerk handed them a list of approved identification.

"I've got my drivers here." Charlie said and handed it over.

"And I need to rummage through my purse for a moment." Elizabeth said in hopes to buy some time to come up with a plan.

"Charles Robert Finley. Date of birth June 7th, 1917." The clerk looked at Charlie for confirmation. He had been watching Elizabeth over his shoulder and he hadn't heard the clerk.

Elizabeth turned around and began to sift through her purse. She pulled out her wallet and flipped through all the small receipts and papers that had filled it.

"Excuse me. Are you Charles Robert Finley, date of birth -" the clerk asked again.

"June 7th, 1917. Yes, that's me." Charlie said when he had refocused.

A small, strikingly yellow piece of paper caught Elizabeth's eye. On it was written, "you're welcome dummy" and stuck to the back was a birth certificate. It was clearly fabricated, but Elizabeth didn't care. She turned back around and handed it across the counter.

"Elizabeth Lillian Whitley. Date of Birth October 21st, 1918." The clerk read aloud.

"I guess." Elizabeth said, trying to quickly do the math in her head. "I mean yes."

"You're 28?" Charlie whispered to her as he casually kissed her cheek. Elizabeth simply shook her head. She remembered that she was never the best at math, and clearly didn't get better in the future.

"Alright." The clerk handed them a piece of paper. "There is a waiting period -"

"Are you sure?" Charlie said. "I know Judge McFaren. I was wondering if he was in today."

The clerk rolled her eyes at him, and mumbled something about entitled and shotgun under her breath. She directed them down the hall.

"Wait here okay?" Charlie said and kissed Elizabeth on the forehead and slipped away into the office. A moment later Charlie stepped back into the hallway and ushered Elizabeth into the office.

"It's nice to meet you, Miss Whitley." The judge said and extended his hand.

"Not for much longer." Elizabeth said, leaving the judge confused. "I mean I won't be Miss Whitley for much longer."

"Charles explained your emergency situation. I understand, this isn't my first quickie wedding." Judge McFaren said. While the judge gathered his things, Elizabeth quickly gave Charlie a questioning look trying to suss out the reason for their 'quickie wedding.' She pointed to her stomach and Charlie shook his head, she pointed at him and received a nodd.

"I'm being shipped out." He mouthed to her and she nodded and gave a quick thumbs up.

"Would you like to exchange vows?" Judge McFaren asked when he had turned back around.

"I didn't plan anything." Elizabeth confessed. "I mean I have a lot I can say, but I didn't -"

"I love you Elizabeth." Charlie said cutting her off and took both of her hands in his. "I promise to be there for you, no matter how long that may be. I promise to always listen, even though I may not understand. I will always be there to pull you out of traffic and to carry your books. I love you Elizabeth, no matter what our future may hold, I am yours, every part of me."

There was a long pause while Elizabeth tried to edit down what she had wanted to say.

"Elizabeth?" The Judge said, "it's your turn."

"I know." She said with a nod. "I just need to think about it. Once I start talking I'm going to find it hard to stop. I just have so many wonderful things I can say about you Charlie." Charlie gave her hand a reassuring squeeze.

"I never wanted to share the responsibility that was me with anyone, until you. You are so understanding, no matter the nonsense. You laugh at my jokes no matter how bad they are, and you eat my cooking no matter how burnt. You calm my every worry, and with each look you make me feel seen. I'm in this with you, 100 percent. Unless you're dead tomorrow, then this never happened." The judge let out a little gasp and Charlie laughed, knowing full well the meaning behind her words. "I promise to argue with you about the mundane things. I promise to always answer your questions, no matter the answer. I promise to stay." Her words hung in the air between them, heavily. "I love you Charlie, no matter what the future may hold. I am yours, every part of me." Elizabeth finished with a smile.

The judge read through the legalese, but neither Charlie or Elizabeth were listening. They were lost in the words of their vows.

"You may now kiss your bride." The judge said and Charlie wrapped his arms around Elizabeth's waist and dipped her into a deep kiss.

"We're married." Elizabeth said when they stood in front of their house, she twisted the door knob and pushed the door open. But before her foot crossed the threshold, Charlie bent over and scooped her up.

"We don't have a lot of tradition, let me have this." Charlie asked when he saw the disapproving look in her eyes.

"Anything for you, Mr. Finley." Elizabeth said and wrapped her arms tightly around him.

"Welcome home, Mrs. Finley." He kept her in his arms and kicked the front door closed behind them, and carried her to the bedroom.

Elizabeth took a moment to look at herself in the mirror. She didn't look any different and she didn't feel any different. She struggled to pin down the feeling, but something was different.

As she inspected herself Charlie slipped into the mirror frame standing behind her.

"You look beautiful, Mrs. Finley." He said as he wrapped his arms around her tight.

"Do you feel different?" Elizabeth asked him. Charlie pondered his answer as he slipped off her coat and gently started to kiss her neck.

"A little bit." He confessed. Charlie worried that she was doubting their decision.

Ever since he had proposed and she confessed the truth, they had both promised to be together but still be careful. But he knew Elizabeth had never quite let go of the idea of staying with him if it meant him losing his life. No matter how many times he told her he'd die with or without her, she was never convinced.

"I think I love you more now." He said in attempts to distract her.

"I didn't think that was possible." Elizabeth joked. Her hand moved up to run her fingers over his face, which was nestled into her neck.

"Neither did I." He planted kisses all around her neck and shoulders. He slid his hand down her arm and raised their ring bearing hands so they were side by side.

"We've waited a long time for this. We've earned this Elizabeth. We've earned the right to be happy."

He caressed her from fingertip to shoulder before wrapping his arm back around her. He slid his hands slowly up the front of her body from her waist to her breasts. He took one in each hand and gave them a gentle squeeze. Her hands followed suit, placing hers on top of his, giving him permission to continue. His kisses on her shoulders and neck grew hungrier as they searched for her mouth.

Elizabeth arched her back, pushing her breasts further into his hands and causing her backside to grind against him. She felt him grow stiff as she did so. The more she moved against him the harder he pushed back.

Charlie's hands made quick work of her shirt, untucking it from her skirt and lifting it over her head. Elizabeth wrapped one of her hands around behind her and began to fumble with Charlie's belt. Following her lead Charlie attempted to slip his hand down the front of her skirt, but it held too tightly to her skin. Not wanting to waste time fighting with a button, Charlie slid his hand down her legs, gathered the fabric of her skit in his fist and lifted it, stopping when he reached the fabric of her underwear. Elizabeth spread her legs slightly, encouraging the direction his hand was moving.

This is what is different, Elizabeth thought as Charlie pushed aside the fabric of her panities and touched her wetness with his fingers. Passion. Every touch, kiss and bite, had a new fire behind it. A new passion that had come with committing themselves to each other. Their passion was sparked by the new optimism of Elizabeth's permanence that came with their vows.

This realization pushed Elizabeth's needs further. His fingers moved in quick circles making Elizabeth's knees weak. As much as she would've liked to let him make her drip, she wanted him to feel the same. Elizabeth turned and quickly dropped Charlie's pants and underwear. His erection sprung up into her hands before his pants hit the floor.

Charlie watched as Elizabeth dropped to her knees and started stroking him. From where she was she could see him drop his head back and breathe deeply. Elizabeth took him into her mouth slowly, sucking the tip and continuing to stroke the shaft with her hands. The further she took him into her mouth the more audible his moans became.

After a few minutes, overcome by a need for more, Charlie lifted Elizabeth to her feet and properly removed her clothes, until they were both wearing nothing but their new wedding bands.

Once they were in bed, Elizabeth climbed on top of Charlie and guided him inside her. She began to rock her hips, feeling him move in and out of her, until his movements matched hers.

Elizabeth ran her hands up Charlie's chest and grazed his nipples which caused him to vocalize his pleasure and to thrust harder into her. Elizabeth continued to flick and squeeze his nipples until her name escaped his lips.

Following suit Charlie ran his hands up her naked body, grazing his fingernails over her as he went, until they reached her breasts. He massaged her breasts firmly, before he began to roll her nipples between his fingers. With every twist he could feel her tighten.

He sat up and wrapped his arms around her. His lips caressing her collar bone and breasts. His hands on her back were gentle but he held her so tightly that she couldn't move, and he took control of their pace. His new position allowed him to fill her more, and with every thrust a new wave of pleasure rushed through her.

"Charlie." Elizabeth moaned, his name escaped her lips as just a whisper.

His name on her lips sent a shock wave through his body. Elizabeth felt him release inside her, pushing her closer to her end and her hips began to move faster. Charlie reached between their bodies to find her little nub of nerves to push her over the edge. Her shoulders went rigid and her breath began to shudder as waves of pleasure rolled through her body before she collapsed on top of him.

Charlie stroked her hair as she lay on his chest, and they stayed like that until they fell asleep.

That next morning Elizabeth pulled the picture from it's hidden place to see that the picture had changed, Charlie's children had faded and Elizabeth sat, middle aged and alone. She quickly ran through the house and threw it in his face with panic.

"Okay." He sighed, calmly. "Back we go." He reached for his coat.

"What are you doing?" She asked as she headed towards the bedroom.

"Going to the courthouse to undo it." He said, confused.

"Come with me. There is a much easier way, much less bureaucratic." The two of them walked back to the bedroom and dug out the watch they had tucked away last year.

"Back we go." She repeated his words.

"We?" He said excitedly.

They discussed what it was that caused the change. They narrowed it down to the moment they decided to go to the court house.

"Maybe I'm not meant to exist here," she sighed and looked at the ring on her finger.

"You're meant to be wherever I am." He said, trying his best to reassure her. She gave him a quick kiss on the lips and spun time back 24 hours before she had let go of his lips. Charlie looked around in wonder.

"What the -" he exclaimed. He looked at Elizabeth.

"You said you've always wanted to try it." She said with a laugh, while Charlie felt and looked as if he was about to be sick. He quickly took off towards the bathroom, slamming the door behind him.

Elizabeth had been nervous about taking him through time, no matter how short it was. "This is going to save a lot of time," she called to him through the door and he let out a chuckle. "Pun not intended but a happy accident." She continued on with her apology.

"I thought that if you came with me you wouldn't forget and try to make me marry you all over again, and I won't have to explain what happened. But now that I've taken the time to explain this I have kind of voided that whole situation." Elizabeth stood outside the bathroom door, corrected picture in hand.

"It worked. Everything is set right." she called to him through the door.

"That's lovely dear." Charlie's voice echoed clearly inside a toilet bowl.

"I love you." Elizabeth said, trying her best to hide her laughter from his suffering.

"I love you too." He said before another wave of illness swept over him.

*****

By late summer of 1948 two things were in full swing, Alice and Freddie's wedding and Alice's movement, 'We don't work? We won't marry!' When Elizabeth went back and told Charlie the truth, she had erased the timeline where the book club revolution had existed. Regardless, Alice still had been determined and now the movement was in full swing attempting to revoke the Marriage Bar in the Cape.

"NO!" Alice called out from her makeup table. Before Elizabeth could run from the bathroom to the bedroom to check on her, Alice had flown down the stairs and out the door.

"Alice!" Elizabeth called as she stormed down the street. "What the hell are you doing?"

"I'm not getting married." She yelled in distress. "How horrible does it look?" Elizabeth didn't respond, not entirely sure of what *it* was Alice that was referring to. "Me, the flippin poster child for the Marriage Bar rebellion getting married?" She reached up into her hair trying to tear out her veil. "I won't do it. I won't get married."

"Oh yes you are." Elizabeth said demandingly. "You're just being stubborn and stupid. You're getting married. You already put this off for a whole year."

"What if Freddie is a horrible husband? What if he doesn't want kids? What if he changes his mind and doesn't want me to work? What if he is conservative? What if I am a bad wife?" It had become evident to Elizabeth over the years that the Finley kids were extremely good at asking long streams of questions.

"So that is what this is about?" Elizabeth chortled. "Oh Alice! You have nothing to worry about."

"How are you so sure?" Alice looked at her eyes distraught, looking for a reason. "Can you see the future?" Elizabeth knew that Alice was stressed and worn down, but Elizabeth couldn't stop herself from letting out a large solid laugh.

"HA!" She quickly stopped herself, throwing her hand over her mouth, knowing Alice would push the response further. Alice was taken aback by Elizabeth's response. She raised her eyebrows.

"Is there something you're not telling me?" She crossed her arms, standing her ground, not letting Elizabeth pass until she spilled what she knew.

"I can't." Elizabeth hesitated, unsure if it was a good idea to expand her group of secret keepers.

"Well then clearly it isn't -" she trailed off in a pool of tears.

"I know, okay." Elizabeth confessed. Alice's tear soaked pouty eyes looked up at her asking for more. "I just know." Elizabeth sighed. Alice dropped her head again, dejected.

"Damn it! Fine." Elizabeth pulled Alice up off of the ground and led her by the hand back to Charlie's house. As they walked, panic began to build in Alice.

"Wait? Where are we going?" She said when she realized they were moving the opposite way, away from the church. She began to dig her heels in and slow down their walking pace.

"You want to know how I know don't you?" Elizabeth said, turning to her. "Or we could just go back and you can get married." She crossed her arms awaiting an answer.

"I want to know." Alice said, settling on the decision. Elizabeth turned and continued walking. "But if you convince me to change my mind, we won't have enough time to get back!" She called out to her trying to catch up. Elizabeth waved her off with a laugh.

"Trust me, we'll have enough time. You'll see." As they walked, Elizabeth began to explain the story of the watch. Alice trotted along beside her, listening in disbelief. The story took up the time it took them to reach Elizabeth and Charlie's house. Alice hadn't had a moment to ask questions or respond to the story before Elizabeth had pulled the watch out of the drawer and placed it in her hands.

"I've been there. I'm from there. I know." She finished her speech and sat down on the bed, prepared for an onslaught of questions.

"Prove it." Alice said, handing the watch back to her.

Elizabeth rolled her eyes saying, "You and your brother." In this situation she wouldn't be able to use the environment to assist with her proof, so she did the only thing she thought possible. She held the watch in front of Alice's face and spun the dial back 15 seconds and she quickly ran to the other side of Alice.

The Elizabeth that Alice had been watching, waved and faded away in front of her eyes. Alice gasped in wonder but it turned into a scream when Elizabeth tapped her on the shoulder from behind.

"Holy!" Alice said, gasping.

"Enough?" Elizabeth asked and Alice responded with a nod. "I have been there. I've seen the pictures. Shit!" Elizabeth said, realizing. She opened the suitcase and pulled out the picture she had taken from old Charles. She handed it to Alice who tossed it down after clear inspection. It was still the same picture that she had originally taken, the only difference was the date and the existence of Elizabeth.

"I guess I'm getting married." She announced and headed out the door back towards the church.

When they arrived back, Elizabeth popped out the watch, grabbed Alice by the hand and began turning back time so it appeared that they had never left. After she stopped spinning the dial she looked to Alice, who much like her brother, looked and felt as if she was about to be sick. She keeled over on the sidewalk vomiting onto the green lawn in front of her.

Luckily, but unluckily for them, Charlie rounded the corner to find Alice bent over and Elizabeth holding her hair back from her face. Charlie stood back a distance shaking his head in concern.

"Time travel side effect." Elizabeth said to Charlie. Charlie nodded and then quickly changed his attitude and looked at Alice.

"You know?" He exclaimed, shooting a judgy look at Elizabeth.

"You know?" Alice retorted to Charlie before the next wave of nausea overcame her and her face lowered back towards the ground.

"I'm getting her down the aisle. I'll do whatever it takes." Elizabeth said, rubbing Alice's back and shooing Charlie away.

*****

After Alice's wedding, time raced away again. Charlie and Elizabeth continued to live their lives as two happily unmarried people. Since Elizabeth had found her 'birth certificate' she had been able to become a real citizen of her new time, including a bank account, proper access to health care, and a driver's license. Charlie and Elizabeth fell into a routine and things had moved more smoothly, until the winter of 1950.

It was a rare occasion that the snow fell in the Cape, but when it did the entirety of the city forgot how to drive; people moved too quickly, forgetting that the roads didn't care about the urgency of their travelers.

Elizabeth sat behind the wheel of Charlie's car, trying her best to navigate the slippery route between their house and the school. In front of her, a car's back tires had begun to subtly spin out. Trying to brace herself for the ice ahead, she lightly tapped her breaks, but she didn't slow. The back tires began to slip and swerve.

Elizabeth did her best to correct the slide and keep going at a slow pace, but the ice had other plans. The car grazed over another patch of ice, sending the front of her car in one direction and the back in the other. She spun on the road a full three hundred and sixty degrees, and then sideways towards the edge of the road. She turned into the skid hoping to catch it and turn back, unaware that the vehicle behind her was following in her path at an unbreaking speed. As her tires hit piles of snow, slush, and ice on the shoulder of the road she slowed, but the car after her did not. The speed of the car sliding behind her crashed into her, and both cars rolled over the side and down into the ditch, one on top of the other.

Across town at the coastal training centre, a young officer made his way running through the bustling building asking for Commander Finley. He slowly made his way, being directed and misdirected. The longer he searched the more nervous and sweaty he became. After forty-five minutes he finally reached the commander's office. He stood outside the door, and knocked rapidly until he heard someone call out inside.

"One second, one second," the voice rumbled. Charlie welcomed the boy into his office, and made his way back to his desk. He sat back down and continued about his paperwork. The officer stood in the door frame, hands folded behind his back. Charlie looked at him and waved him forward.

"I was -" the young sweaty officer stuttered. "I was told to find you right away and give you this." He outstretched his arm and handed Charlie a small, folded, square paper. Charlie eyed the boy cautiously as he opened the paper.

From: Region Medical Center
Message:
        There has been an accident.
        Elizabeth Whitley is here.
        Come immediately.

Charlie threw down his papers, grabbed his keys and hat, and rushed off of the base. The slick roads caused his taxi ride across town to take much longer than he would've liked. He sat in the back of the taxi, panicking, pleading with the driver to pick up his pace.

When Charlie arrived he rushed through the busy hospital wings calling out for any nurse that would listen. At last someone stopped and recognized he was there.

"Elizabeth." She said and pulled out a clipboard and looked at him for more information.

"Elizabeth Whitley." He paused to inhale. "I'm looking for Elizabeth Whitley." The nurse began shifting through the papers on her board. "I was at the base and I was told she was in an accident. Where is she? Is she okay? Everyone here is ignoring me and won't tell me if she is okay?" He rambled on, speaking faster and faster as he did.

"Mister?" She asked, a kind and patient look on her face.

"Finley. Charles Finley. I'm her boyfriend -" He paused and shook his head. "Fiance-" he paused again, "I just - I love her. Where is she?" The nurse nodded.

"Follow me Mr. Finley." She said and extended her arm behind him and guided him forward. They walked for a moment, Charlie rambling the entire time about where he was and what he was doing when he found out, wishing that somehow he had been with her. She stopped outside the waiting area, and motioned for him to take a seat. He sat down, running his fingers nervously through his hair.

"You'll have to wait here." She said and Charlie shook his head in disagreement, and stood back up.

"No." He said and followed after the nurse. "Where is she?" She gently placed her hand on his shoulder and returned him to his seat.

"All I can say is that she is with the doctors now." She slowly lowered him into the seat trying to reassure him.

"All you can say?" He stood again crossing his arms. "You don't know? On that magical little chart of your's you have no more information. It just says 'she is with a doctor.'" He extended his neck, trying to look over and gather more information.

"Mister Finley," her voice was firmer now, "you cannot see her now. It is out of the question. You have to stay here."

"Fine." He said retreating into his seat. "But can you at least tell me if she is okay?" The nurse could see the panic and worry in his eyes, something she had become very accustomed to seeing on the faces of people in this area.

"I'm sorry," she paused and sat next to him, "I can't tell you anything. It's hospital policy. Unless you are family, we will have to wait until she wakes up or until family arrives. Okay?" She asked the question but spoke too quickly to let him respond. "When the doctors are done, I will come and get you." The nurse slowly began to walk away, causing Charlie to jump up and call out.

"But she doesn't have any family here, I am her family!" The nurse kept walking, making no attempt to look back or give him a second chance. Charlie sat back in his seat, and let his face fall into his hands and his mind wander with worry.

Every so often the nurse would walk in and everyone in the room would perk up with hope and worry that it was their turn to receive news. Slowly the room thinned out as people were rushed off the rooms of their loved ones.

An hour later, from his seat against the wall, Charlie caught sight of Alice, Freddie and Lennie came running into the waiting area, heads frantically scanning the room looking for him. He jumped up and waved them over.

Alice ran to him, wrapped him up in a hug, and began drowning him in questions, to which he could only answer, 'I don't know.' Finally he put an end to her questions with, "I'm not family, so they won't say anything until she is -"

"Oh nope!" Alice denied him, turned and walked away to find a nurse or doctor she knew. Freddie and Lennie sat down on either side of Charlie, trying their best to wipe away the concern and worry from their faces. The three of them sat in silence for a brief moment before Alice had returned with the nurse in tow. Alice walked the nurse in front of Charlie, and gave her a nod encouraging her to speak now or lose her tongue.

"She was in a serious accident. When the police arrived it took them some time to get her out from under the wreckage. She has been unconscious since they found her, she had a collapsed lung, and she has some broken bones that need to be reset. That is all I can say, but at this moment, she is stable." She finished and the four of them sat eyes wide, staring at her waiting for more.

"That is *ALL* I can tell you Alice." The nurse said, shooting a glare in her direction before walking away. "You know the rules. Family only."

"She is stable." Alice said with forced cheer in her voice. "It's a good thing." She reached out and held Charlie's hand. "She'll be okay." Her voice shook as she spoke, unsure if she was saying it to reassure him or herself.

Hours later the nurse returned to the sitting area, holding her board tight to her chest. She knew who she was there for, but she looked at the board rather than looking at their faces.

"Whitley, Elizabeth." She called out. "I'm looking for the family of Elizabeth Whitley." The four of them shot up from their seats. "She's awake, and she's asking for you."

Relief covered their faces and they walked hand in hand behind the nurse as she slowly led them down the hallway. When the nurse opened the door Alice, Freddie and Lennie took a step back to give Charlie a moment with her first. The smell of sickness and disinfectant washed over him as he entered causing his relief to vanish and shock him back to the seriousness of the situation.

Charlie approached her bedside, and gently took her hand in his. Her body was badly bruised and scraped. Her ribcage was tightly wrapped in bandages, and both of her limbs on the right side of her body had braces under their bandaging to hold the newly set bones in place. Her breathing was staggered and supported with an oxygen mask.

He lifted her hand to his lips. She turned to look at him and tried her best to smile.

"What took you so long?" She joked. Her voice was coarse, but she gave him a sarcastic look through her scarred face.

"I thought I was the one who had the car accident." He retorted through tears, as he tried to lighten the mood. The two exchanged a sigh of relief. He gave her the option to wait to be surrounded by her friends but she told him not to be silly. He waved everyone into the room and they quickly all gathered around her bed. Before she could be swarmed by questions she took her chance to explain.

"The roads were icy. I tried to stop. Another car hit me. But I am okay." She said reassuring them all, putting an end to any questions they would ask.

"Well that settles that." Charlie said and clapped his hands reaffirming her decision.

The five of them sat around for almost an hour joking and laughing about anything that would remove them from the uncertain situation they were surrounded in.

After Alice, Freddie and Lennie said their goodbye's, Charlie returned to his seat at her side. He sat more or less quiet, holding her hand and stroking her hair until she fell asleep.

Moments later the nurse arrived again. "I'm sorry Mr. Finley but visiting hours are over."

"No." He gently let go of Elizabeth's hand. He pleaded with the nurse through a yelling whisper. "I just got here. You can't tell me to go."

"I am sorry sir, but you're not fam-"

"I'm not family, you've made that very clear." Charlie said, throwing his hands up in frustration.

Charlie walked home from the hospital, the cold biting at his face. With every step he worried that she would wake up and he wouldn't be there. He stopped briefly at home to grab a few things and a shower. He was only gone from the hospital for 2 hours before he was back in the waiting room.

The nurse who had sent him away watched him pace the room for 15 minutes before he settled into a chair, opened a book and promptly dozed off. She felt badly for how she had treated him earlier that day, she could tell he was in an overwhelming pain. She grabbed a spare pillow and blanket and brought them to him.

"The second she wakes up, I'm in there?" His words were a question, but his tone was demanding, "Also, thank you."

"Have a good sleep Mr. Finley." The nurse said and walked away.

"I've had time to think about it," He said the next morning after the nurse had let him back into the room.

Elizabeth knew what he was thinking about, car accidents weren't something they took lightly with the known future looming in front of them. She opened her mouth to shut him down but he continued speaking.

"I don't care what the future says," tears began to gather and hang on the bottom of his eyelids. "I'm never leaving your side again."

She opened her mouth to argue, but he shook his head, shutting her down. She didn't need to know what he had been through, but she could see the fear in his eyes. She shut her eyes admitting defeat to him. He opened her hand, and placed the ring in her palm.

"You don't have to marry me," he sighed, "But please, wear the ring." He kissed her on the forehead as she fell back asleep.

The next morning Elizabeth woke again to find Charlie pacing around her hospital room.

"Good morning, handsome." Elizabeth said. Charlie let out a little jump of surprise.

"Good morning, beautiful." He stopped in his tracks, moved to her bedside and kissed her gently on the forehead. "I brought some of your things and then I had an idea." Charlie kissed her once more and began pacing around the hospital room again, unpacking Elizabeth's bag.

"Yeah?" Elizabeth said. She was getting dizzy watching him move around the room searching for something.

"Where is your watch?" Charlie had taken all of the contents out of her suitcase. "I assumed I had packed it.

"Why does it matter?" Elizabeth questioned, her mind was foggy.

"You can just go back and undo all this." He moved to her jacket hanging off the wall and tore through the pockets.

Elizabeth realized that she hadn't thought about it, and worry rushed over her. *Who had it now? What are they going to do with it? Did I just mess up everything?*

Am I going to be in trouble? How would I go back? Wait, If it's gone, it means that I would have to stay.

"Charlie. Stop." Elizabeth said when she had made her decision. "It doesn't matter."

"You're hurt, of course it matters." Charlie was still frantically moving around the room.

"Charles Finely, stop and sit down." Elizabeth raised her voice which stopped Charlie in his tracks and brought her to sit on the bed by her legs.

"If it's gone," Elizabeth began.

"Then you're stuck like this, hurt, in pain." Charlie finished for her.

"Yes, but that's not all." Elizabeth raised her eyebrows at him, hoping he would put it all together himself, but Charlie was still focused on her injuries.

"If the watch is gone," he said and he ran his hand over her casted leg.

"I have to stay." Elizabeth grabbed his face and turned it to face her. "What's a little pain in exchange for a happily ever after."

Charlie nodded and accepted her decision. The two embraced and breathed a sigh of relief now that the dagger that had been hanging over them was no longer there.

Chapter 20

Recovery was slow and tedious. Elizbaeth arrived home later that next week, and found that Charlie had Elizabeth-proofed the house. He had rolled their bed into the living room, lining it up in front of their small black and white tv. By her side of the bed he had piled books, records, and a myriad of snacks that she enjoyed so she wouldn't have to climb out of bed for anything.

As they walked through the door into the room, Elizabeth looked at Charlie, eyebrows raised in distress.

"Why?" She said, and gestured to the redesign.

"Bed rest. Doctor's orders." Charlie said with a stern look on his face and he helped her into the bed. He began quickly rambling as he ran around the bed tucking her in. He talked her through the list of things the doctors told them back at the hospital for a quick recovery. "Coffee?" he asked, and turned to the direction of the kitchen before she could answer.

"No. Stay." Elizabeth reached out, grabbed him and tried to pull him back down into the bed with her. He extended his free arm towards the kitchen.

"I stay when you ask." She batted her eyelashes and he caved crawling in beside her. Elizabeth opened the blankets to their bed and wrapped them around him.

She convinced Charlie to go back to work shortly after their return from the hospital, but only if she agreed to check-ins throughout the day from Lennie, Freddie and Alice. Elizabeth didn't argue about the visitors, without mobility she was going to become very bored very quickly while trapped in the house. Despite Charlie using them as cannon fodder to relieve his panic, Elizabeth appreciated the company.

During her morning's with Lennie, they would mostly discuss girls, his successes and failures, trying to pin down exactly why he hadn't landed one yet, or as he liked to believe, one hadn't landed him yet.

"I'm a catch," he would say, defending himself, and every time Elizabeth would laugh and nod in agreement. She was the only reason he had managed to find dates over their years together. They bonded over a similar sense of humour and passed the time telling jokes, playing cards and other games he would bring along for her to try out.

Everyday when he would leave he would beg her to leave Charlie for him, and would say he wished he was the one to catch her before she hit the pavement the day they met. And every day she would shut him down, shake her head and say, "You know damn well I'm just too much for you to handle." He would wink, tip his hat and head out the door.

During lunch with Freddie, he would whip them up sandwiches, soup or pasta, depending on what was on hand, and they would eat, watch the news and read the paper. Until she had had her accident, she and Freddie we're by no means close friends. But after weeks of having lunch together they quickly realized that they shared a lot of the same liberal political and social views, which for Elizabeth was refreshing considering what a conservative time they were living in.

Having their sit in everyday allowed them to realize that aside from political and social beliefs, the two of them had something unique in common that they didn't have with the others. They were engaged to each other's best friend. They would talk about Alice and Charlie, sharing their horror stories, jokes, tips on how to deal with them. In no time they became comfortable enough to be vulnerable with each other, and discuss their concerns and weaknesses in their relationships.

The more time they spent together, the closer they became, forming a solid support system within their group of friends but only for each other. They would roll their eyes and scoff when Lennie would say something backwards and conservative. And they had each other back when dealing with their loves, being a fly on the wall providing them with helpful hints and supportive advice when their relationships hit speed bumps.

During her afternoons with Alice, Alice would catch Elizabeth up on all of the town gossip over large cups of tea. And every time Elizabeth would push for more gossip, Alice would scorn her for her nosiness, but continue on providing as much information as she knew to tell. They would talk for hours about weddings, engagements, and Alice's latest union battles. While Elizbaeth lay in bed, Alice was out still fighting for equal pay, and trying to overturn the Marriage Bar.

If Elizabeth could walk, she would've been out there walking a picket line or handing out fliers alongside Alice, doing whatever she could to ensure that change would happen. But even though she was restrained to her bed she created catchy slogans, folded pamphlets, created petitions, and absolutely anything else she could do to lend a hand to the movement.

Her evenings with Charlie were romantic, quiet and close. He would return home from work every day carrying flowers, chocolates or a small present.

"You don't need to do this." She would tell him every time when he placed the evening surprise in her lap. "I'm here, perfectly fine." He would kiss her on the forehead and brush off her denial.

She didn't understand that he did it all because of the accident. He was constantly reminded of the tick-tock of the clock running down their time together, and he would do anything and everything to make her comfortable.

They would spend their time together in bed wrapped up in one another, talking about their days, reading books, and watching television. They continued with their tradition of her telling small stories about the future. He would lay next to her eye's wide with wonder as she talked about the quick paced, high tech world she was from.

One night after she had wrapped up her story about flying across the country in the planes of the future, looked up at her from his position where he was laying on his side, his head propped up on his hand.

"Why did you ever leave that all behind?" His question caught her off guard. She knew everyone would wonder that about her but no one outside herself had ever asked. She smiled, reached her unbandaged arm towards him and placed her hand under his chin.

"You of course." She bent to kiss him but the bandaging on her ribs prevented her. He lifted himself to meet her lips.

"Really?" He asked slightly pessimistically.

"From the moment I met you, there was no going back." He kissed her again, pulling her closer, wrapping his arms tightly around her. His lips moved their way from her face to her neck to her collar bone, sending a tingle through her whole body.

"Ow!" She twinged as his arms rubbed against her bruised ribs. He shot back like a bullet, fear across his face.

"I'm sorry." He held his hands back as if he was being held at gunpoint and looked too nervous to touch her again. She smiled and grabbed his hands to lower them.

"It's okay." She said trying her best to reassure him. "You can touch me. Just not so tight next time." She moved closer to him again, bringing his arms back around her.

Every night they would say they loved each other. Charlie held her a little closer afraid she would shatter into pieces or slip through his fingers.

The time she was alone was brief, but lonely. She had grown so accustomed to having someone around that when no one was there she counted down the minutes until someone would arrive.

One day, as she lay confined in the empty house between Freddie and Alice's Elizabeth check-in shift, she thought about how grateful she was to be trapped in that bed.

She decided that being there, unable to go out and interact with the rest of the world, was possibly the best thing that could've happened. She gets to stay here, living her life with the people she loved, while having a zero percent chance of ruining the future.

As lonely as being alone was, it gave her brief moments to appreciate just how lucky she was that the watch led her here, wherever the watch may be.

After a few weeks of living displaced in the living room, Elizabeth was able to convince Charlie to return their house to the way it was before the accident, and attempt to go back to living life normally.

The first morning after their house reset Elizabeth awoke to chatter. Elizabeth could hear the voices in the living room. She slowly slid her way out of the bed, and dressed. If Charlie had known she was awake he would rush to her side to assist her as she walked. Elizabeth knew she was strong enough to walk without him, she had completely regained her ability to walk days ago, but it was at a very slow waddling pace.

She hobbled her way down the hall towards the voices. She could hear Alice, Freddie and Charlie discussing the new shop opening downtown.

"When does it open?" Elizabeth said casually as made her way nearer the room.

"We're going out to celebrate!" Alice said, jumping up from the couch when she saw Elizabeth enter the room, free from assistance. Alice ran over to her with a huge smile on her face, and she stood confused by the unsure urge to hug her.

"It's walking, Alice. Not a reason to celebrate." Elizabeth replied when she was released and reached the room.

"You're still here. Alive and standing. We're celebrating." She squished up her nose in excitement helping Elizabeth walk the rest of the way to the couch.

She began listing off plans for a big dinner out and then dancing.

"Stop." Charlie interjected before Alice could get too deep into her ideas. "She's not ready yet."

"Next week?" Elizabeth offered and Charlie groaned in disappointment while Alice let out a small squeal of joy. "After my doctor's appointment on Friday?" Elizabeth negotiated with the both of them trying to keep the peace.

"Fine." They agreed, both sighing in unison.

When the celebration day arrived, Elizabeth left the doctor's office to find the four of them waiting anxiously out on the street. Elizabeth shot both of her hands triumphantly into the air and called out, "All clear!" The group erupted with an over the top cheer and high fives all around. Charlie ran to her and scooped her up into his arms, spinning her around.

The celebrations were cut brief when Alice clapped everyone to attention. She began to deal out everyone's orders.

"Dinner, 6's, Connelly's." Everyone nodded in agreement. "Dancing at 8." Nods all around again. "After drinks?" Freddie let out a cheer. "Our house."

"Lennie," Alice turned to him. The stern look on Alice's face had him looking taken aback, "No weird girls." He opened his mouth to defend his female choices, but he caught the eye of Elizabeth. She raised her eyebrows in defence of Alice and he quickly remembered their talks during his daily check-ins, and nodded his head in agreement with Alice.

Elizabeth had laid out a dress on their bed, but she stood a few feet away from it, with her finger tapping her lips as she pondered her choice.

"You're going to look stunning no matter what." Charlie said from the door as he stood and watched her. As if following a habit, he quickly moved across the room to her side.

Since her accident Charlie had been helping her with everything, including getting dressed, so Elizabeth wasn't surprised when his hands moved to her hips and quickly slipped off her shirt, the cold of the room caused her to shiver slightly. With her shirt off neither of them wanted to let this moment go to waste. Charlie quickly discarded his own shirt and wrapped his arms around her. He held her tightly while he kissed her, warming her body with his own.

The two of them had been keeping their sex life at an arm's length while she was healing, but now with the doctor's approval the fire had been reignited.

"I'm not sure about this." Charlie suddenly stated.

"I know it's been awhile, but I still know what I'm doing." Elizabeth joked.

"I don't want to hurt you." He clarified.

"Doctor gave me the all clear." Elizabeth reminded him.

"For this?" Charlie asked demandingly

"Yes, I specifically asked if I could get freaky with my fiance. You think I'm joking but I'm not." Elizabeth said before pushing him down onto the bed.

"How about this?" Charlie said and quickly swapped their positions. He lifted himself above her, ensuring that the only thing that could touch her was the gentle caress of his lips.

He kissed his way down her body, his lips touching any piece of exposed skin. When he reached her waist, he slipped his fingers in the waistband of her pants and slipped them down over her hips, taking her underwear with them. Charlie slid his hands between her thighs and spread her legs as comfortably as they could go.

He lowered his face between her legs and gently kissed her inner thighs. Slowly his slips made their way to her center. He ran his tongue up and down over her lips, gently grazing her clitorus with each pass, making her twitch. Watching her body twitch with pleasure pushed him further. He gently slipped his fingers inside her, slowly pulsing them in and out, while his mouth sucked and flicked over her.

Elizabeth writhed in pleasure. She grabbed him by the face and pulled him up into a kiss. She reached for his belt, but he pushed her hand away.

"Let me take care of you." He whispered, and put his hand back to work. He laid with his head up by hers, kissing and nibbling on her lips and neck, while his fingers worked inside her. He could feel her growing tighter and pulsing with every movement of his fingers.

Her breathing was growing faster, not wanting to make her move too much and bring her pain, Charlie moved his thumb over her nub while his fingers curved in and out of her causing her to moan and dig her nails into his shoulder as she was overcome with the release of pleasure.

"My turn." Elizabeth said after taking a moment to catch her breath and then she firmly pushed Charles onto his back.

"You're right. Your turn again." A crafty smile bloomed on his face as he grabbed her and gently flipped her onto her back. Charlie positioned himself above her, and lifted one of her knees so it bent up towards her chest.

He locked eyes with her before he entered her. Elizabeth let her head fall back and inhale deeply as she took a moment to adjust to his length inside her. With her head back, Charlie seized the opportunity to kiss his way from her neck to her lips knowing that the sensation on her neck would drive her mad. Charlie's motions were slow and deep. With every thrust Elizabeth grew tighter, nearing her second climax. Charlie lowered his head to her nipple and bit it gently, pushing her over the edge.

He wrapped his arms around her and rolled them over once more. With Elizabeth on top, he wrapped one arm around her waist and the other held her head. Their lips did not leave each other, and their motions fell back into sync. As Elizabeth bucked her hips she could hear Charlie starting to unravel. Her name, passionately escaping his lips through heavy breaths. He held Elizabeth tightly to him as he released inside her. The sensation of him throbbing sent her final wave of pleasure through her body.

"I love you Elizabeth." He said and planted a kiss on her forehead, his arms were still wrapped around her waist, holding him on top of her.

"I love you too Charlie." Elizabeth allowed her head to rest against his chest. From where she lay she caught sight of the clock. "Shit, we need to get ready."

"Knock knock." Lennie said as he opened the door and let himself into their house. Charlie came into the hall to greet him a moment later. "You've got mail." Lennie tossed a small brown envelope at Charlie.

"Wow, what service!" Elizabeth said when she joined them. "All the way from the base?"

"It was on the door." Lennie said.

Elizabeth watched Charlie quickly tear open the lip of the envelope. She could see a big lump form in his throat when he looked in.

"This is for you." There was a sadness in Charlie's voice as he spoke. Elizabeth quickly moved to his side and he shook the contents into her hands.

Elizabeth's heart was filled with disappointment when the gold metal of the pocket watch touched her skin. Attached to it was a note, *"Don't be stupid. Don't lose this again. You're going to need it."* The words were foreboding and Elizabeth and Charlie shared looks of uncertainty.

When they arrived at Connelly's they were all dressed in their very best. The boys had donned their crispest suit, and the girls dressed in flirty full skirt dresses, Alice in white and Elizabeth in a dark navy. Alice had been strict on the formal dress code.

"This is a celebration," she stated over the phone to each of them, "we are all together, all healthy, and it's about time we had a nice sit down meal together." No one ever dared to cross Alice when she was in party planning mode.

They stood outside the restaurant and Alice gave each of them a once over. Straightening Freddies tie, tucking Charlie's tie and shirt collar into his coat, and scolding Lennie for forgetting a tie all together. After she had gussied them up she asked a passer by to snap their picture with Alice's camera.

Suddenly Elizabeth was met with a foreboding feeling. Something about this evening felt final to Elizabeth, like a going away party. She looked around the table at her friends laughing to tears and she felt as if her time there was coming to an end. She subtly shook her head and tried to push the nonsense idea out of her mind.

The dinner rush had ended and a larger part of the floor had been cleared creating a space to dance. The group moved to a booth on the edge of the dance floor while a band set up shop on the small stage at the front of the restaurant. By the time the music had fired up the entire place was jumping with people, crowded wall to wall. It didn't take long for the five of them to rush the dance floor.

The evening was passing too quickly and before they knew it, the band had decided to take a break and put on a record to create some background sound while the guests sat and stood around the hall visiting.

Elizabeth sat at the edge of the booth leaning back into Charlie's arms listening to Lennie recount his latest endeavor with a woman who was seated a few booths over. As she listened to his disastrous tale she let her eyes wander around the room, watching people as they interacted with each other. She had always found it entertaining to watch how people acted when they didn't think anyone would notice them.

She had her attention focused on a man trying to casually pick his nose in hopes that it would go unnoticed by his date, when a few tables across the way a woman caught her eye. She had poker straight brown hair, but her hair had been held back out of her eyes with a bright pink ribbon. Her eyes were water blue and sat very close together on her delicately thin face. This wasn't the first time this evening that she had caught her eye, but that wasn't why she seemed familiar. She couldn't put her finger on it, but there was something about her, Elizabeth felt compelled to talk to her for Lennie's sake. The woman seemed to be all alone, so Elizabeth marched over, intending to invite her to come and join their group.

"Hi." Elizabeth said, stationing herself across the table from her. "I'm super sorry if this is strange, but my friend over there keeps staring at you." She pointed towards Lennie, who was luckily enough looking in their direction. He waved when he saw her pointing. "I was wondering if you wanted to come and sit with us?" She had completely forgotten that it was 1951, and people now-a-days were much friendlier and trusting than where she was from. The stranger nodded, picking up her things and following Elizabeth across the hall.

"Everyone," she announced as she reached the table, "this is -" She fumbled, realizing she had never even asked the poor girl her name.

"Peggy." The girl smiled as she introduced herself. Elizabeth's face had gone cold. She motioned for Peggy to sit down and then quietly that she was going to go find

Alice. Elizabeth had retreated across the dance hall while realization hit harder.

She found Alice by the bathrooms and dragged her to empty seats across the room. The two sat in silence, Elizabeth watching Peggy and Charlie talk and Alice watching sadness grow on Elizabeth's face. A lump had begun to form in Elizabeth's throat. She leaned into Alice, "What do you know about her?" Her voice was shaky as she pointed in Peggy's direction.

"Margaret?" Alice clarified and Elizabeth nodded. "She's nice. Smart, athletic, comes from a very wealthy family, and very very sweet." Elizabeth bit her lip trying to process the situation.

Was this the moment? She thought. She looked around.

This is the place. She looked at the two of them laughing at a joke Freddie had no doubt told. *That's her. His Peggy. His Peg.* She called back the memory of Old Charles telling her about how he met his wife. Never thinking that she would be the one to introduce them.

"Would she be good for him?" The lump in her throat grew.

"She is very brilliant, definitely would keep Lennie on his toes." She eyed up Elizabeth, starting to understand what she was asking.

"You're not asking for Lennie. Are you?" The two girls' eyes met and for the first time Alice noticed the growing pain in Elizabeth's. "Are you okay?"

Elizabeth stood up and pulled Alice with her. Elizabeth squeezed Alice tight. Her tears started to drip down her face onto Alice's shoulder.

"Thank you. Thank you for everything. You know," she smiled. "I didn't have a lot of friends. Actually, when I decided to stay, I didn't even give two thoughts about leaving them behind. But you, I'm gonna be lost without you Alice. Who am I gonna call when I freak out about men, or keep me from nosing into other people's business, or," Alice motioned for her to stop, but she had so much to say. "And even if I'm gone, keep fighting the fight, okay, you're gonna change the world Alice. Also, Fred loves you Al, like really loves you. He doesn't say it, but he does. You guys are going to be together for a long time." Elizabeth chuckled, and Alice's eyes filled with tears.

"You took me in, made me feel so welcome, let me fall in love with your brother." She stopped. "Charlie." She looked at him one last time, she could feel her heart shatter in her chest, and she felt the pieces settle like a lump in her stomach. "Please take care of him. You'll be sure she'll be good to him, right?" She started to collect her things.

"I don't understand. What's going on? What are you doing?" Alice grabbed her by the hand.

"I know it doesn't make sense, but I can't be here anymore. I can't explain it. It feels like the end of a good movie or a book. Like you know you want more, but you know this is exactly where it is supposed to end, that if it kept going the new ending would be horrible. The absolute fucking worst." Elizabeth said remembering Charlie's body on the road. "It's time for me to leave." She wiped her eyes dry before looking up at her. A concerned look was in her eyes, and Alice could tell that this was serious and was more than just the cold feet and nervousness that came out after their engagement.

"Please, tell him I wasn't feeling well. He can't know I've left. Keep him distracted for an hour or so. That should be enough, I just need some time to go home and pack my things." She trailed off, debated whether or not to explain her sudden exit. "He'll explain." She motioned in Charlie's direction. She was too afraid to look at him, knowing that seeing him would make her change her mind.

"Promise me." Elizabeth grabbed Alice by the shoulders, "Alice, promise me." Alice nodded. The two hugged one last time before Elizabeth took off out the door.

Alice quickly ran into the bathroom to compose herself before returning to the table.

"Where's Liz?" Freddie asked as she sat down.

"Went home. She wasn't feeling well." She tried to say as casually as possible. She didn't want to lie, especially to Charlie, but the look Elizabeth had given her when she asked her to promise was strong, she knew that Elizabeth was doing what she thought was right.

"No." She grabbed his arm. "She'll be fine. Drank too much. Just needed to sleep it off." Her short sentences made him suspicious of her, but before he could ask any more questions Alice took him by the hand and dragged him out onto the dance floor.

Elizabeth ran the entire way back to the house. She grabbed the suitcase out from under Charlie's side of the bed and began throwing in her clothes, pictures and any other memories that could fit into the suitcase.

She rushed through the hall to Charlie's study, rummaging through his desk to find a pen and a piece of paper. She positioned herself at the desk, took a deep breath and began to write.

Charlie, my Charlie,

I'm sorry. I'm so sorry. I'm sorry that it has to be like this, and I'm sorry that it has to be now. We knew that the other shoe would drop, one day this would end, and I would have to leave. But somehow it still feels too soon, like our story isn't finished. I'm not ready to let you go, but I know now that I have to.

Please, tell everyone how sorry I am, and how much that every second we had together meant to me. I'm certain and scared that they won't understand, they will be hurt but please explain to them that I had never intended to go so suddenly. I never wanted to hurt anyone, especially you guys.

Charlie, never doubt that I love you. I never thought I would want to share my life with someone, it always seemed too hard. But with you, living was easy, loving was easy, being myself was easy. Thank you for being responsible for me, and letting me share that with you. I am so sorry to break our vows (though technically we undid that), but I can't stay. I won't let you die Charlie. I can't.

I know I will never let you go, but please don't let how amazing our time has been together, don't let that hold you back from the wonderful life I know you are going to live.

Live and love, and please never regret what we had for one second. One day I hope you will forgive me, and understand. I will see you again, I promise.

I love you Charlie, with every part of me,

I'm yours, 100%

Elizabeth

The tears streamed down Elizabeth's face as she re-read what she had written.

Alice sat watching the clock, waiting for that hour mark to pass. Time was ticking much too slowly. It had only been 35 minutes when Alice slammed her drink down on the table. Freddie and Lennie sat in the booth on either side of her and let out a startled yelp when the glass hit the table.

"Move!" She yelled at the both of them shooing them out of her way so she could get out of the booth.

"I'm sorry. I can't do this." She called out to apologize to Elizabeth, wherever she was. She marched out onto the dance floor where Charlie was dancing with Peggy. She grabbed him by the shoulder and turned him to face her. "She's leaving."

Charlie opened his mouth in confusion.

"Elizabeth. She's not sick, she's leaving." Alice said firmly. Panic flew across Charlie's face. The moment Alice dropped her hands off his shoulders and he ran.

At the house, Elizabeth tore off the bottom of the paper and wrote 2012 on it. As she tore she noticed the ring. She sighed at the sight of it. She tried to pull it off her finger, it sat stationed in its position despite her vicious tugs.

"I can't take you with me!" She cursed through her tears. She stopped and looked at it. The diamonds sparkled in the twisted white gold setting. She considered taking it along, but staring at it, it felt like the diamonds were cutting into her glass heart, scraping and breaking her, with every sparkle. She knew anytime she caught sight of it, it would cut her deeper and she would never be able to let her life in 1950 go.

She sucked on her finger and began to feel it begin to loosen. She slipped the ring off her finger and wrapped it around the letter, placed it on his pillow and headed down the stairs. She tucked the 2012 she had torn off of her letter and hid it in the face of the small clock in the sitting room. She didn't have to doubt that he would figure it out, because he was the one that told her. She swung her coat around her shoulders, placed the watch in her pocket and calendar in her pocket and walked out of the house.

Charlie flew down the streets and alleys, cutting through people's yards, taking the quickest route clear across town as he ran. He stopped only once at an intersection and waited for the steady stream of cars to pass.

"Please don't go, Elizabeth." He panted, bending over resting his hands on his knees. "Please." He looked to the sky pleading. "Let me say goodbye." The line of cars faded and Charlie began running again, moving faster than he had before.

As he turned down their street he saw her. She held her suitcase tightly in her hand, head bowed, staring at the watch in her hand.

"Elizabeth!" He called out. She turned and their eyes met, and he called out again, something she couldn't hear. She almost dropped her things when she saw him, wanting to give up on the safety of the future and cave into his arms.

She blew him a kiss, turned her eyes back to the watch in her hand, and spun the dial. He was almost there, he reached out his hand to touch her face. He watched her disappear right before his eyes. He dropped to his knees and she faded through his fingertips.

For how long Charles sat on the pavement, he didn't know. He simply sat, waiting for her to fade back into existence. The moon was high above him, when he heard the sound footsteps approaching behind him. He turned hoping to see her standing there, but all he saw were his friends.

"She's really gone?" Freddie asked, it was clear Alice had tried to explain the confusing situation before they arrived.

"At least you got to say goodbye." Alice said, unknowing the pain she caused with her words.

Charlie said nothing to them, his whole being was filled with a broken rage. He stood, walked into the house and slammed the door behind him.

Alice, Freddie and Lennie didn't leave. From where they stood they saw papers, books and furniture fly past the windows, and they could hear Charlie yelling. The three of them simply stood on the sidewalk, each of them processing the confusion of Elizabeth's sudden exit in their own way.

Eventually, calm settled inside the house. They didn't need to speak, they knew what they had been waiting for. The boys walked towards the house, but Alice grabbed them by the hand and whispered, "not yet, give him a minute more."

10 minutes after the calm, Charlie turned to see them as they entered. In his hands he held Elizabeth's letter and massive round, lightweight steel industrial style clock which he had just picked up off of the floor from where he had thrown it earlier. Lennie and Freddie quietly began correcting the furniture, while Alice tended to her brother.

His eyes were red and puffy, his shirt ripped, and his hands bleeding from where his fists had landed in fury. "What am I supposed to do now?" He said before he collapsed into tears on the floor.

Chapter 21

At first, Elizabeth watched the dates on the watch change, as she spun the dial. As she spun she turned and looked to the spot Charlie had faded from, her breath caught in her throat and she gave into the pain she was holding back.

Elizabeth dropped her bag and collapsed. She felt as if she would shatter right there on the curb, if she allowed herself to give into the emotions she felt bubbling up inside her. She forced herself to put all of her emotion into a tiny box and lock it up inside herself. She allowed herself to stay there, only for a moment, to calm down. She wasn't sure for how long sat still and silent on the sidewalk. She only removed herself from her defeated position when people had begun to walk past her and give her looks of concern.

She picked up her suitcase, wiped some of the dirt off her clothes, making herself presentable for her walk through town. As she walked, she looked at the date on the watch, May 30th, 2012. She had overshot her arrival time by five months.

"Damn it!" she cursed, moving her thoughts from the heartbreak she was feeling, to the panic of explaining to her family and friends where she was for the last five months, and why she appears to have aged six years in those five months. She thought for a moment about dialling back some more so it was as if she never left.

"Fuck it." She said deciding not to. "It doesn't matter."

When she arrived at her apartment, she was overwhelmed by dejavu of the last time she stood at this door. To the rest of the world it was five months ago, but to her had been in a whole other lifetime. Before she entered she wondered what she would find. Maybe this time the room would be covered in cobwebs, would there be mail piled behind the door and messages overflowing her inbox. Once again, there was nothing.

"Really?" She said, throwing down her suitcase on the couch. "Five months and nothing." As she walked around her apartment she began to notice strange things. Her mail had been collected and piled on the coffee table, any messages from her phone had been neatly scribed and piled too. Someone had been here. She quickly spun around cautiously, expecting to see someone walking around her apartment. Then it hit her, *her* apartment, that was the most peculiar part, the fact that she still had an apartment.

"I haven't paid my rent in five months." She panicked and glanced around the room, ensuring that all of these things were hers and she hadn't mistakenly entered someone else's home. "I shouldn't even have an apartment anymore." Confused, she continued around the room looking for suspicious activity. She walked into the kitchen and her eyes were drawn to a large, bright yellow sticky note on her fridge. It read,

Elizabeth,

I noticed some things had changed, thanks.

I wasn't sure when you would be back, so I took care of your place for you (rent and what not.)

Also, don't worry about family, I let them know too.

      -Liza

Ps. If they ask, Europe is really nice this time of year.

Elizabeth breathed a sigh of relief when she put the letter down, making note to do the same when her turn came. When the thought crossed her mind she felt the sudden need to sit down, she quickly moved into the living room and settled herself on the couch to think.

"Will my turn come?" She asked, talking to herself out loud. For the first time she thought about her actions and how it will have changed things.

"We always go back," she reassured herself, "Did me staying change that? Will it stop? Did I leave enough hints that he'll understand that I will come and visit? Did I change Charlie's future?" She began to panic once more. She felt her tiny box of emotions creaking open, and she reminded herself to lock it. She wasn't ready for that yet.

She stood up to pace around the room while she thought. But she stood up too quickly and became lightheaded. She fell forward and caught herself on the table. As she stood, half bent over the table she spotted another big yellow sticky note, it read,

May 31st, 2012, Hotel on Beach street, 1:00 pm. Be there

    - Liza

Elizabeth quickly ran to the watch and checked the date, 10:55 pm May 30th, 2012. She breathed a sigh of relief that she hadn't missed it, whatever it was. She quickly flipped through the rest of the mail and messages on the table before letting herself head to bed.

The next morning while she dressed she cursed the fashion of 2012. She tossed the skinny jeans she was trying to squish back into the closet and reached for her loose fitting black skirt and white t-shirt. As she examined herself in the mirror she was pleased that vintage was back in style because she wasn't quite ready to part with her clothes from 1950.

Typically when she looked in the mirror it wouldn't take long for Charlie to find her, wrap his arms around her waist and kiss her on the cheek, but that wouldn't happen this morning. Elizabeth's knees grew weak and she crumpled down to the floor. She sat there crying and holding herself. She looked up from her position on the floor to see yet another yellow sticky-note strategically placed at the bottom of the mirror.

It sucks. Lock that shit back up. Get up, ~~you're~~ we're better than this. 1:00 pm, be there.

- Liza

"Heartless bitch." Elizabeth whispered and then made note not to be so cynical in the future and pulled herself up off the floor.

She sat at her kitchen table, slowly having her morning coffee and toast watching the time slowly tick by, impatient for whatever it was Liza had told her to attend. She followed the notes instructions and arrived at the hotel at five to one. She saw a large crowd of people winding their way through the entrance and into the conference room. Rows and rows of chairs filled the large, square, mahogany floored room, all facing a large black draped stage.

By the time Elizabeth had arrived the majority of the chairs had been filled and people stood talking amongst themselves. She quietly slipped in and found a seat at the back of the room to herself. She tried her best to blend-in in hopes that no one would try to strike up a conversation with her, because at this point, she still had no idea exactly why she was here. Slowly people started to move to their seats and Elizabeth managed to peek her head through the crowd to the front of the room.

Standing atop the large stage were rows and rows of flowers and a casket. Above the casket, dead center stage sat a photograph of Charlie. Not Charles, but Charlie. Young, uniformed, fresh home from the war Charlie.

"My Charlie." She thought, and with that thought the emotions from yesterday swirled and bubbled up in her again. She quickly closed her eyes and looked away, trying her best to push those emotions back down. "Stop it, we're better than this," She tried to jokingly calm herself.

The ceremony in his memory was long, his children and work friends spoke. They reminisced, and told their favorite stories about their lives with him, but Elizabeth heard none of it. She couldn't bring herself to look at those who spoke, or the guests in the room, afraid of who she might see and what she might feel. From the moment she saw his picture there was a loud ringing in her ears that she couldn't seem to block out that would occasionally be deafened by an uncomfortable 'air sucked out of the room' level of silence.

As the ceremony came to an end the sound of bagpipes echoed through the large wooden room as they walked the casket containing Charles Finley's body down the aisle and out of the room. The family slowly filed out behind it and Elizabeth stood hidden in the back row. Elizabeth bowed her head trying her best not to make eye contact with the family, her heart was already breaking from losing Charlie, she didn't need to see the possibility of a family that was taken away from her too.

As she walked home afterwards she took the long way back to her apartment, to walk past Charlie's house one last time before moving on with her life. She stood in front of the house thinking. Remembering the evenings spent laughing, her bedridden afternoons with friends gossiping about town and the news, and how their house - she stopped herself from continuing.

"His house." She corrected herself as she called it *theirs* in her memory.

"Excuse me?" A voice said behind her. Elizabeth startled, jumped and turned around to see a tall delicately faced man standing on the sidewalk behind her.

"Oh, sorry." She apologized, casually tipping her head and stepping out of the stranger's way.

"Are you Elizabeth?!" He said through excited confusion making Elizabeth feel concerned.

"Yes." She replied nervously. "How-" her thought was cut off by the man's frantically waving hands. Through the waving of his hands she recognized him, well part of him at least. She was transfixed by the deep chocolate eyes staring back at her. The moment of eye contact was brief before he spoke.

"Wait here! Wait here please!" He ran up the steps and into the house. Elizabeth stood waiting on the sidewalk, looking around nervously debating whether she should or should not leave. Before she had come to her decision the man came barreling back out of the house with an envelope gripped tightly in his hand.

"Here," he said through panting breaths when he reached her. "This is for you." Elizabeth hesitated, unsure if she should take it. "It's from my grandpa Charles."

"What?" Elizabeth's eyes shot up to meet him at the sound of Charlie's name.

"He told me about you before he died." He explained. "Said that you would be at the funeral, and that if he knew you at all you would linger here afterwards, and if I had the chance I had to give this to you." Elizabeth's eyes were hazy with confusion, asking for him to explain more. "I saw you at the funeral, at the back. I wasn't sure, but here you are." He fiddled with the envelope between his fingers, holding onto it, as if too afraid to let it go. "He wrote it the day before he passed." At last he gave in and extended his arm, handing it to her.

"How very Back to the Future of him." She replied, eliciting a laugh from the both of them as she gently took the envelope.

"Yeah. I guess so." the man said, watching her waiting for her to open the envelope and read it.

"Thank you." Elizabeth said as politely as she could hoping that he would go away.

"I'm sorry for asking this, but who are you?" He looked at her curiously.

"You wouldn't believe me if I told you." She said squishing up her nose with a smile. She slipped the letter into her purse, she took one last look at the house, sighed and began walking down the street. The young man stood there watching her as she went.

"You're her aren't you?" He called out chasing her down the street. "When we were little he used to tell us stories about, ah, how did he say it?" His brown eyes flickered as he snapped his fingers trying to spark a memory. "This marvel of a woman who could travel through time."

"Sounds like he has a really active imagination." Elizabeth shrugged and gave him a wink before continuing down the street leaving him there staring at her in awe.

Elizabeth waited to open the envelope until she was in the solitude of her own apartment, unsure of what it would say and how she would react.

When she arrived home she gently placed the envelope on the table and began to clean her apartment. She told herself she was doing it to ensure she had minimal distractions and so she could focus on what he had to tell her. But in reality she was doing it so she could put off reading his final words; she just wasn't ready to say goodbye all over again.

Eventually, after having cleaned the kitchen, bathroom, and vacuumed the floors, she couldn't ignore it any longer. She settled herself on the couch and gingerly opened the envelope. Her breath caught in her chest as she pulled the letter out and saw his handwriting scrawled across the letter.

Elizabeth, my Elizabeth,

In my last days I look back on all the fond memories of my life and I see you. In the times we were together, and I even see you in the times we weren't.

There has not been a moment of my life that I haven't wished to share with you. Even though you had left, you were never really gone. Everywhere I looked I saw you books, movies, any small time travel reference in popular culture. Anytime a person spoke with passion I would see you in their eyes, as you did whenever you discussed, well, anything. And everywhere I looked I hoped to see you. Living in the before, wandering the streets not knowing that one day you would stumble back and we would go through that all over again.

I don't have the words to express how much you mean to me. As I write this I remember the letter you left me, and you were right in everything you said, as always. Our love is one for the record books, others may not think so, but you bent time for us to be together, I think that speaks for itself.

I want to thank you for everything you gave me. Those years with you then, those days with you now have made my life. The time we have spent together changed me. You opened my eyes to all the possibilities of the world.

After you were gone I was scared that you would be lost, because I was lost without you. I gave up on everything for a while, please don't do that. Promise me, you will never regret what we had, and how we had it.

I love you Elizabeth, with every part of me, never stopped.

Yours, now and forever,
Charlie.

When she finished the letter she sat still and blank. She looked for the envelope to return the letter to. It had fallen off of her lap as she read and was lying under her coffee table. Elizabeth slid onto the floor reaching for it. As she grabbed it she felt something heavy shift inside. She tipped the envelope onto its side and the white gold ring that used to adorn her finger fell out of the envelope and into her hand. Attached to it was a white string and tag, it read,

- *Forever yours, Charlie.*

She sat on the floor, looking at the ring in her hand, silent in her disbelief.

"Okay." Elizabeth told herself. "It's time." With a deep breath she began to let herself feel it all.

A feeling moved through her body, and her disbelief was shaken away and replaced by a crushing vocal exhale. She took a deep breath, and her entire body shook, as the reality that her adventure then was really over. Her sadness quickly turned into rage. She lifted herself from the floor and began to move furiously around the apartment throwing anything that reminded her of her life before into a garbage pile.

She spotted a stack of newspapers and was hit by the first wave of pain.

"No more Freddie." She said blankly as she picked up the papers and threw them violently against the door. From there she caught sight of a deck of cards on her bookshelf.

"No more Lennie." She grabbed them, tore them to pieces and let them rain like confetti on the papers. She quickly moved from the pile to her suitcase tearing it apart. She didn't stop until she had removed any evidence of Alice.

"No more Alice." She yelled, throwing flyers, pictures and clothes against the door. She turned to find more Alice memorabilia when she saw a photograph laying at the bottom of the suitcase. She pulled it out to find her in Charlie's arms, dipped in a kiss below the ferris wheel at the carnival.

"No more Charlie." She whispered, almost completely silent, the words barely escaping her lips. Every thought hit had her harder than the last until she reached Charlie. Despair washed over her like waves moving against the sand with the tide and she collapsed on the floor picture and ring in hand. All of the emotions she had kept too tightly trapped inside her were finally unleashed. The tears came flowing down her face and her sobbing rattled her body with every breath. "What am I supposed to do now?"

As she lay weeping there was a sudden knock on the door. Elizabeth lifted her head but placed it back on the floor too drained to move. There was a knock again.

"We know you're in there." A voice called from the other side of the closed door. Elizabeth recognized the voice, and lifted her head to respond.

"Well you're wrong," she called out, "no one's home." Her solemn response elicited laughter from the unknown visitor in the hallway. Elizabeth had no intention of getting up and opening the door. "Go away, please," she asked politely and dejectedly.

"Hard way then," the voice said, sounding as if they had rolled their eyes. There was a moment of silence before Elizabeth could hear the jingling of keys. She looked up from her halo of tears as the door slid open a crack. She tried to see who was pushing against the door, but the tears had made her vision hazy.

"What is on the other side of this door?" The voice gently gave the door a shove, but it barely budged. She shoved again, harder this time. When she pushed the pile of Elizabeth's torn up and tossed memories, moved out of the way. Elizabeth looked up again from her defeated position. She blinked her eyes frantically, trying to push her tears aside to get a clear view of the person coming through the door.

When she thought her eyes had focused, she stopped and blinked quickly again to ensure what she was seeing was real. It wasn't just one person marching through her door, it was four.

Four women stepped over the pile of things in the doorway and began to make themselves comfortable in the apartment. One gathered chairs and placed them in a circle in the living room. One rushed into the kitchen, poured five glasses of wine and carried them in on a tray and placed them on the living room table. The third woman casually shut the door and stood staring at the pile with disappointment on her face. She dropped down and began picking up the photographs and clothes from the pile and returned them to their proper place in the suitcase.

While the last woman dropped down on the floor and lay adjacent to Elizabeth. When Elizabeth saw the face laying in front of her she felt two feelings waft over her. The first was relief, Liza had been the one to push in the door and scramble over to lay on the floor in front of her. The second feeling was concern, Elizabeth couldn't quite put together the reason why she was here. Before she could ask, Liza spoke,

"Are you doing okay?" Elizabeth didn't need to answer the question, she simply let her eyes flash around the room and then she raised her eyebrows as if to say, "Really?"

After some begging and dragging Liza managed to lift Elizabeth from the floor and onto the couch. She sat on the couch staring blankly ahead, uninterested in giving any recognition to the other women in the apartment.

Slowly the women entered the room and sat with Elizabeth.

Everyone in the living room seemed so familiar with one another that Elizabeth had begun to feel like a guest in her own home. As she looked around the room she slowly realized how silly her thought was. She looked from woman to woman quickly realizing that every set of eyes that she looked into she saw were her own looking back.

Elizabeth paused and wondered what those eyes had seen, her eyes in their bodies. Traveled further back or forward? Had they been on adventures Elizabeth had no idea about? Had they seen love again? Had they seen Charlie again? The group of them sat in silence for minutes that seemed to drag on.

"A meeting of the Elizabeths?" Elizabeth finally said breaking the ice, hoping her sense of humor wasn't lost as she aged. They all let out a subtle laugh, and appreciated the start of their discussion, but it quickly teetered out back into a brief silence.

Elizabeth sat wondering when they were all from, but everyone in the room seemed to have a firm handle on who was who and Elizabeth didn't want to seem out of the loop. Luckily for her, not a second after that thought had left her brain, the woman who collected the items from the floor spoke up.

"I'm E." She said. Elizabeth assumed as much. Her long grey iconic hair was familiar to Elizabeth, and slightly aged skin singled her out as the oldest in the room. "I'm 75 years old, and I just arrived back from Ancient Egypt." Everyone oohed and ahhed, slightly trembling with anticipation of their future travel.

"The first." Elizabeth said, slightly bowing with recognition and admiration. E smiled back and sighed, longing for those youthful days when she had so much adventuring ahead of her. Elizabeth opened her mouth to ask a question, but E quickly raised her hand in protest.

"No, I will not fill you in on the adventures in your future. It's cheating." E turned to the woman on her right but someone else spoke up. The women turned their heads to E's left, where a woman with glasses was seated.

"She's right. It is cheating." She leaned back and crossed her arms, nodding in agreement. "Eliza. 56. Traveled back from 1800 to be here. Missing out on a monumental election." She finished almost begrudgingly. When she finished speaking there was a slight laugh from the woman to Elizabeth's right.

Sitting next to Elizabeth was a middle aged woman with dark pixie cut hair. She reminded Elizabeth of her rebellious teenage years, when she cut off all of her hair and pierced her nose, and thought the only thing she could do was to stand up to the man.

"Always so righteous those two." She said and rolled her eyes. "I'm Beth, 45, I've been to the future. And it's awesome." She finished speaking and tossed her feet up on the table. This action caused all of the women in the room to straighten up in their seats and give her a look of disapproval. This elicited a chuckle out of Beth who withdrew her feet from the table.

"Traveling to the future," E called out in a puff, "you shouldn't be tempting fate like that!" She raised her arms, flailing them with anger, causing Eliza to follow suit.

"Oh calm down Mom!" Liza said, chiming in at last. "You know me," she said, throwing a wink to Elizabeth. "I'm you," she paused, confused. "You're me." She tried to correct it. "When we last met it was very clear that you were me, but now, we are very close in age, all things considered." She paused, giving Elizabeth time to think and process. *"How much had she changed by staying? How differently would things play out from here?"* She thought to herself slightly panicked by her actions.

"This is unfamiliar territory for all of us really." Eliza announced, seemingly impressed by the situation.

"But, you're me." Elizabeth said bashfully, embarrassed to have pointed out the most obvious thing. "How is any of this unfamiliar?"

"We have the memories, but none of us lived what you lived." Beth clarified.

"If that had been me, I would be in worse shape." Liza announced reassuringly. The group nodded in agreement, at which Liza was insulted that they had all agreed so quickly.

"How does all of this work?" Elizabeth asked, motioning to the situation of all of them being in the same room. E took control of the room having had the most experience out of all of them. She explained how none of them were from the same timeline which means all of them have and will somewhat live different lives.

"In my timeline there was no one to tell me what I should or should not do. I had to decide for myself. And when I went back and made the decision it created a slightly different world than the one I came from. It made the world that Eliza was born into." E tried to explain it in as simple terms as possible, so everyone could follow. "Even though we share the same name and DNA, none of our lives will play out exactly the same.

With that Elizabeth felt defeated again. Being with all of these women had made her hopeful for her future was brighter, and she would eventually move on from what was here.

"So, none of you can be of any help?" She asked dejectedly.

"We do get to see him again, you know." E offered out trying to brighten the hurt for Elizabeth and lighten the mood. For the first time in their conversation, Elizabeth had felt hopeful.

"But it's never like before." Liza interjected, wanting to clarify exactly what E was saying. "We see him, that's all."

"When?" Elizabeth asked, curious to know what her future would hold for her and Charlie.

"I saw him at the nursing home." Liza shrugged knowing that Elizabeth already knew this. "But he never let me know if he knew or not." There was a pain in her voice. "He was an entertaining old man, and even though he never said it, I think he knew. He would always be nicer to me than he was with the others." She leaned back smiling with the memory.

"I go back to the moment he proposes." When E said it a light turned on in Elizabeth's memory.

"You're the little old woman, holding on to him, begging him for something." she exclaimed remembering that night. That memory created a domino effect in Elizabeth's mind. "AND, you're the little old lady that yelled at me. You pushed me down outside the corner store and told me to leave."

"I wouldn't say old!" E retorted, offended, but content with her actions. They all let out a good laugh, and continued explaining when and where they saw Charlie. Beth saw him and Alice when they were younger growing up in the Cape.

"They were walking down the street with their mother." As she spoke she seemed as if she regretted that moment. "I finally understood what old Charles meant when he talked about living in the before. It's hard." She finished leaving it at that.

Lastly Eliza spoke up. She explained how she went back to see him and his wife. While she told the story, it became clear to Elizabeth that this was the first time anyone had heard this story before. All four of them were poised on the edge of their seats, completely wrapped up as she explained.

"I wanted to be sure it was the right choice." Eliza looked down at her feet. "Leaving, you know?" She paused trying to find the words to explain. As she spoke she seemed ashamed of what she had done. "They were just married. I saw them walking on the street. I was walking towards them, I looked away hoping he wouldn't see me. But-" she sighed "he saw me. He recognized me." She shook her head embarrassed. "He looked so confused and hurt. He called out my name, and I heard his feet try to chase after me, but I just grabbed the watch and left." Silence fell over the room when she finished speaking, everyone too emotional to respond.

"Be careful." She looked at Elizabeth, eyes burrowing into hers. "Seeing him again, it isn't perfect. It is so much harder than you think." There were tears in her eyes, and as Elizabeth looked around the room, all of them had glossy tear soaked eyes.

"Well." E said standing up. "I think this is enough sadness and confusion for one day." She grabbed her bag and headed for the door, the rest of them following suit. "I'm sorry we couldn't be of more help, or any help for that matter." She said before hugging Elizabeth and sliding out the door.

"You'll feel better eventually." Eliza patted her on the shoulder. "You've got to feel the pain to move on."

"When I left," Beth said when it was her turn to go, "I wallowed. Wallow, until you know how you want to end it. Then, go anywhere in the world. You've got all of time in the palm of your hand." She gave Elizabeth a high five and headed out the door. Seeing how optimistic and adventurous Beth was gave Elizabeth a small twinge of hope for the future. As much as she would've loved to have lived her days out with Charlie, adventures throughout time seemed like a solid second place choice.

Elizabeth turned to see Liza standing in the middle of the apartment looking around at the mess. When Liza caught Elizabeth staring, she grabbed her by the hand, drew out her watch and slowly turned the dial back. Elizabeth watched in awe as all of the mess she had created slowly made its way back to its original space.

"You did what no one else could do. You stayed, and then you left when it was harder than ever to do it." Liza pulled her in tight as she made her way towards the door, and gave her a big squeeze. She held her there for a moment. "Thank you," she whispered, "They don't want to admit it but, thank you. You gave all of us a little more time with him. Even if it is just a memory, it's nice." She squeezed her once more and headed out the door closing it behind her.

After everyone had left her, Elizabeth stayed in her apartment and wallowed. The time passed slowly, days and weeks a blur of nothing. Nothing in her life felt right, a large part of her was missing now. To her almost six years had come and gone, but to everyone else she was only away for a few months. She stayed cooped up in the apartment, trying to think of some reason to leave, but none were compelling enough.

A few weeks after being sequestered in her apartment, living off take-out delivery food and Netflix, she woke up one morning feeling as if she finally knew what she wanted to do to allow it all to come to an end. She grabbed her coat and rushed out the door.

She slowly made her way through town, and as she walked she allowed herself to be overwhelmed by the sights and sounds that reminded her of her friends. She wanted to take Beth's advice, she knew how she wanted it to end and she knew how much it was going to hurt.

Elizabeth stood outside the library breathing through the pain. "I may as well take all of the pain at once and then let it go." She told herself over and over before she entered the building. With every step she was hit by painful memory after painful memory.

She looked around the library, it had been updated, but it still smelled of old books and had the same brown paint that it did on her first day here with Charlie. In the distance she spotted the window where he confessed his love for the Hobbit, and they found something in each other at that moment. "All at once, and then let it go." She whispered.

She asked the librarian to direct her to where they stored the archived newspapers. The gentleman was confused, but Elizabeth explained, "googling it won't be enough."

Luckily everything had been stored on computers so she simply had to search for their names and obituaries to find the dates she was looking for, but she dug through piles and piles of paper until she found the physical copies. She knew what she was hoping to find, that they all had lived happy lives, and were better off without her around.

"Charles Robert Finley, 92, died saturday May 26th, 2012, at Cape Regional Medical Center after a brief battle with heart disease.

He leaves behind his three children Theodore, Freddie and Elizabeth (husband, Patrick Swan). As well as his two grandchildren, Charlotte and Grant.

Born and raised in the Cape, he lived a simple life until being drafted by the navy and later the United States Coast Guard. Prior to retiring he took pride in working with the Training Center for the United States Coast Guard.

Family and friends remember Charlie as a loving, caring man who loved to travel, having visited Canada, Australia, and all of Europe. He could dance a storm around the room, and tell wild stories, most notoriously memorable being the tale of the time traveling girl.

Funeral services will be held next friday, May 31st at 1:00pm at the Beach Street Hotel."

"Alice Helen Finley-Marcus, 90, died monday November 14th, 2011 at her home surrounded by her family after a long battle with ovarian cancer.

She leaves behind her husband Freddie Marcus, and their three children Henry, Helen, and Robert.

Alice was a staple of the Cape community, since she took up her nursing post with the clinic and later the Regional Medical Center. Every patient who passed through her care, remembers her, kind demeanor, charming attitude, and beautiful smile.

Her greatest prides in life included rallying with the nurses and fighting to establish workers rights for the nurses and women of the Cape.

Funeral services will be held friday November 18th, at 7pm, at the beach where her family will spread her ashes on the beach front. In lieu of flowers the family asks that you please donate to the Cape Nurse's fund."

"Frederick Grant Marcus, 91, died tuesday November 15th, 2011 at his home, only one short day after the loss of his wife. He leaves behind his three children Henry, Helen and Robert.

Frederick, or better known as Freddie, moved to the Cape at the age of five. When he and his family first arrived young Freddie did his best to show his disapproval for his family's move by terrorizing the townsfolk. Much to young Freddie's disappointment he never left the Cape, but also in attestment to his luck in life he also found friendship, love and his greatest pride and joy in his life, his children.

Funeral services will be held friday November 18th at 7pm at the Cape beach, his ashes are to be spread in conjunction with his wife, Alice Finley-Marcus."

"Leonard Cornelius Knox, 92, died thursday February 2nd, 2012, at the Cape Regional Medical Center after a sudden heart attack.

He leaves behind his wife, Audrey Knox, and his five children Janet, Elizabeth, Warren, and the twins Frederick and Charles. As well as his 9 grandkids, Elijah, Robert, Beckett, Craig and Sanders, and Libby, Barry, Cedric, and Ronald.

Leonard, or Lennie as he was better known, will be remembered as a constant, caring and misguided soul. All of his wives and children describe him as a man with nothing but love to give. Born and raised in the Cape, he lived his life until he was drafted into the United States Navy, and later the Coast Guard, with friends Frederick Marcus and Charles Finley. After the war Lennie remained in the Cape, working alongside his friends with the United States Coast Guard training center.

Funeral services will be held saturday February 4th, at St. Mary's Cemetery."

Elizabeth leaned back in the chair, her face wet with tears. She felt satisfied now, knowing what had come of her friends. She was proud of the things that they accomplished, but it was bittersweet as she wished she could've been there to see them through all of it.

She pictured Alice sitting on the picket lines and speaking at town meetings, demanding equality and justice. Freddie with his children on his shoulders, chasing them through town, and showing immense pride with every tiny little thing they accomplished.

Lennie at his first wedding, second, and most likely his third beaming with pride each time, and the four of them hoping that he finally landed the right girl that time.

Charlie travelled Europe, Australia, and Canada, all of those places they planned to visit hand in hand. Watching his eyes shine in wonder every time they landed on new ground.

She tore the articles out of the newspapers and placed them into her pocket and headed to the library exit.

"Excuse me," the man behind the counter called out and pointed to the papers peeking out of her pocket. "That's vandalism, and theft." He said huffing and puffing. "Give those back right now or I'll,"

"You'll what? Ban me?" A huge smile grew on her face before she melted into tears again. "Too late, I'm already on it. 1940s, look it up." Another outburst of tears ran down Elizabeth's face as she left the library, leaving the librarian baffled and confused.

As she made her way to her car she fumbled with the keys when a rusted gold key hanging on her chain caught her attention. She stopped in her tracks and stared at it, holding it to her face, analysing the words engraved across it, 'HOME.' Elizabeth climbed into her car and stared at the key some more, as she did she tried to figure where this key came from. Her home? Charlie's home? A box hidden in her apartment?

She slowly drove her way through town when it dawned on her,

"Home!" she said slamming on the brakes and swerving to the side of the street, "Her home. My home?" She quickly made a u-turn and rushed back in the direction she came.

She pulled up in front of two familiar houses. She stood, leaning against the car staring at the two witnessing both her past and her future at the same time.

"Weird," she whispered as a shiver passed through her body. She slowly made her way up the steps towards the yellow single-story house. She stood on the porch and glanced in through the windows, trying to spy if anyone was home. She turned towards the door at the sound of a paper fluttering in the wind caught her attention. She walked towards the door key in hand and pulled the note off of the door. It read, *"From me to me you"*

She slid the key into the lock and was relieved when she turned the key and heard a click and felt the door swing open. Everything was just how it was when Liza lived there. The pictures, the books, the furniture, everything.

"Well, I guess this is home now." She sighed looking around. She decided it would be stupid to turn down a free and destined house.

After an evening of vigorous packing and unpacking, she awoke the next morning to see the pocket watch staring at her from it's spot on her bedside table. She picked it up and tucked it away inside the drawer.

Elizabeth headed into the kitchen, brewed a pot of coffee and went about setting her morning routine; breakfast, coffee, tv. After a vigorous marathon of her favorite shows she missed while back in time, she turned off the tv and her eyes wandered to the vast bookshelves piled against the wall.

She crossed over towards them and began to scan the books on the shelf. She ran her fingers over the books reading the titles as she went. Her fingers came to rest on a rather large, hardcover, travel book titled, "History of the World."

"Well," she said, a history book open on her lap flipping through the pages. "When do I want to go next?"

Chapter 22

Years had passed since the day Elizabeth left her life behind. She had gone on many adventures through time since she left 1951. She spent her days bouncing around from era to era, coining herself as a Time Tourist. She wrote down her adventures and kept all of them in piles of journals tucked under her bed. On occasion she thought of publishing them one day, when the world was ready for it.

Elizabeth plopped down on the window bench, coffee and "History of the World" in hand and stared out the window. Her eyes gazed around and down the street watching the people pass by. She flipped through the pages of the book and thought back on her almost 14 years of time tourism. She decided her favorites had been the 1920s, 1880s, and 2050; but nothing ever held a candle to the life she had built in 1945.

Her eyes landed on the house next door as she thought of him. She didn't pine for him, he wouldn't have wanted that. She had managed to find some kind of romance in every time she visited, but none was ever love or was as perfect as what she had had with Charlie. A smile filled her face and a pain hit her heart whenever she thought about it.

She continued to flip through the pages. She removed her bookmark from page 175, *Ancient Greece* from where she had just returned. As she turned the pages she thought about the other Elizabeth's, the ones that came before her. They had told her how they had gone back and saw him, and spent time with him.

"Why can't I?" She thought and her eyes shot over to her watch on the table. It called out to her, like it was beckoning her to glance it's way. She sat, staring at the watch, chewing the inside of her lip, pondering the thought that had bounced through her mind from time to time.

"No hesitating." She told herself. She quickly scooped up the watch and her coat and headed out the door.

She stood out on the street and spun the dial back until the date read 1965. When she had arrived she looked around, the houses stood in the same position, and the people still went about their way with little recognition to the woman who just appeared on the street.

She slowly walked up the steps of the porch to Charlie's house, nervously shaking with every step.

"If he is home, I'll stay." She told herself firmly. Elizabeth had done her research. She had hoped that 1965 would be the perfect time. They would still be similar in age, his children would be older now and Peggy had passed. "The future is pretty much set now, the family is built and Peggy has passed." She reassured herself with every step.

She knocked. No one answered. She took a deep breath and knocked again. Again nothing.

"Third time's a charm," she said, knocking harder this time. Sadly, still nothing.

She sighed, turned and walked down the steps towards the street. Her head hung low, defeated, as she fished the watch back out of her pocket. She turned back to the house one last time, swearing to leave it all behind for good when she was back.

Before her fingers could reach the dial a voice called out from down the street.

"Elizabeth?" The voice echoed out again. "No! Don't go!"

There he was, running down the street towards her, just as he had done the night she had left. She had no second thoughts this time, no doubts about anything. She had no time to return the watch to her coat pocket, as his arms came wrapping tight around her, and his lips crashing onto hers. The watch flew out of her hand and onto the street.

"But what - how?" He said kissing her again, hands gently holding her face close to his. He rested his hands on her face

"Does it matter?" She said with a smile, looking deep into the chocolatey eyes she thought about every night before she fell asleep.

"No." He said with tears in his eyes as they frantically looked over her face longingly. "You're here. How long do I get you?" He began rambling off questions, trying to determine what exactly she was doing there in his arms. "What about everything?" he said, remembering the implications of their relationship in the future.

"Fuck it." She said and he shook his head back with shock and gusto falling to laughter like he always did when she would curse. He lifted her up, wrapping her legs around his waist and carried her into the house.

That night the two fell back into each other with ease and the next morning, it felt as if she had never left. Elizabeth puttered around the kitchen making breakfast and looked at the pictures of Charlie's kid that hung on the walls, trying to piece together what has happened since she left.

Suddenly there was a knock on the door.

"Hey!" Elizbaeth called out in a panic to Charlie, who came swooping into the kitchen after her.

"Good morning!" he said, kissing her on the cheek. "I've missed having you here." He kissed her again. "What's going on?" He said.

"Someone knocked on the door." Elizabeth informed him. "I was going to answer it but -"

"It's probably the kids." Charlie finished her thought. He had explained the night before that the kids had spent the weekend at his parents. "Come on." He grabbed her by the hand and led her down the hall. "I intend on keeping you here this time, so you'll have to meet them eventually. They're going to love you."

Elizabeth peered through the pane of glass on the door and on the other side of the door were Charlie's parents, the kids, Alice and Freddie. Before they turned to look through the window Elizabeth dropped to the floor.

"Did they see me?" She asked. She looked up to Charlie who merely smiled and waved.

"Nope. And good effort." He extended a hand down to her. "Just a second." He called out through the door as he helped Elizabeth to her feet. "You okay?"

"It's Alice, Freddie, and your parents. I want to meet your kids, that's easy. I didn't disappear on them 14 years ago with no excuse. But I don't know if I can face

Alice and Freddie." Elizabeth rambled in a panic as Charlie led her to the sofa.

"Breath." He told her. "It's fine." He tried to reassure her. "I mean, yeah, maybe, it'll be fine."

"That's really helpful Charlie." He kissed her on the cheek and went back to the door, leaving her sitting nervous and alone.

"Sorry." Charlie said when he opened the door. "Just surprised it was all of you." He tried to stop the kids from running away before he could explain but they dropped their coats at the door and took off through the house.

"Sorry dear, we should've called. But we ran into Alice and Freddie and thought we could all go for lunch. Grab your coat." Charlie's mom said. She stooped down to pick up the kids coats, called out to them and then headed back to the car.

When his parents had left, Alice and Freddie stood on the porch looking apologetic.

"Sorry. I tried to stop her. But you know mom." Alice said entering the house and scoping her brother up into a hug. Alice's voice echoed into the living room and caused Elizabeth's stomach to do guilty backflips.

Elizabeth stood, hidden out of Alice and Freddie's sight. She had travelled all throughout time, but she didn't have the nerve to face Alice and Freddie, they didn't love her like Charlie did and they may not be so easy to forgive her.

"We were walking here and we spotted this on the street. It's older, and clearly broken, but," Alice paused a moment to fish something out of her purse.

"I think someone drove over it." Freddie continued to explain.

The kids made their way into the living room to find Elizabeth sitting, clearly eavesdropping on the conversation by the door.

"It's rude to listen to other people's conversations." The oldest of the three said when they found her.

"Did your Dad tell you that?" Elizabeth said, and the three of them eyed her up, but they nodded. "He's pretty smart right?" They all nodded in agreement, and Elizabeth continued. "but let me tell you a secret-"

"It's been years, but I knew it when I saw it." Alice explained, and Elizabeth's eyes popped at the sight of the rusted, gold, pocket watch as it hung from Alice's fingers. It had fallen from Elizabeth's hands when Charlie grabbed her, and she hadn't cared to worry about it. "You have some explaining to do brother. Is she?"

Following habit Alice and Freddie had begun to walk into the living room, not knowing Elizabeth was there waiting.

"Theodore, Fredd and Elizabeth eh?" Elizabeth said, and shook the hand of Charlie's daughter. "That's my name too."

"What?" Little Elizabeth said with surprise and excitement. "I've never met anybody with my name."

"I know a whole boatload of Elizabeths. Welcome to the club kid, we're all cool." Elizabeth joked, while little Elizabeth tried to understand what 'cool' meant.

"What?" Freddie said, being the first to spot her sitting on the couch.

"Hey." Elizabeth shot him a smile, trying to pretend that she had never left, and gave him a small wave, and turned back to her conversation with the kids.

"What?" Freddie said again, more confused.

"What's wron-" Alice said when Freddie grabbed her by the elbow and swiveled her to see what he was seeing.

"Hey Auntie Alice," little Elizabeth waved, "Do you know Elizabeth, we share the same name. We're in a club now. It's cool." The two Elizabeth's gave each other a high five, and a large prideful smile burst across Charlie's face.

"Wait, what!"Alice said again and stood frozen, watching dangling from her fingertips. She looked from Freddie to Elizabeth, and Elizabeth to Charlie and then back to Elizabeth. "How are you...here?" There was a confused anger in Alice's voice.

Charlie took a moment, wanting to avoid a fight and sent the kids out to wait in the car with their grandparents.

"Wait, what?" Alice had no other words, even though Alice knew Elizabeth's secret she had never expected her to come back.

Charlie gently took the pocket watch out from Alice's hands and passed it to Elizabeth.

Elizabeth turned it over in her hand and let out a gasp. The perfect glass that had encompassed the steadily ticking hands of the watch had shattered. The crisp white face and sharp black numbers now were cracked and faded, and both hands from the face were missing. The time controlling dial had cracked and would no longer turn.

"I guess I'm sticking around." She said giggling with excitement. She showed the watch to Alice.

"To stay?" Alice said, tears forming in her eyes, and Elizabeth nodded. "I've missed you so much." Alice pulled Elizabeth into a tight hug and threw the watch at Charlie.

Charlie's face sat blank for a moment before he pushed Alice aside and wrapped his arms around Elizabeth and lifted her to his lips. Freddie stood watching, completely confused.

"About damn time." Charlie said as their lips met again. Elizabeth and Charlie sat with their foreheads together, sharing a quiet moment of relief.

"Can someone please explain?" Freddie asked because Alice still stood mouth open with confusion.

"There is a lot of explaining to do." Elizabeth said. Her eyes were completely apologetic but she couldn't hide her enthusiastic smile.

"Why don't we explain over lunch." Charlie said, wrapping his arm around Elizabeth and guiding the group out of the door. "Like old times."

Elizabeth and Charlie kissed another time before locking the door behind them. The two melted into each other as if they hadn't had a day apart in their lives.